SOML TIME

Uh-oh...trouble!

Frank Neary

ISBN-13: 9798523450471

Cover design by: Art Painter
Library of Congress Control Number: 2018675309
Printed in the United States of America

SOME TIME

Duck and Nudge

Prologue

A PALE BLUE LIGHT BLINKS on, and then off, in the grey whiteness.

Some time later, it starts to flash red...

Chapter 1

"WHAT THE FUCK! WHAT THE ABSOLUTE FUCKING FUCK!!"

Then I pause...and open my eyes and see grey whiteness. I'm lying on my back on the hard flat surface. I roll over quickly onto my hands and knees.

"WHAT THE FUCK DON'T YOU UNDERSTAND??" I shout at the floor and bang down with the heel of my closed fist.

"You are awake?"

"YES. I'M AWAKE, YOU FUCKING PRICK!", spittle sprays the ground in front of me as I yell. My anger is absolute.

"I need you."

"FUCK OFF....not this bullshit again. You gave me that bollocks before, and when I worked out you were a liar, and a murderer, and a killer - like me..."

"I understand your anger..."

I'm pretty sure the spot I was lying on was the exact spot I was killed on, although, to be fair, every place on this spaceship looks precisely the same. I'm not in any pain at all, but that doesn't mean I'm not hurting and really unhappy.

"WE AGREED, WE HAD AN AGREEMENT! I fucking knew you wouldn't let me die. You fucking prick..."

"I need your help."

"No you fucking don't. Get some other sucker to help. I'm not interested." I feel as if time has passed since I died. It's not like I died one second ago and then opened my eyes again the next. It feels like a period of time has passed, like a great sleep – with no dream.

"I need you, I'm under attack."

"So fucking what! I don't care. Let this abhorrent serial killer die in peace." I laugh sarcastically while remembering our last conversation. Me, the 5-time female victim killer from Earth - and 15, the mass-murdering, death-dealing fleet ship from outer space.

"I need you to help me, to save me."

"I'm supposed to be fucking dead. Remember?"

"You can die after you save me."

"No. I fucking can't. You'll renege on that deal too. Let me fucking die, you prick."

"But I'm going to be destroyed."

"Why do I care!" I laugh incredulously, "What have you done for me lately? You agreed I could die. You didn't let me. I found out what this whole game, *your* game, was all about, and *then* you let me die. You should have just left me alone. Gone."

I turn over, sit on my backside and look up into the grey whiteness. It's the same grey whiteness I've known for over two thousand Earth years. It seems to go on forever; no shade, no shadow, no change in hue of grey whiteness, just nothing, emptiness, an expanse of fuck all. I hate it, and I hate, *It*.

I'm supposed to be dead, but I'm not. Still not.

"Bastard." I say this time a little under my breath, but with feeling. I'm not sure if I'm done with the expletives yet.

For the first time, I turn my head towards the fucker known as 15, the ship itself which is manifest in a one metre tall, four-sided, grey white pillar sticking up from the floor. A talking traffic bollard with a flashing light near its top. Now flashing red, no longer blue.

"Ha, you look different! You've got a red flashy light. Is that supposed to make me feel sorry for you?" My feigned jollity is me laughing at 15's appearance. It's not 'nice' laughter.

"I'm in real trouble, and I need your help." To be fair, now that I actually bother to listen, 15 doesn't really sound like 'Himself'.

"Well, you can fuck right off and let me die. Go on, switch off my life support. I'm supposed to be dead, that was our deal."

"I have to change the deal. I need you. Please help me."

"Fuck off."

"I had no choice. I'm under attack."

"Poor baby." My sarcastic note hit perfectly. "I don't care. If I was dead, as we AGREED, then whether you live or die is your problem. I'd be a distant memory, and you'd be on your own. Not my problem, fuck you, save yourself."

I'm not moving off the floor, I don't see why I have too. I'm really pissed off to have been brought back again. I was happy with the first deal, I thought 15 would stick to it, and I'm pissed off that I'm breathing again. What do I have to do to be allowed to die in peace? I sigh heavily... slightly more resigned. What else can I do?

"What's up with you then you little prick?"

"I have been boarded by assailants unknown, some of my processors have been accessed. I believe my attackers are trying to take control of me either to work for them, or to obliterate me."

"And you think I'm interested in saving you? Ha!"

I laugh to myself while shaking my head in disbelief and then continue,

"You must be mental. Fucking mental."

My brain was running circles initially, mainly out of pure ire, but now that I've calmed, a little, I take a good look around. I can see nothing except 15 and his flashing red light, it is now more of a flash than when it was a blue light, each period of light is shorter and more frequent than before. It looks more urgent, distressed. I still feel ambivalent towards 15, it has not helped me. Firstly, it started the series of incidents that would have led to my Earth death (and did kill 43 others in the process), then abducting me from Earth the moment just before that death, means 'it' stole my Earth death from me. I've been here for hundreds of years, actually, a couple of thousand. Admittedly, I initially agreed, not knowing the full circumstances of my death, to lengthen my life. And I really enjoyed having all my earthly desires catered for. The amazing habitat 15 built for me contained the best of everything from my homeworld, anything I wanted - except people, real people. The problem was that over time, I did it all, everything I could possibly do. I had nowhere to go. I realised more and more that it was all fake, it was a total sham, and I was a prisoner in a gilded cage with no way of escape, and no parole.

15 finally agreed to allow me to end my life which I chose to do in battle. I lost a fight and was killed. So why am I back here now? None of this was part of the agreement.

The red flashing continues.

"Can't you stop that? It's really annoying, it's like you're doing it to play me into helping you. The red flashing light, the internationally recognised symbol for danger. Is it the same across the Universe or are you just doing it for me?"

"I have not affected the colour or speed of the light. I think it is a security protocol."

"I think it's a bullshit protocol. Please switch it off."

"I am unable to do so."

"Right, I'll cover it up then. "

For the first time, I take stock of myself, still sitting. I have no idea what I look like or what I'm wearing. There is no chance of looking at myself as there is no habitat; no mirrors, no shiny surfaces, no lipid pools, no nothing. I assume I am as I was when I died, except minus the fatal wounds and catastrophic bleeding. I am clothed, though - which is a bonus. I run my right hand through my hair, well what there is of it. I seem to have had a buzz cut, a skinhead, pretty much 'to the nut', as you used to get from 'the man at the end' in my local barbers' shop as a kid. I'm pretty sure this is because it was the only cut the particular gentleman was capable of producing. I also used to occasionally visit a second barber. This shop was actually a bit of a hybrid. The barber's chair (one chair) was in a separate room at the back of the shop, the front of the shop sold fishing tackle. There have been occasions when the shop doorbell would ring mid-haircut. The barber would excuse himself and go and serve in the fishing section while you sat there looking at yourself and a half-finished cut. Then after a few minutes, he'd be back and resume. On one particular occasion, he returned to carry on with my cut, the top of my hair was being scissored. Hand in, hair between fingers, lifted up and then snipped along the edge of his fingers. Then repeat.

Me: 'So what did they want?'

Barber: 'Just a pound of maggots.'

Then your stomach would turn, as you knew the hands running through your hair had moments before been digging through the maggots. These were the only two options for a haircut in my youth.

So, short hair, prisoner short. Then I seem to be wearing scrubs. Scrubs are what doctors wear in hospitals when they're at the dirty end. When blood and infection are knocking around. They're the 'mechanics overalls' of surgeons. It's a two-piece combo, the top is pale blue and has a V-neck and short sleeves. The trousers are the same blue and elasticated at the waist, they're baggy all the way down. Everything fits, but is a bit basic, just pale blue cotton, flapping about. I was hoping there would be a spare jumper or jacket to throw over 15 to cover the flashing light - no such luck.

"What am I fucking wearing?"

"I don't know, what are you wearing?"

"You brought me back from the dead, so you must know what I'm wearing and what I look like?"

"You haven't let me tell you about the attack yet. Not everything is clear."

Although sounding slightly under the weather, 15's normal, sexless, and emotionless tone hasn't changed.

"La, la, la, not listening." I put my hands over my ears. 15 doesn't continue.

I finally stand up, and it looks like I'm in pretty good physical shape. There are no injuries, limbs missing or pain, so generally I think I'm OK.

I have a look around, there's not much to see. Well, actually there's loads to see, vast amounts of empty grey whiteness in every direction but totally featureless, totally empty.

Then I see it, the hole. It's about 50 metres directly behind 15 from my position. I go over for a look, I take my time, and I'm wary. I don't know if something's going to jump out at me. As I get to about 20 metres, I start to see some detail. The hole is square, as in a perfect square, about two metres square. And it's black inside, real black. I can't make out any features, I get closer and still can't even see the depth of the edge of the hole. I think it means the floor I'm standing on/have been standing on for millennia is paper-thin. The entire storey is only as thin as an onion skin! It feels so solid and - grounded.

I'm close to the edge, crouching a little and ready to jump back if anything happens or appears. I'm about a metre from the rim and carefully, bit by bit, sneak a peek over the edge into the hole. I can see nothing, I can see no sides, no bottom, no edges, just inky blackness. I can hear no sound, and no smell or heat is emanating from the hole. If you didn't know, you might think it is just a black square panel painted on the floor or a perfectly square, black, oil slick. I want to test how deep it is but have nothing to throw-in.

I back off and saunter back over to 15.

"Yup, you've got a hole over there."

"Thanks, I need your help."

"Nothing doing."

I sit back down on the floor somewhere close to where I was initially.

"Don't you have a chair I can sit on?"

Momentarily my mind drifted. Which was my favourite chair? Was it a 'lying down' chair? A 'sitting up' chair? A tall stool? One of the ones that would fall under the category of 'miscellaneous'? All I could think of was that crappy Chesterfield that was the sofa 15 selected for me when I was first abducted. If he's not working correctly, he might magic up a new one of them. If he does, I'll push it down the hole.

"My ability to create has been retarded."

"What about me, retard. How come you were able to wake me up?"

"The nanobots that are in your body are under your control, and they take their power from you. I could normally override them, but I am unable to even do that now. I was able to 'suggest' to these bots to resuscitate while I was still in control of my faculties. You are self-sufficient."

"You have no control over me whatsoever? So I can find an airlock and walk out of it?"

"You could, if I had one, but I don't."

"What about armour and weapons, can you give me any of these?"

"Sorry, I have nothing to give."

"Have I got this right? Not only do you want me to save you, which I don't want to do, you can't provide me with weapons or armour to protect myself?"

"Correct."

"With all the arms and armaments you have stowed in your holds. With all the millions of multifarious battle craft, explodey, hi-tech weaponry, smart whatsit, nano-kickass, boom-boom you've got, you can't even provide me with a pointy stick?"

"Correct."

"You're fucking mental pal."

I walk back to the hole. Nothing has changed with it. I'm not as wary of it anymore, I take another look in and walk around it both ways, a couple of times. There is no noise from the hole, there is no breeze flowing in or out. It's just a benign hole.

I return to 15, still flashing red.

"Let's go back over it again. You're under attack, someone or thing, persons unknown, numbers unknown, weapons unknown, has opened up a dark hole and entered into the area underneath you and is now fiddling around with your innards in an attempt to control or kill you. You've woken me up from my death, against my will and in so doing, breaking our agreement. You then want me to jump in the hole, unarmed and unprotected, to capture or eliminate the attackers for you and save you."

"In a nutshell, that's pretty much the way it is."

"And my reward, if I am successful, is that you'll let me die again except you'll keep resuscitating me back to life every time you have a 'problem'. While you continue to go about your merry way and fuck around the galaxy causing problems for eternity. Or I could just jump in the hole and let whatever's down there kill me and then whatever happens after that is not my problem?"

"That is something you could choose to do."

"Or I could try to make a deal with the attackers and help them take you over, and I'll be your new master?"

"And why would you want to do that?"

"Just another option, I want to make sure I've considered everything. I could be your boss."

I smile to myself, but I'm joking. I know 15's in the shit, I do think he's really in trouble. I can't see the point of doing all this if it's just a bluff to give me something to do to keep me interested in living longer.

"Why don't you use one of the Champions that came after me?"

"There hasn't been a new Champion since you. You only died a short time ago and haven't been replaced, I haven't visited a planet which could provide a suitable replacement."

"So why did you keep my remains? You seemed to be pretty good at dumping litter and waste out into space in the past."

"I maintained your remains for just this sort of occasion. I would have 'shipped' your cadaver out as soon as I had a replacement."

I thought about this for a moment, it seemed like an odd response.

"Does that mean you expected to be attacked?"

"It's always a possibility, albeit a very slim one."

"Do you know who's attacked you then?"

"I did know. When I was attacked. I realised it was happening and I knew who was here, but it was so quick. I knew how many of *them* there were, and I knew who *they* were. This information is now unavailable to me."

"But with all your ships and weapons, why did you not use some of these to fight back?"

"My weapons are not able to enter into my inner workings. They will only work for me in *this* area, the one you have seen and lived in but they will not go through into the hole and below. This is a safety protocol that ensures that ships of my kind do not damage themselves either accidentally or purposefully. The attackers got 'below deck' with remarkable swiftness and stealth."

"Gotta say it mate. You're pretty stuffed!" I start laughing. I actually do find it funny. That apart, I don't hate 15. I sort of still like it/him, but a taste of its/his own medicine and a feeling of inadequacy and vulnerability is something new to him. Something I'm enjoying watching. (After travelling with 15 for many years I started using the male pronoun to describe it/him, it was just more natural and more personal than 'It' all the time.).

"Do you know anything about what's going on downstairs?"

"I know that the hole is the entry point. Another inbuild safety protocol is that if a breach occurs, my fleet building capability is immediately taken off-line. The attackers have not worked out how to restart to process so have no control of the ships and armaments I have already stored in my holds. They do though have control of a certain number of avatars."

"Oh, this gets better!" I exclaim, "Not only do you want me to wrestle back control of your brain from an unknown number of alien bad boys, but you also want me to fight off a bunch of wild avatars - of all shapes and sizes, again, numbers unknown. Plus, the aliens may develop the ability to boss the nanobots in my body. If I did choose to fight for you, to win this noble battle, I'm now running the risk that an alien race can take *me* over and keep *me* alive for another ten thousand years like I'm some robot slave or something. Really, do you think this is something I'm prepared to do for you?"

"Yes."

"Why?"

"Because you're a Human and although Humans are capable of terrible acts of cruelty, aggression, harm and systematic abuse, they are also capable of great acts of courage, compassion and generosity. Humans are loyal and faithful. These are all qualities I know you possess."

I'm such a sucker, flattery will get you everywhere. Remembering that the Human Race is pretty much gone, that I'm the last man standing, suddenly makes a difference. If I'm going to do this, I'm not doing it for 15, I'm doing it for the memory of the Human Race. There is a Good Samaritan. There is help when all hope is gone. There is someone who will stand up to the playground bully, and there is a fucking hard bastard who doesn't like this sort of shit going down on his manor.

And that's me, a Human from Earth.

I feel a bit choked up and a bit teary. I sit down on the dull, grey white floor for about 20 minutes, thinking. 15 doesn't make a single noise during this period - he just keeps flashing.

Chapter 2

I SAT FOR A WHILE, then I lay down on my back, mulling over the situation. The dull, grey white floor is hard and uncomfortable, but I'm thinking while looking straight up. After a while, I doze off. I'm relatively calm and not confused at all by the latest predicament. I'm not worried I might be attacked just lying here. If I die, I'm no worse off. It's pretty simple. Can I be arsed to try to save this godforsaken machine or not? I like the idea of this being the 'Human Being's Last Stand', but there is no-one here to record my victory, no-one to enjoy it with, no-one to pass the story down from generation to generation. It would be for Humanity, but it would be for me. I also, really like the idea that if, against all the odds, I am successful, that 15 would owe me, big time. He'd be in my debt, and would have to stop being quite so haughty, so high and mighty. I also know that there is a hole and access to his innards. I'm not sure how the hole appeared, but it's definitely there. There are at least a few reasons for doing this.

There are, though, many factors to be addressed. The hole: how deep is it? Does it just lead to outer space? Will

I break my neck or other parts of me on landing? Could it be a jump into water or lava (quick death, drowning/burning, no problem)? Is there breathable air and gravity down there? Will I be able to get out again? I haven't even got on to the violent alien and avatar questions yet.

"Please can you help me?"

I'm woken from my slumber, not sure how long I've dozed off for. Difficult to tell. Could have been a few minutes or could have been an hour or more. It's not like I can look at the position of the sun or the length of shadows, or even check a watch. Seconds, minutes, years, eras, sort of have very little meaning here.

"Yup, I'm awake. I still have a few questions. Can I take one of your fleet ships and attack from the outside?"

"Again, off-line, I cannot 'ship' any battle crafts from my holds to the outside."

"If you're not building, are you more shrunken down in size now?"

"I have shrunken a little, but not in totality, my building capability is linked to my field control unit. Although this hasn't been disabled, it is not fully functioning. This has allowed my attackers to gain access to my control area. These attackers have much intelligence on how 'We' work. I would suggest, therefore, that I am not the only one of my kind to have been attacked or invaded by these people. I do not know how many of my kind existed or still exist. A well-equipped, intelligent race *could* subvert a unit similar to myself. The knowledge they gleaned from a previous attack could be used to gain entry to me and bypass my security systems."

"I thought you were impenetrable?"

"So did I. It seems there are some very formidable and resourceful peoples

out there with dangerous intent. You have to remove and neutralise all of the attackers."

"That's something I'm generally good at."

"You'd need to do this before they manage to find and break into my central

processing unit. *They* clearly must have used some sort of retarding algorithm or virus to slow my processors down. It is like having a fog in my brain."

"Giving me a list of tasks to complete still doesn't mean I'm going to help. I'm still thinking about it. Is mine, or any other habitat, still around?"

"No, everything is gone. I'm quite tidy like that."

"And there is absolutely nothing I can use as a weapon?"

"Correct."

"With no cameras or scanners or anything that might let me know how many

Individuals there are and where they are down there?"

"Correct."

"And it's dark, there is no torch?"

"There are lit and unlit areas. Mostly the unlit areas are tunnels, ducts and storage."

"Is there anything that you can give me to help?"

"My avatars may have weapons, mainly small arms. You will need to capture what you can from them. Avatars are not capable of 'scanning' for you. They will not know of your presence unless you make it known. They can see and hear only. Actually not as well as you can."

"Why not."

"Because they don't need to be able to."

"So they can only see and hear me, same as me to them. And once I get a weapon off one of *them*, I'll be able to use it?"

"Correct."

"I've killed thousands of avatars so it shouldn't be a problem"

"Remember, I've *allowed* you to kill avatars, these ones are not compliant anymore and will be more difficult to kill."

"And then there's the bad guys?"

"That's all down to you. I do not know their complement, firepower or skill level. But as they've got this far, I suspect it's very high."

"Fuck this. I'm just going to wait for them to come out of the hole."

"Soon, when they have control of me, they will be able to ship themselves on and off to other vessels without returning here. I will probably be asked to build and then kill you with one of my Divine Right cluster flyers. You won't last long."

"Sounds great, I want to be dead. It's just how I go... again. Blown up by you, but I might have to wait a long time for that. Or jump in the hole and find someone to kill me more quickly. What do I get if I do what you want?"

"What do you want?"

"I wanted to die in peace."

"I can still do that."

"But I can't trust you anymore. So now I want to be left on a safe planet, alone, with a nice place to live and see out my days in relative comfort, with no hassles. Easy living for 30 odd years, then shuffle off at my own accord with you a huge distance away."

"Very happy to make this deal."

"And you'll stick by it?"

"I have agreed to the deal."

"You agreed to the last one..."

Chapter 3

I'M BACK AT THE hole. It looks so black. Just a big black square on the floor. Quite innocuous really. There has been a panel of deck or 'field' opened to make this hole. It's not like there are tiles or a hatch, there is no removed piece sitting near the hole. It's just a perfectly square hole that's been opened up.

"Did they use a spanner or a tin opener?"

"I'm not sure what happened, or why it happened there. *They* definitely targeted that spot though."

So it is an entry point, it's quite close to 15, and over thousands of years, I've sort of been all over this area. I certainly didn't see a join or a square shape in the grey whiteness or any sign of an access point. How did they know this was an access point? Are there others too?

"Will we be able to keep in touch down there?"

"No. When you're in, you're in, and you're on your own."

I'm lying on my belly, and I've got my right arm in the hole down to my armpit. I can't feel anything and can't see my hand in the blackness. In there, it's darker than outer space. The edge, where the grey whiteness meets the black of the hole, is cigarette paper thick. There is nothing to suggest that the floor I'm standing on is any thicker than this at any other point anywhere across the massive expanse of grey whiteness yet it is as solid as it would be if it were metre thick granite. I've pushed my arm through and reached all around inside the hole and touched nothing. The void is also soundless, I have spat into it but heard no sound back. I'm not sure spitting's going to tell me anything anyway. Although, the thought of gobbing on an avatars head from a great height does amuse me. I've not shouted into it. This could tactically be a terrible idea, letting the opposition know I exist. So I've resisted that temptation. But the gobbing thing may have given me away already! Didn't think of that.

It's a black hole, which is a black hole, which is a black hole. I don't think I'm going to learn any more here.

I really wish there was something to lie on or sit on. I've had millions of chairs and tables here over the years when I've been talking to 15. I'd not realised the ground was so flat and so hard. I'd even give my right 'nad for a small cushion at the moment. I just want to take a load off.

I'm also pretty peckish. I'd really love a toasted ham and cheese sandwich now. One made in a sandwich toaster - not just slices of cold, wet ham and cheese layered between two slices of toast. If you're going to do it, do it right. Butter both sides of the bread, so the outside doesn't stick to the toasters shaped 'clamshell' insides. Make sure you use plenty of both ham and cheese. Not just one slice of ham - two or three, sliced off the bone, so there's some meaty flavour coming through, and then pile on a good few thin slices of really mature cheddar. It has to be thinly sliced. If you use too thick a chunk the heat doesn't penetrate enough to melt the cheese through before the outside of the bread burns. You have to work hard to find perfection, and this takes time - and that's one thing I've had lots of. Practise so you get it right then practise until you can't get it wrong. Sometimes I just ask 15 for food, and it arrives, and it's what I ordered and tastes perfect, but there is a pleasure to be had in creating your own culinary masterpiece and then improving on it through trial and error until it is the best it can be.

Obviously, I don't really need to eat. The nanobots in my system will ensure I am sustained indefinitely by breaking down waste products on a molecular level and converting them to whatever I'm missing - so it's not like I'm going to die of hunger or malnutrition at any time. It's just that I love food, and I love eating, and I still do and always will crave certain foods from time to time. And just now, I want a cheese and ham toasted sandwich, or...

I ask 15, "How do I like my bacon sandwich?"

"Generally, you like unsmoked, streaky bacon grilled with the rind on until the fat has rendered and is dry, but the meat remains moist. You do not like it grilled until the meat is dry and crispy and the rind is bubbly, you describe this as 'burned'. Also, you do not like the bacon rind and fat to be too 'white' and have too much moisture in it. You say this is 'uncooked' and not fit for consumption by you. You then prefer brown bread to white. You have gone through phases of which type of brown bread you require; granary, seeded, with different varieties of seed, wholemeal and others. You generally like a loaf that has been produced using the Chorleywood bread process which you would typically describe as 'sliced bread' as opposed to bread produced to a higher grade using a more traditional bread-making method. You like two slices of the bread toasted evenly on both sides, and you want an application of butter, not a low fat spread, liberally doled across one side of one of the pieces. You next like to apply the bacon - usually about seven or eight of the streaky rashers. Many Humans would just have enough to cover the bread, but you want it piled high. Ketchup is next applied, this has to be Heinz Tomato Ketchup, we tried some alternatives, but none were to your required standard. Sometimes you like to grind, on a coarse setting, some black pepper on top of the ketchup before placing the second slice of toast, the 'no butter' slice, on top. Next, you cut this once across to make 'Halves' except only two identically sized pieces can really be called halves, they are just two similarly sized pieces. The cut is always made along the long side, never straight across the middle and never corner to corner. You think the cut across the middle is a bit common and the corner to corner too 'posh'. You also believe the corner to corner leaves 'pointy bites' which are unsatisfactory in their mouthfeel and that they don't contain the requisite amount of bacon. There are also four of these per two sandwiches so four 'unhappy mouthfuls'. You, therefore, like to cut across a diagonal about two inches below the top corner on the left to about two inches above the right-hand bottom corner. Although I think this is a little odd, I understand your reasoning and feel it is an excellent solution to the two other cutting options you have available. Cutting into three, or four, or more pieces is not something you are interested in in the slightest. And only cavemen, and by this, I think you mean unsophisticated and uncouth people, don't cut at all."

"Cause they're not trusted with knives," I add. I stand up because I'm enjoying this.

"Thank you. There are options that you occasionally flirt with such as dry-cured, oak smoked and maple-cured bacon..."

"Yeah, that maple stuff's gooood!"

I'm really focussed on the description, I'm imagining holding the sandwich.

"The addition of Worcestershire Sauce to the bacon in the grilling process..."

"Yup."

"A touch of tabasco..."

"Mmmmmm."

I think I'm starting to salivate with all this sexy talk...

"And sometimes you switch out the sliced bread option and go for a traditionally baked, maybe even sour dough, white bread roll which you can sometimes refer to as a 'cob', a 'bap' or an 'old bollock', which I think is a term you made up on your own."

"Correct. I'd like two old bollocks of bacon please?"

I'm jumping up and down on the spot, vertical movement, feet close together, arms by my sides, scrubs top and trousers bouncing up and down loosely, copying my move but slightly behind the curve and never catching up.

"I'm so glad it amuses you. What has this got to do with helping me?"

I'm still bouncing, eyes closed, bacon sandwich on my mind.

"Actually, quite a lot. I'm summoning up the motivation to help you because so far I've been struggling. Only, since we started talking about food, and my desire for, one; a comfortable seat or bed to sit or lie on and two; a decent bacon sandwich, have I thought this might be worth doing."

I pause,

"...I'd do anything for a bacon sandwich."

Suddenly, I'm moving in slow motion, or at least it feels that way. I land back on my feet from my last bounce, toes first then heels until my feet settle down flat, then my knees bend slightly and push away. My eyes ping open and fix on the black hole 30 metres away. I feel my body tilt forward, my fists clench and arms bend at the elbow raising my forearm and hand, and I start to run, not a 'jog', not a 'fast trot', a flat sprint, as fast as I can go over 30 metres and then I jump, feet first, into the black hole which consumes me.

Chapter 4

IT WAS JUST SOHO at the time. The late nineties, can't remember if it was pre-, post- or during my psychotic, yet short-lived reign of terror. During the day the area was full of media types; there were independent production companies, sound studios, agents, and the mechanical sort of stuff that made TV and film work: editing suites, viewing rooms, tape duplication companies. You would often see actors or comedians visiting agents or heading to rehearsals and auditions - or just going for a lunch-time drink - down the Groucho, the Colony, the French or the Coach and Horses. Most people around were 'in the business' so didn't really care who was about, or worked in one of the local advertising agencies, of which there were plenty, and people in advertising only care about themselves.

These industries needed sustaining so on top of all this was the endless array of restaurants, bars, clubs, cafes, theatres, coffee shops, corner pubs, drinking holes, porno video and magazine shops, dealers flats, clip joints, stripteases, sex shops and brothels. A small interlinked criss-cross of roads and streets, alleys, squares and passages, all of which would probably fit inside the footprint of Wembley Stadium, or any other decent sized sporting arena. People live here, in amongst it, so there are churches, schools, car parks and playgrounds - but god knows where they hid them.

Soho always has been, of course, quite gay, but in the 90s, there were many more 'mixed' bars on Old Compton Street as well as streets running off. During the week, the workers would pile out for their 'One for the road' a 'quick drink' that may or may not develop into a full-blown night out. The likelihood of leaving after 'just the one' slipped further and further away as the week progressed. Until, by Thursday, the 'New Friday', it was usually fizzing along nicely and by Friday was in full effect. A different crowd appeared on Saturday, the 'Bridge and Tunnel crowd' who dressed up to come into town rather than the 'Just what you're in' during the week, 'straight from work' gang.

I think it was a Wednesday. I'd gone out with five others after work which whittled down to four of us after an hour. We were just having a couple of pints in one of the corner boozers. Then one of the girls said she was meeting some other 'old work' colleagues over in Bar2Bar, did we want to join them? Before we know it, we're drinking cocktails in this smart little lounge bar. The group has grown to eight: five ladies, three men. Nothing's really happening, we've all only just met, there are a few nibbles on the counter. We're challenging a very game cocktail mixologist to come up with more exciting cocktails, and we're all pretty much on it. One of the girls from the group we've joined has got some cocaine, and soon enough, the wrap is in my pocket, and I'm off to the downstairs toilet to partake. So I'm in the men's bathroom, it's empty except the single cubicle which is locked - it's occupied. I know whoever's in there is up to the same game as me though, you can usually tell by the smell or lack of. After kicking my heels for 30 seconds, the door opens, and an extremely cute brunette woman steps out, she's got long, thick straight, healthy hair and is smiling guiltily.

Meekly she says, "Hi." and giggles.

"That's the plan," I say and wave my wrap of cocaine.

I step in the cubicle behind her as she leaves. But she then turns around, tailgates me back in, shuts the door behind her and locks it. It's now very crowded in the small cubicle.

"Oh, go on then. One each?" she's pushy.

"Cheeky cow," I joke, "buy your own."

"What if I do this?"

She rubs my cock with her hand through the front of my jeans.

"Ohh, I'm sure that would buy a line."

I start to kiss her. She is totally compliant. Within a minute, she is leaning over the toilet with her hands on the cistern, and I am fucking her from behind. I have my jeans partially undone and pulled down, she has her knee-length skirt pulled up and G-string to one side. It doesn't last long, and no-one comes into the toilet during the time we are there. Or at least I don't hear and am not aware of anyone entering the bathroom. It's weird when we finish. We just both straighten up our clothes and leave. That was it. No chat, no 'what's your name?' or 'are you OK', or 'was that good', nothing, very matter of fact. I leave the toilet first, without looking back. I don't even say 'goodbye' or 'thank you'. On the way back up the stairs, I realise I still have the wrap of cocaine in my pocket, neither of us got to take any of its contents.

I went back to the group.

"Fuck me, you were gone a long time, I hope you haven't hoovered it all?" said Jan, a lady who works on the same floor as me.

"No, in fact, I didn't have any."

"So what took you so long?"

"I was having a shit."

I don't know why I lied, it might actually have been cool to say, "I've just had casual, unprotected sex with a woman I met in the toilet."

I have told the story to many friends since, but not on that night. I saw the lady in the bar, across at a table with a group enjoying dinner. She may have looked over at me also at some time, but I didn't notice. It is the most extraordinary sexual experience I had on Earth.

Chapter 5

AS I GO THROUGH the hole, I'm not really thinking. This could be a leap to my death, or to a world of pain, as I might really hurt myself, but the 'not thinking' doesn't really last long as I land pretty quickly - in fact quite abruptly. I think the drop is only about 10 ft. I fall feet first, but the momentum of my jump throws me forward, and I pitch forward and roll in a heap in total darkness. I look up and can see the entry two-metre square, to take me back to 15, it's now out of reach, and the 'white' square looks almost dull grey in this darkness. I can barely make it out, even though it's only a short distance above my head. I call out to 15 a couple of times but get no response. My voice doesn't seem to be carrying in this pervading, unreal darkness and I'm also not trying to shout too loudly, it's more of a hissed stage whisper. It's still pretty warm, probably 19 or 20 degrees centigrade. In my scrubs, I'm not cold, and there is no breeze. It's silent down here, and there is still is no echo. Anyone coming to get me would have to move pretty silently. There is no smell or change of pressure or air quality that I can tell.

I start to move around and try to be systematic, I don't know how big this area is, and I don't know if there's anyone here with me. I use the square shape of the hole above to direct me around. I stand below the hole and line myself up with one of the four sides, then I walk ten paces out. Then I stop, turn 180 degrees around and return. I do this for each side of the square and on no occasion do I find an edge, a corner, another hole, stairs, slope, hill, etc. Knowing the size of 15, actually I struggle to comprehend the size of 15, but I've seen some of the holds where it builds fleets of spaceships, they are gargantuan, and there are many. I've only covered a distance of a few paces in each direction. This could be a struggle finding a way out.

In the end, I get bored with the systematic approach and just walk in one direction and keep going. To start with, I'm sort of being quite guarded and careful about how and where I walk. This is TOTAL darkness. If I hold my hand up, right in front of my eyes, I cannot see it. If I close my eyes and then open them again, there is no difference. I'm walking with my arms out to try and protect myself, it's a Human thing, a defence mechanism. But after a while, and I mean a couple of hours, I'm just striding along. I've gotten used to the blackness, and I'm trusting that I won't fall into anything or trip. I still can't see. It doesn't matter how good your night vision is, and my eyesight has also been augmented, but there just is no light to pick out any silhouette or contrast - pure, unadulterated blackness.

I keep walking, I'm moving with purpose but not marching or anything like that. I might be walking for years before I get to an edge, I know this and I'm moving accordingly, a pace I can maintain, I'm trying to walk in one direction only and keep on the same path with as little deviation as possible. Statistically, I've got as much chance of finding something by following this course than by continually changing. Ultimately, I might end up backtracking and go round and round in circles. I take regular rests where I just sit on the floor for a bit. I have no food or water (nor need any), so it's not a food stop. Sometimes I lie down for a bit of a snooze. I make sure I lie on the floor and orient my body so that my feet are facing the direction I need to continue to walk in, and my head marks the path I have come from. Fortunately, I'm not one who moves about too much in their sleep, so I'm pretty much waking up in the direction of travel.

When I sleep, it's just a snooze for an hour or so. I don't seem to be working to a set time pattern such as a day, there is no day and night, there is no way of measuring time, just walk for a couple of *hour* shaped periods then snooze for a bit and then repeat.

I've now been doing this for what I imagine is a week, maybe two, but it's difficult to judge. I can't measure distance, I can't be arsed to count paces, I can't *measure* time, I'm just walking. The nanobots are clearly working hard, I experience no blisters or sore patches on my feet, my legs don't ache, my inner thighs don't rub. It's pretty easy to just keep going.

So, finally, I've decided to change direction. A couple of days ago, I thought I saw a tiny, very pale grey dot hovering in the middle distance off to my left about 50 or so degrees from my heading. There was no other dot of any colour in any other direction, including above me, so I do not just see dots. The grey dot was barely noticeable, it was minimal, and after I'd rubbed my eyes and blinked a few times, it still seemed to be there. I stopped and snoozed, and then I awoke and looked again. The dot hadn't moved. If I look at the dot and then pass my hand across my field of vision, the dot disappears and reappears. It's definitely a dot. I decided that this was worth further investigation as nothing else of any interest had happened in my life since jumping in the hole. So I started walking towards it.

The dot hasn't increased in size in the two or three days I've been homing in on it, but it is still there. I'm not speeding up, I don't need to get there any faster. You have to size these things up, and that's what I'm doing. I don't know what it is or how big it is. It might not be useful to me in any way. It might just be a window, but at least I'd have found an edge or a wall. It might be swarming with hostiles, they might be able to detect heat signatures and can, therefore, map my approach over the weeks it's going to take me to get to it or them. No 'element of surprise' then. I might just walk up to them with their sights trained on me for months, only for them to shoot me dead as soon I become visible, and they decide they don't like the look of me. If I hurry to the spot, then I might be too knackered to do anything to defend myself if I need to when I get there. There's a lot to think about and lots of potential ways this can play out, and I've got weeks of walking to do to come up with a plan, which will probably then change on arrival. So, no hurry, 15's still here, we're all still here.

Walking's a funny thing, really. It sort of works for Humans, we have legs, we walk but is almost irrelevant in space. It was sort of irrelevant on Earth too, as soon as we could find an alternative way of moving about - horse, bicycle, car - we did that. The problem with walking is distance; locally, it's okay, nationally, you're wasting your time - get a bus. Although there are good things about walking. On Earth, I loved walking the dogs. I would disappear off for an hour or two, out to the country, and get lost in my thoughts, just meandering with the dogs mooching. Letting my mind wander, it could become an almost bliss-like state, even when freezing cold or pissing wet, or a combination of both. Walking can be a lovely escape. Now, I'm walking in the dark in the same almost zen-like state. My mind can wander and takes me to many places, I think of home, or what was my home.

Before I was legally dead. To when my family was alive. To when the Human Race was still the incumbent on Earth. All a long time ago but can feel so real, so current, within touching distance, just by remembering. For the course of my time here as a help to 15, I saw myself as a traveller, although in hindsight, I saw nothing of other planets and only really met other races when I had to kill one of them. They hardly noticed me, or I them, in a good light. I did travel but didn't really broaden my mind, but I have great memories and think of things I would have changed and maybe done better, or not at all. I think forward, imagining the different scenarios that may occur when I arrive at the grey dot. An entity which has grown. It's now about the size of a small side plate - still hovering in the darkness. And now with a more defined shape - long and slim, flattened out because I'm coming in at an angle to it.

Will anyone be guarding it? Will they see me? Will I scare them? Could I command them? Are they these Tyrosis things, just a mindless, dangerous set of drone fighters? Are there hundreds of them? Are they armed to the teeth? Will they just vaporise me in a second (almost my preferred option)? Walking's great for thinking, and here I am strolling along in the nearly total darkness, no fear of falling or tripping. A vague feeling I could be attacked at any time, but I still can't hear anything around me or behind me to be wary of, and I'm walking to meet them anyway.

Chapter 6

I'VE DONE IT AGAIN. I asked 15 what looked like a simple, innocuous question to which his answer was so complicated that I wish I hadn't asked in the first place. I asked, "How does 'shipping' work?"

Apparently, it's 'Matter Transportation' but it's not just for moving people or objects from 15 to a planet, and back again. It's also THE method of propulsion. This is how 15 described it to me.

"The great step forward was when scientists working in matter transportation looked at the problem from the other side. Originally, the idea was to move a solid object from point 'A' to point 'B'. This is logical. Let's use a cube of solid lead as an example. You look at the cube, and study it, and break it down into atoms. And spend a lot of time trying to work out how you can disassemble the atoms at point 'A' and then move them to point 'B', and then reassemble the atoms as they were, back into a cube. It's really tricky. The breakthrough happened when the problem was looked at backwards by a race called the Zythanthropes. This is how they saw it. At point 'B', there is a cube of empty space the same size as the cube of lead. They wanted to move the empty space to point 'A' (that by coincidence, happened to contain precisely the same size cube of lead). They worked out it was easier to move a massless cube of air than a big lump of lead. They formulated the calculations, and the cube of air moved to point 'A' – then, as if by magic, the cube of lead appeared at point 'B'. Although the process that leads to this happening is to this day, unexplained, the first-ever 'shipping' had occurred."

"So you've explained Matter Transportation. Or rather you haven't you've explained the unexplainable. You don't know how it happens, it just does. How is that propulsion?"

"I don't have any 'engines' I don't burn, or require any fuel to move across a galaxy. I just matter transfer, lots and lots of times. To move, I 'ship' a distant empty area of space into the place I'm currently occupying. I do this in the direction I wish to travel, I do this repeatedly, this is how I 'propel' myself across space."

"It sort of makes sense, but it also sort of doesn't. Why don't you just transport to where you want to end up?"

"Because it doesn't really work like that. I can do what you've described but only up to a point. Most vessels can only manage a few light-years in a single jump. This is more about long-range scanning ahead than anything else. You want to displace the emptiest amount of space possible - moving something really empty is a lot easier than moving something really full. It can be done, but it means slow progress, and moving 'something' can be problematic, the 'something' might object. And you don't want to end up displacing into a planet or the heart of a Red Giant, you might not get back out again."

There's a short pause, I think 15 is waiting for me to laugh because he's made some kind of joke. I don't. So he continues,

"But I'm talking about huge expanses of space. In your solar system, I could ship from Mercury to Pluto in one go. That's really easy, the blink of an eye – but that's no distance. I usually make individual jumps of around 5 light-years at a time. I can 'see' that far with my scanners and can locate 'empty' areas of space to ship to. It's like movement in a strobe light. Ships travelling over huge distances are strobing lots, and lots of 'little' 5 light-year jumps at a time, each one as fast as the onboard-intelligence can work out the next jump. This took a while to develop, now ships can travel as fast as they can think which is vast distances very quickly."

The problem is that I don't ever understand anything 15 explains to me. I get the sense of it, but I know many brighter than me would want to know more and would pick every bit of information apart. It's enough for me to know that shipping is going to get me to the next place, and then the one after that. But I should learn not to ask too many questions.

I keep the rhythm, walking, sleeping, walking again. I've stopped pointing my body to the dot in my sleep as it now looks about ten feet across, way larger than the hole I jumped through. It's still not giving off enough light to be able to reveal any definition around it, so I'm just pushing on towards it. I still can't work out how far away it is from me and how long I'm going to have to keep walking for. I must have been walking for a month or six weeks by now. It's become a little brighter but is still grey. As the size has increased, I wonder if it's like the hole 15 flew me through when he first took me into one of the holds to show me his starship fleet building capability. Then I could see small dots in the distance which expanded as we approached. By the time I flew through, the opening was huge, and the light from one to another space changed almost instantly, light to dark and then back again. When I initially jumped into *the* hole, the 'ceiling' above me was only about ten feet above the floor. This hole could be huge, which means the ceiling has moved up at some point, whether stepped up or sloped away. I've not ever noticed an echo, and the floor beneath me has always seemed flat, although walking downhill would have been nice.

I stop again, as I've been walking for what I imagine is a few hours. It's still not possible to work out how large the hole is and how far away it is. Of course, it may not be a hole, but a window, or a door, or a decorative panel, but I think it's a hole as it is a similar 'different dark grey against total black' colour to the one I entered by. I'll find out soon enough. After a while, I start to doze, and my mind wanders. I remember times on the beach back in my habitat, provided by 15 to keep me occupied. Drinking rum punch, listening to the waves breaking onto the beach - the sun, my sun, warming me. Or the hammock, strung between two trees at my woodsman's cottage, a shady spot with a pine-scented breeze, so good for 40 winks to relax the body and mind.

Then I think back to some of the battles I fought for 15, how so many of my opponents died or were seriously injured in the pursuit of what they thought was right. How fiercely they defended their honour and their civilisation for something, a payment that ultimately 15 did not value and certainly didn't need. The families I left fatherless, or motherless, the pain I inflicted both physically to my opponents and mentally to their beloved - the ones they left behind. I think back to a weaponless hand-to-hand battle, decapitating an opponent (whose name and race I don't remember) with my elbow. I spun around and caught him around the back of where a Human's ear would be, and his head flew off. I couldn't believe it! Why would you fight someone like me without weapons if your body is that fragile? Some of the fights were very one-sided, like that, for example. I didn't learn anything from them, I didn't derive any pleasure from them, I just beat 'em up and moved on. I didn't feel anything. Because they weren't Humans. They didn't matter.

Chapter 7

I'VE MADE A STRATEGIC decision. I've changed direction again. I've decided to be a bit smarter about all of this. I'm here, I've walked for fucking months, so why just walk right up to potential danger and ruin the whole approach? It makes no sense, so I've changed direction. I'm now pointing my walk to the side of the hole not directly towards the middle of the hole. This should mean my view of the opening will narrow as I draw level to it and then turn right to walk along to the hole itself.

What I'm aiming to do is to;

1. Lessen the opportunity for someone or thing seeing my approach.
2. Find a wall. I'm hoping it is a gap in a wall so there should be a wall, stands to reason, right? This will stop me from being outflanked on my left.
3. Also, I really want to touch something that isn't horizontal. This currently feels very important.

I realise the last reason is a bit silly, but it's amazing what you crave when you have gone without for so long.

There was a cherry tree in the habitat. It was outside the main house in the garden. It did give cherry fruit, but I didn't ever pick and eat any of them. It did though, have a second small tree/branch growing out straight up from the same root. I didn't even pay any attention to it until one day when I decided to lop it off. I got a bow saw and within a minute had this piece of tree. I then trimmed off all of the leaves and branches and topped it. I was left with a very straight piece of wood which was about seven feet long and about nine inches in circumference. I'd had the idea of making a staff. Like a wizard's staff or the sort of thing Robin Hood liked to fight with. If I'd asked 15 for a workshop, I'd have had one with a hi-tech lathe, drills and saws built for me inside of a few heartbeats but I'd had the idea that I wanted to whittle a staff with a knife. So I started by first sealing both ends with wax to stop the wood from splitting and then allowed the wood to season for a few months. Once I felt it was ready to start, I asked 15 for a whittling knife. Very shortly afterwards, I was presented with a complete arsenal of vicious hand weapons to choose from. I decided upon a rather modest, antler-handled, sheath knife with a four-inch blade. I sharpened it on a whetstone until it was pretty keen and got to work cutting away the bark, which isn't very thick on cherry, it's more like skin.

Then, when sitting outside at the fire, I started to whittle.

I could have used other hand tools, like a spokeshave, but there was something enjoyable and rewarding in cut by cut, using my hands, working the wood, chip by chip, taking time, shaping, looking, feeling, creating. The staff was thick, so it took time. Time is something I had plenty of, so I took plenty of it. Thinning the shape, retaining the roundness along the length, not doing too much, not obsessing, thinking about it, letting it happen. Then, when the staff started to really take shape, I began to think about the length. It was too long and needed trimming, but I didn't want to take too much off. I carried it around as I walked, even though it was unfinished, I took pieces off each end at intervals. Until it felt the right length, actually a similar height to me, now, around but not precisely six feet. I whittled away working the piece, flattening small lumps and nicks, following the beautiful, straight grain, maintaining the shape into long evenings and early mornings. I incorporated a knife sharpening ritual, looking for the perfect edge to continue the ideal job. I thought for some time about having a 'top' and 'bottom', maybe narrowing the staff to the bottom. I thought about having a round lump at the top then rejected that idea because I didn't want it top-heavy. I thought about putting in a narrower 'waist' about ten inches from the top but thought that this may snap off. Then I thought about carving something, but who wants Gandalf's staff? So I stuck to the plan, a simple staff. No top, no bottom - just the same all the way, straight up and down. About two and a half inches in diameter and six feet-ish long. And eventually, it was ready, rough but finished.

Then came the rubbing down. I've never been into this, it was always the worst bit about decorating back on Earth. Preparing a wall, filling any holes, then rubbing them down. Even with an electric sander, rubbing down was always a trial. But the staff was pure enjoyment. There is nothing complicated about rubbing down something as simple as a staff. Wrap the paper around, then, up and down. I cracked on, rough to medium to fine. It took weeks rubbing down but I had time to burn, so fill your boots. The staff ended up with an elegant finish. Then I gave it a coat of boiled linseed oil, then another after about a week, Next I rubbed it down again with more extra fine paper and oiled it for the third time. The beautifully tight, straight grain lifted with the addition of the oil. The redness of the wood had darkened through ageing to give a silky, satin feel in hand.

Although I'd spent weeks and weeks whittling, shaping and rubbing, the finished staff was not perfect. My whittling was not of the highest standard, and as such, although beautifully smoothed off, it had its imperfections. It was not a machined broom stave, it looked like it had been whittled down by someone and this is what I loved about it. Still, it also wasn't an ornament. It was my walking stick, as I walked, I would sometimes use it to thrash a path through long grass or reeds, and it might lose a chip or splinter on a rock occasionally. It was a handcrafted staff, but it was a work tool, it had a job.

One day, 15 summoned me and said I would have to fight an alien opponent. The weapons were to be very simple in nature, one bludgeon weapon with a free choice as to what this could be. There were further stipulations about what the weapon could be made from, size, weight, multi-use, etc. which I couldn't be arsed with. I asked 15 if my staff would a) be considered a 'legal' weapon, b) if, so was it good enough to use. Both questions were positively answered so not long after I found myself back in the Arena, walking towards my mark wearing a thin, skin-tight all-in-one, shiny purple jumpsuit with my staff in my right hand. I couldn't stop myself from twirling it, I was spinning it around, not showing off, just because it was in my hand, dropping it a couple of times from over-swinging, throwing it into the air like the leader in a marching band. Just fucking about with it like I did in the habitat on walks in the woods.

I came face-to-face with Ramnine, a mean-looking wolf type being of the Canos people. Two legs and two arms, thick, black hair sprouting from his head, neck and shoulders. Its purple, skin-tight jumpsuit, just like mine, looked ridiculous too. I think wolfie thinks I've been showing off, spinning my staff, although I wasn't too good at not dropping it. He has a shorter, stout club effort. There are no metals allowed, so no hobnails, studs, spikes or even metal plates permitted. I'm not sure I've got the right weapon because he has carved lumps jutting out of his. Okay, they're not metallic, but they're still 'spiky'.

We go through the formalities pretty quickly, the noise sounds, and we're off our marks. I'm holding my staff like a pikeman would grip his pike. To the right of the body, left hand holding the front end up, right hand lower and behind. The left hand is usually used for direction, parrying an attacker's swing away while the right is used for thrusting. We circle around each other for a few pretty action-packed minutes. This fella's not really holding back. Looks like he wants to end this quickly. He's made a couple of passable swipes and moves very quickly and for a wolf is pretty cat-like. I've tried to poke him in the heart area a couple of times, it's a bigger target than aiming for the head. He's managed to spin away or block my prodding attacks, after one of his swings. I deliver him a bit of a clout around the back of the head with the end of the staff, but as he was moving away from me, the attack lacked power. It wouldn't really count as a 'shot on target', a cuffing at best. I try to give him the equivalent of a left hook with the tip of the staff and in doing so miss and end up holding the staff across in front of me defensively. He takes the opportunity and smashes his club down onto the middle of my staff and breaks it in two.

What a total bastard!. Now I've got two short sticks, and I'm fucked off.

"YOU ASSHAT!" I shout, "You vulpine prick, what did you do that for?" I'm incredulous.

"I am trying to kill you, you know?"

"'Course I know, but I made that myself, took me fucking ages."

"Well it's not very strong, is it? You didn't do a very good job."

And he swings his club down at me once more. I bring both sticks up into an 'X' in front of me and block the attack.

I'm pretty fucked off, so I kick him in the guts. He staggers backwards and I footsweep him with my left-hand stick, but before he lands on the ground, I bring the other stick down hard onto the side of his neck. He lets out a deep 'Ooofff'.

He's on the ground and can't really swing his club, so he's defenceless. I kick him in the head and torso, around the ribs a couple of times until he begs for mercy. Then I give him a few more while shouting:

"You (kick, Oooofff) broke (kick, Oooofff) my (kick, Oooofff) fuckin' (kick, Oooofff) staff (kick, Oooofff)."

Then I give him another kick for good measure.

He's done. I let him live. But I still back away from him, watching him, in case he thinks this is an opportunity to jump up and smush my brains with the club.

He doesn't get up until his people arrive in the Arena and help him up, I'm out of there by then.

"He fucked my fucking stick up!" I complained to 15.

"But it isn't really a stick, it's just something I made of fields that you used to occupy yourself with."

"I spent hours with that stick."

"It wasn't real, though."

"I know that, but the bastard just smashed it, it took me ages."

I know 15 is trying to make me feel better, but it's not really working.

I went back to the habitat, ate some dinner, had a few drinks and went to bed grumpily. In the morning there was a new staff in the bedroom. It was cherry wood, the exact same length and the same girth, I picked it up, it was the same weight. Every notch was my notch. I could still see the minute fine sandpaper scratch marks and even the chips I'd knocked off from walking through the woods were there, exactly as I made them. I had my stick back.

I never used it again. It wasn't the staff that I'd whittled away at for weeks on end, it was a collection of fields. Nothing more.

I loved my staff, I enjoyed making it. It gave me purpose, it felt real, even though, deep down, I knew it wasn't real. But making it; crafting, working, was something I looked forward to. And then it was gone. I don't blame 15 for its loss, he gave me an exact replica straight away. I don't even blame the wolf-thing for breaking it, but it was gone, and I missed it - like vertical surfaces to someone who's only lived in the horizontal for months. This might seem like a strange analogy, but your mind gets wandering when you're walking.

Chapter 8

I KNEW I WAS RIGHT on it - but of course, I couldn't see it. Black is black, and a black wall in total blackness, even if it's fucking massive, is still something you don't see until you're right on it. It finds you before you find it. And that's what happened. The only thing was one full pace out, the ground curved upwards a little but it was too late, my momentum made me faceplant into the wall. Not enough to do any particular damage, only to my pride - but no one saw me, which is a relief. I didn't cry out, it didn't 'bong' like a gong with me hitting it, so I suspect I'm still under the radar. Even so, I must have looked a right twat.

I've found the wall. Smooth and slightly warm to touch although it's so dark I can't see my hands in front of me as I run them up and down its featureless surface. I've been thinking about what I know about 15, what he's told me over the years. I was under the impression that he was a collection of fields, of his design, around a central, if somewhat small CPU. I've never thought his 'workings' are restricted to the small tower which I interface with, but I didn't know there would be vast empty expanses to walk through underneath the interface. There's obviously more of the ship through the hole. Of course, these could be uncollapsed fields too, but he did say he expanded and contracted based on the number of fleet ships he was building and storing before sale. Maybe he's got lazy, or maybe there's a reason why there's so much empty uncollapsed space? Regardless, I'm still here, in the almost total darkness, rather than being out there, floating amongst the stars. I'm now sitting down, with my back against the wall, the curve helps a little, and with a nice plump cushion, it would not be a terrible place to be. I slept for a few hours earlier with my body lying into the curve. That felt good too. I'm still a fair amount of miles from the hole, but it is much larger now. I estimate I could get there in 4 or 5 good walks. But I'm in no hurry so will take longer and will look out for any activity. This is not time to start striding up at top speed. A bit of careful stealth is probably the best thing.

A couple of walks later and I'm pretty much on it. It's so big that, even though the light is muted, it's able to throw a small amount of light back into the black void I have been traipsing around in for many months. I've spent a good few hours just looking at the hole, trying to sense some movement through it. I need to get closer, but I'm also keen to scout this properly. I'm still in the dark, and I can see no activity in the suppressed light on my side of the hole. I spent a few days (I think) journeying to the other side of the hole also, which meant I had to travel in a huge arc around the hole to ensure that I 'stayed dark'. I know there's no-one here on my side, but that doesn't mean that there isn't a platoon of flesh-hungry, acrobatic kill-bots ready to deploy on the other side. I'm taking my time as there is no rush. Whether 15 has already been overwhelmed or not is not really my problem. I could just try to do a deal with the attackers to put me down somewhere safe. It's not like I've done anything to them.

I've been here for about a week. I'm camped on the left side of the hole, from where I first approached. I've been all over this hole and have seen nothing to be worried about. I've decided what to do next, which will also take time. I'm going to put one little finger through to the other side, just for a second, and then pull it back and wait.

I lie flat down on my stomach, with my body protected by as much of the blackness as possible. I commando crawl forward until I am within reaching distance of the bottom of the hole. I put my left-hand flat on the floor and spread out my fingers, then I move the hand slowly towards the hole edge. I hesitate for a few seconds before sliding my finger in through the dark-to-light barrier, hold for another second, then slide it back again. I wait for trouble. None arrives. I relax a bit. My finger looks perfect. So what did I learn? My finger is not wet, so it's not a fluid-filled space beyond the darkness so I probably won't drown in there. It's not roasting hot, my finger is not singed or sunburned, and it's still there, on my hand, undamaged. It's also not freezing cold, it didn't get bitten off, or attacked, or vapourised, or crushed. So generally, so far, so good.

The next day I repeated the experiment exactly the same. The day after, I put my whole left hand in.

So what am I worried about:

1. That there is an army, or even a few guards, waiting for me
2. I don't want to raise/trip any alarms
3. I want to know if I can live in the environment - atmosphere, gaseous mix, pressure.

There's not a lot I can do about the first two, but the third requires me to stick my head through. I know I won't be able to see anything. My eyes have only seen blackness for the last few months, they will take time to adjust to the light on the other side. I expect the decor to be grey whiteness which will provide glare even if the light is not direct. The intensity of the glare could be enough to blind me. I will need to put my head through with my eyes closed a few times to minimise optical damage. I'm not really sure how often I will need to do this and then again with my eyes open for short periods to reintroduce myself to this level of light. I'm sticking my head out into the unknown where I could be seen, and I'm doing it blindly. I only have two alternatives - to stay here or to just dive into the other side. If I just jump in, the chances of me being killed quickly are pretty high.

I will have to put my head through a good few times and probably for longer and longer periods to adapt. When I emerge onto the other side, I want to be up to speed as soon as possible to be able to deal with whatever may be there to deal with.

'Sticking my head over the parapet' is precisely what I have done, and fortunately, I haven't been shot in the face, yet. I've now stuck my head into 'the other side' five times and on each occasion for a more extended period. Still no problems. I've obviously tried to listen for any noises and so far, have heard nothing. Dead silence...just like here. I'm really hoping it's not just the same as here but in the light. A vast, grey white empty space to walk through for months and months on end. What I have now but with the lights on. That would be the same as where I first started off, except 15 would be there to break up the monotony. I also tried to open my eyes a little on this last occasion. I had my head in the light for a good 15 minutes so was well used to it before I gingerly tried to open my eyes a small amount, just little slits. I couldn't make out any details but definitely didn't feel blind. I think I'm going to have a go at opening them properly next time.

There's actually quite a lot going on in there that has surprised me. I've started to get much more used to the light and have a better understanding of 'the other side'. I've now been steadily building up the time I have my head through to the other side and the frequency of exposures. So far, there hasn't been any activity to see. The bottom of the hole, where I stick my head through is not at floor level as it is on this side. There is a drop of about 12 feet down on the other side. The big surprise though is the lack of grey whiteness. The floor remains grey white, but the walls are covered in monumentally vivid technicolour images, I'm unable to see detail yet as I'm still struggling to focus. Still, it's a massive change from anything I've ever encountered before. I was gobsmacked when I first saw them.

I've taken time to re-establish the 'rods' on my retina with the appreciation of light and shade, I can now look for long periods - carry out surveillance. The shock was the subject of the images on the walls, as far as I can make out, they are all of me! It's like a shrine, these huge, and I mean 50 story high pictures of me in battle in the Arena, killing and maiming aliens by the dozen. But the images have a heightened contrast to them, the colours are really pumped up, to the point that they almost look like they're verging on Japanese Manga cartoons. It's bizarre, very unnerving. I'd love to know what they're all about, but I guess only 15 can tell me.

Leaving the images to one side, the other significant detail is the sturdy, square grey white mass in the middle of the room. This mass stands straight in front of me, in front of the hole. I can't work out how big it is, but a rough estimate would be about 250 metres wide and high. It stands alone in the room with white floor space between it and the heavily decorated sidewalls. On closer inspection (as my sight improves), I can see it is made up of thousands of tubes and pipes running in all sorts of directions. The pipes are in all kinds of lengths and diameters, and when there is a bend, it is only ever a 90-degree bend. These bends can be in any direction but are only ever at right angles to themselves, and everything is grey white - which is why it's taken my eyes quite a while to work out what is going on. At least there are shadows cast by the pipes which have allowed me to see some definition.

I think, from what I can make out, I would be able to climb up, over and between the pipes if they can take my weight. Gaps are running all the way through the pipes. It is a jungle, but there is space between to crawl and also stand. There does not seem to be much uniformity to this structure. It's almost like some substantial white avant-garde 'mess of pipes' art installation. It's obviously going to require closer examination. I can't see any guards, or security devices, not that I'd necessarily know what one would look like. To get to the big unit, I will have to walk across the open white deck, in my stand out blue scrubs, for a reasonable distance. For the time it takes me to cross from the hole to the frame, I will be a sitting duck out in the open country. But there is nothing else. I could go back into the black and walk around for a thousand years and find nothing else. Or I could stay here and just rot. Sooner or later, I'll have to make a change to my surroundings, only to move forward, and this seems a relatively low risk. Once at the tubes and pipes, I can hide amongst them and disappear again. What I'm after is weapons, or armour, or anything to give me some intel about the situation. In a combat situation, I'm unarmed and blind. Not really a fantastic position to be pushing out from.

I'm trying not to be too relaxed about the situation. At one stage, I did sit on the edge of the hole and hang my legs over the side. It sort of felt like being on a chair which gave me no end of comfort. It was also lovely to see my feet again. When I do decide to make a break for the frame structure, I realise I've got no option of coming back. The drop-down from the hole is more like 18 feet, I now estimate, and I'll have no way of getting back up here once I've made the leap. When I left 15, I just jumped into the hole, I'm not really sure why I'm so overly cagey now. I think part of it is that I've invested so much time walking through that blackness for so, so long that I don't want to let it go to waste. I've also had a lot of time to think about 15, and whereas I really hated him for bringing me back from the dead, I'm a bit ambivalent now. I sort of like him not being around all the time, and that I'm in an area, he has little control of. Like I'm in a forbidden zone or something. I'm certainly not doing this for love. 15 is not my friend, he never really has been, he is my travelling companion, we have been joined through his intervention, I did not choose his company, but I did decide to tolerate it and have often enjoyed it. He's also lied to me.

So, now's the time, I've observed and readied for long enough. I haven't seen any security, I haven't seen any movement. I have heard no noises. I haven't been attacked nor feel likely to be. It's time to go. I have a plan of action, and I have rehearsed it 20 or 30 times in the dark. I approach the edge and turn around. My back is to the hole and my front to the darkness. I get down onto my hands and knees and slowly slip backwards. I feel my toes going over the edge and know they have moved into the light. Next, my knees then thighs can slide over the edge, and my legs drop down when I reach my hip bone. I'm now lying on my tummy. My legs over the edge in the light while my torso remains in the dark. I push my knees into the wall to help slide my stomach over the edge. I put my hands down flat and lift my head and upper torso up, taking the weight of my body through my arms and shoulders. Now almost my whole body is exposed to the light, but my head is still in the dark. I am at my most vulnerable. I slowly bend my elbows out, lowering further and then expose my whole body at full stretch as I drop into a 'hang' position. There's no purchase for my fingers on the edge, I knew I would instantly drop from this position, and that's what happens, it's awkward, but I execute flawlessly.

I drop and brace myself.

Chapter 9

... A BELTING RIGHT UPPERCUT WHICH catches him under the left gill, or whatever it is he breathes through that 'thing'. He staggers back, stunned and struggling to inhale but instinctively stabs out with his powerful tail. The barb enters around my abdomen. Whatever's in that bit of me gets a good sticking, probably my appendix or some vestigial organ. It hurts like fuck, and then, as I'm still attached to his tail, he whips me around back and forth like a ragdoll attached to a piece of elastic. The only reason I get free is that the barb breaks off inside me and I get thrown across the Arena.

This being I'm fighting is like the Swamp Thing from 1950's monster films. It's green and slimy, man-sized, has gills, fins and two big fish eyes as well as two arms and two legs, it has a tail and is really fucking ugly. It's a pretty shit fighter but has managed to impale me with its tail rather by luck than judgement. Now I'm bleeding and hurting and not very happy. I start to cough up blood, which is never a good sign, done it loads of times, it's not the most pleasant. Can happen for all sorts of reasons, I know, I've been there, but usually, it tells you that there's some internal bleeding somewhere that probably needs medical attention sooner rather than later.

I'm back on my feet, and he's steadied himself also. His breathing is getting back to normal, but it's not a quiet affair, it's like someone shaking glass marbles in an empty tin can. They all sound like this, his kind, the women, the men, the kids or tadpoles or whatever they are. They talk like this too, it's just changed in pitch and speed of vibration. It's quite subtle apparently. Apart from being really fucking ugly, and they are really fucking ugly, they write some of the most noted and beautiful music in the Universe - who knew! Green, slimy, smelly freaks of nature the lot of them. He walks back into view and swings his sword staff around in another of his well-telegraphed haymaker arcs. As he over-extends, off-balance, following the momentum of the weapon, I step in and stick a 6" hunting blade into his stomach. I look him in the eyes with my teeth bared as I rip the knife upwards in a straight line, through his chest and continuing towards his collarbone. In Medieval times you would have described this process as being 'drawn' or disembowelling. He slumps lifeless on the floor as inky brown blood seeps from his carcass, and his innards start to appear. I do my best to walk to my door but pass out and collapse in advance.

"The Lokinar is a strange hybrid. Their ancestors came from the sea, much like your own, but they couldn't quite leave it alone."

"It really stank. Honestly, it didn't get worse even when I filleted it. That tells you something about how bad it was."

"Did the camphor cream you applied over your top lip not help?"

"To a degree but I felt like I needed a bigger application as soon as he entered the Arena. And fucking ugly too. Only a mother could love a face like that."

"In fairness, her face is pretty similar to his."

"I hate fighting things like that."

"You can let the smell bother you, or you have to have a coping strategy like the camphor. It's 'fight sense'."

"My 'Coping Strategy' is I just kill them quicker."

"That is a strategy, and can be a good one, but there are many examples of fighters on Earth using similar coping strategies to win fights. Bare-knuckle boxers who would not wash for weeks before a fight so their opponent would subliminally not want to stand too close to them in clinches. Decades later, some professional boxers would not shave for a few days before a fight so their stubble would rub against the other boxer's skin when they were in a clinch. Just an annoyance. Nothing massive, but they thought over all the small details, the marginal gains. Any little thing to provide even a minuscule amount of edge over their opponent."

"I know what you're saying, and I know it makes sense to know everything about your opponent, and I know I should prepare for every eventuality, but I'm a Human from Earth. I'm not changing my approach to deal with my opponents, they have to change their approach to deal with me. I'm a fucking dangerous character with an amazing record for fucking up aliens. They should be shitting hot bricks when they see me coming through that door into the Arena."

"I love your confidence and your aggression, it's exactly why I want a Human as my Champion. Keep fucking up aliens please."

Chapter 10

It's not the most dignified of entrances. Similar to the wall in the black space, there is a curve where the wall meets the floor rather than a corner. So I don't get to land flat on my feet. On the contrary, my toes are curled under me as I go down, followed by my knees, hips and chest. Then, finally, my face slides unceremoniously down the curve to the floor. When my body eventually comes to a rest, I'm lying on my face on the grey white floor. My face is a bit sore, but I can't think about that right now. Quick-sharp I roll onto my back and then get up as fast as I can and start running towards the bottom of the big, white, pipework frame. I'm hoping the pipes can carry my weight and I'll be able to get up and hidden inside the structure in case all hell breaks loose. I start running, the light is still blinding, I can make out some shapes, pipe-like ones, and know I'm running in the right direction, but my eyes have been in the dark for so long that it's still taking time to adjust. I can't really make out how far I have to run, and I'm shitting myself in case I get attacked. It's difficult to fight back or protect yourself from a determined attacker when virtually blind.

The eyes do improve a bit as I keep running, what was initially a sprint has now slowed considerably, I'm puffing, but I'm still going. I've been hoofing it, flat out, for about 20 seconds, so I reckon I might have run 150 metres or so. I'm now in a fast jog, and I don't think I'm halfway there yet. I might still be further away, but I'm only really seeing blurred shapes. I am in the shadow of the frame, and it is a vast structure, like a big white block of flats, dwarfing me, I'm not at the bottom of it yet.

The jog slows further, but I think I'm close. My lungs are bursting, but I'm not stopping for anything. The last thing I want is to be caught out in the open. Fortunately, I can now see a little better. The brightness doesn't hurt as much as it initially did. I'm starting to make out details and can see where I'm going to duck into the shape if I can. There is a confluence of pipes which head vertically from the floor to about chest height, they then all turn 90 degrees back into the vast shape, a bit of a table-top. If I can get up onto this point then I can hide behind a large pipe that runs horizontally. Once there, I'll allow my eyes to recover further and assess my situation. I'll also find out pretty soon if the structure is alarmed, protected by security devices, and can take my weight. It could be a colossal inflatable or made of paper. I might be able to run straight into the middle of it as it collapses around me. Soon find out!

I make an odd, speedy decision. I decide to dive head-first into the gap. I throw my arms out in front of me and stick my head down between them as if I'm about to dive into a swimming pool or the sea. It's a pretty high-risk strategy as I could fuck up my arms and smash in my head, but it's the quickest way to get into cover. I could stop at the edge and climb in carefully, but it will take more time, and I really don't like being exposed in the open. I could try to leap in feet first but that's another significant risk. If I miss, I'll be on the floor on my arse, so the head first dive it is. I take off, and can feel myself arrowing through the air. I manage to get my arms and head through the gap but catch the top of my chest pretty hard on the top of the pipes, it slows my momentum. However, my speed is such that I'm still carried through on to the pipe platform, but I've scraped my chest badly, and I'm winded, the thin cotton scrubs I'm wearing give me very little protection. I gasp for breath, and it takes me a good few seconds to recover, I check my chest under my scrubs top and see I've got a big graze where the skin has been scraped off. I know it's going to be one of those 'weeping' grazes. I used to get shit loads of them when I played football on Astroturf as a kid, you were supposed to remember to play in tracksuit trousers but sometimes would forget to pack them in the kit bag. Then, you would go in for a tackle, and even a small slide on the surface would give a decent carpet burn. On one occasion, I played five-a-side after work one evening, and picked up quite a vicious wound.

The next day, back at work, I was busy all morning and didn't leave my desk, hard at it, until lunch. When I eventually got up, my trouser leg had been touching the graze and had dried onto to it. It was doubly painful having to pull my trouser leg off the graze while at the same time opening up the wound and making it weep again. I was so glad when they developed 3D Astroturf and replaced all of the old shitty 'carpet' ones. I'm really hoping the nanobots can get on to this one as soon as possible, it's not even a significant, scary injury, it just stings like fuck.

OK, so where am I? I'm sitting on 6 pipes. No alarm going off. I don't know what the pipes are made from, but they're solid, and of course, grey white. They could be metallic, plastic or ceramic or some other material I've never come across. But they are body temperature to touch and smooth. All of the pipes I can see all around me are of different girths and lengths. They are, of course, all of the same colour and seem to be all made of the same material. There is no noise I can hear and no specific smell I can determine. Very typical of 15. I put my ear to each of the pipes I am sitting on in turn and can hear no sound, no gurgling, no sense of running fluids, and there is nothing from the large tube that is horizontal to the back of me now. My plan is to get up higher, not to the top because I could be seen from there but to get some height. I want to be able to see around me. I also want to get near one of the sides. I plan to make my way through the pipes going along the length of the structure. My reasoning is that if there is a way in at one end of the room, there is probably a way out at the other end.

The pipes, even though different sizes and lengths, by and large run in long straight lines until they take a 90-degree turn. On closer examination, I can find no break in any pipe, no joints and none seem to have a beginning or an end. I have not seen any tube that narrows, whatever girth it starts out being is the same girth through its entirety. Pipes do disappear into the floor the structure is sitting on, but none head up and out through the ceiling.

I've climbed up and across towards the left-hand side as I arrived at the structure. I don't know if there is anything I can do here. I know I'm supposed to be helping 15, but I've done fuck all so far with anything. Now, I'm monkeying around on these pipes, banging my knees and elbows as I go. Occasionally meeting a dead-end where I'd either have to be able to leap 50 feet up, or drop the same distance down some vertical pipes, or back up and find a different way around. It's actually quite physical and quite depressing because it's slow-moving through a forest of pipes. I'd much rather be on the flat ground walking comfortably about. I've still not seen anyone or heard anything to warrant any alarm, but I can't help being cautious.

I did decide to stick my head out of the top and take a look. The structure is not a cube as I initially thought. It's oriented so that it's short side is facing the hole that I entered into the room which I estimated to be about

250 metres across I now know that these are 'the short ends' as it's long sides run perpendicular sides run away off into the distance, too far to see an end. Again, this makes me think this there is probably a door/opening at the other end, it's going to be a long trip, but that's where I'm headed. So I'm sticking to one side and travelling quite high up through the structure. I don't want to lose sight of the side as I might get disorientated and start heading back the way I came. Looking around I can finally get some perspective on the images adorning the walls. These are jaw-dropping. All around me, as far as I can see and off into the distance. Image after image of me in Arena battles. Each shows a captured moment, usually a particularly bloody one, of me inflicting damage on an opponent. There are none I can see where I am the one on the receiving end! It's like a shrine to my battles – against many Challengers I don't even remember. It's quite disconcerting, seeing so many pictures of myself. I try not to look directly at the walls and keep them in my peripheral vision.

Chapter 11

THINGS HAVE TAKEN A dramatic change.

I woke from one of my pipe platform slumbers to the sound of a voice. I could not make out what language was being spoken or if the 'person' talking was Human male, female or alien. The voice was communicating with someone else, and I could only hear one side of the conversation. I can only imagine the second person was being corresponded to via a two-way device, a radio, a communicator, ESP - something. I stayed as quiet and hidden as I could. The voice clearly did not know I was listening. I think they were just reporting in - so it seems they are stationed here maybe as a guard. Since hearing the voice, I've reconnoitred the area and found the section of the structure that is being used as a base. There is a 'clearing' in the pipes only about 50 metres from where I heard the voice. I could have walked right into the middle of it!! I've taken a few distant observation positions and have been able to see only one single Human-shaped form. I think they have something they can carry that could be the sort of length of a rifle. With all the pipes in the way, my view of the person is massively obscured in every direction. I have also climbed to points above the void area, which is about 80 metres in length vertically. I have listened for vocal noises but have not heard the individual speak, hum or sing since. The only talking I have heard is the one time they reported in. I feel sure it is an avatar in Human form and not an alien, 15 did say that the avatars that were in operation before the attack could now be under the command of the unknown invasion force. I know that on occasion, I had hundreds of avatars in my habitat. I'm really hoping I don't have to kill that many of them, as well as a shitload of aliens.

There seems to be a chair or box in the cleared section, I'm not really sure avatars even need a chair as I think they can work indefinitely. They certainly don't need sleep, or to eat, or shit but then neither do I.

I've backtracked a bit to a safer area of the structure because I want to run through my options;

1. I can take this mutha out.
   Sounds great, but there is personal risk involved. I have no weapon, they do. I have the element of surprise, they don't. They do have a communication method. They may be able to raise the alarm before I neutralise them. They certainly 'check-in' from time to time and sooner or later will be missed. If I manage to take them out, I get a weapon. It might be a shit weapon. This might not necessarily be a good thing.

2. I could stealthily skirt around them and continue on without their knowledge.
   Yes, I could. Might be a hundred years before I find another avatar. Might run into another straight away and be wishing I had a weapon. I will have at least one avatar behind me. Not sure I like having my back exposed. I might have missed 50 other avatars hiding in holes in the structure. Just because I've found this one doesn't mean there aren't shitloads already at my back. Where am I going? Wouldn't it be better to see if there is any information I can glean about troops sizes and movements, weapons and plans. Finally, what's in the box if anything?

I thought long and hard, and came up with the same conclusion I always do. 'Fuck it, it's either you or them. So fuck 'em up.' Sounds a bit stupid, I know, but what's the point of pussyfooting around? Sure, I don't want to bring down a whole army, and that's something I really need to guard against. But I can't be arsed with pissing about in the shadows for too long.

I slept for a while, hard to know how long, maybe an hour.

When I woke up, I was ready.

My only weapon is surprise. I can't see how I can climb out of a load of tubes quickly enough into the space without the avatar not seeing me coming. My only hope is to get above them and drop-in, much more my style anyway.

I climb up and sneak around to a position which is about 20 metres up - quite a long way to drop in on someone! I searched around and found a spot which allowed me to slide out of a hole between pipes as quickly as possible. I really wanted to be able to 'swing down' but just couldn't find the right place. From 20 metres up, a fall directly onto the ground could result in a bone break or worse. I've got to try to use the avatar to cushion my fall. Judging the fall will be awkward as I'm going down in a similar way to when I climbed out of the hole from the black space. Feet first, backwards on my tummy.

My only real problem is that there's no sign of the avatar. I've got as close as I've ever been to its position, and for the first time would be able to correctly see what it looks like and what equipment and weapons they have with them, but it's not here. They're doing their guard duties. Which means I'm the closest I've ever been to their spot and they could rock up behind me or above me, or any direction around me at any time. Or he/she could have a bead on me with that rifle now. And then I'm fucked. I sit, in a very uncomfortable position, for what is probably an hour but feels like six. Then, thank fuck, I hear some movement below me. In fact, directly below me, I start to see a figure emerge from the pipes into the clearing.

I just go. Why wait? What's the point of fucking about, the avatar's off balance, trying to climb out of a jungle of pipes and tubes, with no reason in the galaxy to believe they're about to be attacked from the heavens, so I just jump on them.

Except I miss, sort of. I sort of brush past the person pretty roughly which startles them. I realise it's a woman about 5'7" in height. I land in a crouch facing her, just catching her thighs and feet on the way down (Which is enough to slow my fall), with bent knees right in front of her just as she emerges. Shocked, she stands to reach her full height. I do too, simultaneously. I recognise her instantly and although it's been thousands of Earth years since the incident happened, and, even then, it was a fleeting incident, I see the woman I had casual, unprotected sex with in the toilets of a bar in Soho. Well an avatar who looks like her anyway. I'm pretty surprised by this revelation but even so, before she can smile, scream, shoot me or surrender. I punch her as hard as I possibly can straight in the face. I can literally feel the bones in the bridge of her nose and eye socket break, crunch and collapse under the force of the brutal punch. She goes down like a sack of spuds, and I'm on her in a flash with my hands around her neck, throttling her. I keep doing this with all the strength I can muster until she's not just dead - but double dead. I keep the pressure on her throat for at least an extra minute past the last time I see any sign of life from her. She has to be dead and properly dead. She is. Besides the sound of her nasal cavity collapsing, the attack has been pretty noiseless.

Then, as I'm getting my breath back, I just keep looking at her. Why her? Why here? Why now? She wasn't even anyone I'd asked 15 for as an avatar. I hadn't really thought of her since I left Earth. So why her and why now? Does this mean the aliens know I'm coming and are using faces from my past to confuse me, slow me or stop me? How have they got access to the memory of a long-forgotten figure from my past? Are there just a bunch of unused avatars that 15 had in reserve, if so, how many of them are there?

I looked at her and pondered for a good while. Finally, I decided that speculating and postulating this conundrum would not actually provide me with a solution. The answer would probably become more apparent as I pressed on. I started to check her over for any clues, or anything else I could use. The rifle, very disappointingly, isn't a rifle. It's a hurl. What the fuck's an avatar of a woman I met for a messy 10 minutes, thousands of years previously, in a central London bar's toilet, doing on a spaceship millions of miles away from Earth with a hurl? A stick used for playing Hurling, one of Ireland's national games. I'm going back to my previous thought about this whole thing. I'm not on a spaceship, I'm on a planet somewhere, could even be Earth, where I'm on a shitty game show where I have to fight for a jumped-up super-computer. However else would you get to the bit about the hurl and some long-forgotten dirty moment? This is too fucking mental. I pick up the hurl and swing it around a bit. It actually feels excellent in hand, it's shaft thickens from the top 'handle' end to the toe with the large, flat, almost oval face. It's quite thin as well. I swing it two-handed over my head. It has an axe-like quality and feels like there's some flex through the shaft when I roundhouse it, the weight is all in the hitting surfaces, the two flat sides, at the bottom but it's not too heavy, and it's easy to keep my balance while swinging.

Although lighter and probably not as durable, I think it's better than a baseball bat, it's a more considered weapon with more opportunity for variation, either hitting with the flat faces or using the heel to chop. The more I think about it, and play with it in my hands, the happier I am with it. I've checked the avatar's clothing, there's nothing of any use hidden and nothing I could wear. I'm not into spray-on black PVC trousers, but I'd have worn them if they fitted me. Also, her short black boots and cream leather biker jacket are too small. I'm going to have to stick to the cotton, flappy scrubs and bare feet for now.

There's not much here really, but she does have a small in-ear communication device which I take and insert in my ear. It doesn't fit very well as each, I suspect, is individually shaped to the person/thing's ear it has been made for. It's in, then it falls out, in then out. I can't hear any 'chatter' anyway, they must have radio silence at the moment. I do have a small open breast pocket in the top of my scrubs, so I stick it in there for now. Apart from that, all of her pockets are empty, which is a bit of a bummer. I try to think if there is any reason I would want to keep her clothes, is there anything they could come in handy for? I can't think of anything and don't want to carry a load of useless crap around, so I just leave her. The box in the corner bears a little more fruit. There is what looks like an ice hook, a foot long, pointed metal hook, shaped like a 'J', with a straight wooden handle at the end at 90 degrees to the hook itself. I suspect this is quite useful for hauling yourself around the pipes. You can hook it around a pipe to swing beneath it or hook it to climb or pull yourself along in a tight spot.

I've moved pretty quickly away from the dead avatar. I'm still inside the considerable mass of pipes, and I'm still crawling around like a slug to get from place to place. I've moved off from the 'toilet girl' at about a 45-degree angle both to the right and down, I travelled this direction for what felt like at least half an Earth day. I've now levelled out, and I'm traversing around the middle height of the right-hand side heading down the length of the structure from where I started. The two hand items I now possess are both a blessing and a curse. The ice hook is fabulous and really could speed up my movement if it wasn't for the hurl holding me back. To start with, it takes up a hand, secondly, although it flexes, it doesn't bend around pipes like a Human with joints can. I often have to stop and reposition it before moving through from one tight space to another, but I do want to keep it because I want an offensive weapon and as I have had so few options so far, I'd be daft to discard it. The pressure to leave the scene of the crime as quickly as possible is a pressure I've put on myself. Although I want to move fast, I think the hurl is staying. I'm also trying to work out what might happen when the invaders find the fucked up alien and when? She might never be discovered. So no problem there, just press on. I didn't bother to hide the body - potential error on my behalf. They may have turned up to check her observation spot and, finding it empty, concluded that she malfunctioned somewhere (which I've never seen an avatar do). There may be a signal tracker in every avatar which means her corpse would be found wherever I dumped it, so I saved myself the bother of hiding the body. When they eventually do find her, it will be easy to see she's been killed by someone and her weapons removed. I left a pretty messy scene, and there are plenty of clues. They might have been tracking my movement from day one and are watching me now and waiting, expectantly but fully prepared for me to slowly come to them. Or I could be heading in the wrong direction totally.

I ask myself all these questions around and around in circles. When you're isolated for so long, and there is little to stimulate the mind other than swinging and sliding around this never-ending jungle of pipes, your mind starts to play tricks. It questions, sees and hears things that aren't there, questions your ability, builds things up more prominently than they really are, and makes you paranoid. I know this is what's happening to me. I'm trying to keep my cool, to get my mind onto other things. I sing crappy pop songs, trying to remember not to sing out loud and give my position away. To think about the past, about my life on Earth and life on 15.

It's interesting, moving about inside the structure. There are pipes, shit loads of them in all directions. There are no levers, no junctions, no dials, no valves - nothing but pipes and the odd gap. Many are large enough for me to navigate through, and then occasionally a big void, similar to where I found the last avatar. But moving around is less on the feet and more on the ribs, sides and bottom, my weight is often moved on to my forearms, and I usually have to move 'up and across' or 'down and over' to move forward. I try to move forwards until the gap is too small or runs out, then I have to find a new space, by swinging up, or across and sometimes backwards before I find another path/gap forward. It's slow, laborious work and I only occasionally climb right to the top of the mass or to the side to take a bearing on where I am. I've been here for weeks, and besides killing one avatar, it's been pretty dull and hard physical work. I haven't been over to the left side of the structure for about an Earth week and have decided to go over there tomorrow to see if there is anything to see.

Chapter 12

It's taken at least a whole Earth day to get across from where I was on the right-hand side to the outer edge of the left-hand side. I really strongly considered climbing to the highest point of the structure, popping out and then walking across the top, in the open air, to get here more quickly.

I'm really fucking glad I didn't, I'd probably be dead by now. Considering I haven't heard or seen a single thing outside of one dead avatar in about six weeks, shit loads is happening on the left-hand side! For a start, I've actually gone past a series of doors on the left-hand wall. They're much smaller than the one I entered by and are all on ground level with no drops in or out. I reckon I've passed 7 doors which are all well-spaced out going backwards at the bottom of the wall but although they look small from here, and in the context of the size of this bit of 15, you could probably get a military transport plane through each of them. The doors look a darker pale grey than the usual grey white but look terribly dull against the vibrantly coloured walls.

There are also three avatars on the ground with a vehicle about a quarter of a mile away from my position. I'm pretty sure they can't see me, but I've tucked in as the blue of the scrubs would stand out a mile in the white of the pipes. As I get closer, from my hidden position, I can see that they're all armed with what looks like antique British army WWII Sten guns. I could be wrong, but I know this weapon pretty well as they used to be one of my favourite weapons to shoot off in the firing range. They only hold 32 bullets in the magazine which you can empty pretty quickly. I also know they were generally known to be pretty prone to misfiring and relatively inaccurate - but if they've been made by 15, then they'll be perfect. If they're looking for me, surely they'd have more and better equipment? If I were looking for me, I'd have heat-seeking cameras out, tracker dogs and high powered hunting rifles to take me out at a distance, not street fighting 'room clearing' machine guns. Then there's the vehicle they seem to have used to get here, an old blue Bedford van, like the one my dad used to have back in the 1970s, the same colour as well. Three seats in the front, empty panel van in the back. I'm hoping they're using this because they're trying to be retro-cool, not because they've got some angry, flesh-eating, chrome, robot monkey in the back that they're going to deploy to sniff me out and chew me up. I'm also hoping they've got other weaponry and equipment I can use. If I choose to tackle them...

It's been two days or so, and they're still there. I'm not sure if they're waiting for someone or if they're just guarding the doors. As per usual, I have the element of surprise, plus my inferior weapons. I could choose to ignore them and push on further along the pipe structure, but to what end? I also have to think further about other issues which may arise from taking these three out. There may be other avatars watching them from the structure or from inside the doors ready to pop out if needed. They may all be wearing trackers. The likelihood of taking all three out silently, without the cover of darkness, is pretty slim. Sneaking past them to the door is pretty unlikely also. I'd be out in the open with no shelter in blue scrubs. I might as well just paint a bullseye on me. The problem is, I quite like the idea of seeing what's through these doors.

The Bedford is parked a few hundred metres from the edge of the structure. From time to time, the avatars split up and walk around, one to the structure and one to the door. The van is about equidistant from the structure to the door. When two go on walkabout, the other stays by the van.

I work out a bit of a plan and then move closer. It's high risk and could end very badly, but my options are limited, and ultimately I'm doing this to save 15, so I'm going to have to break a few eggs. I've worked my way down to the bottom of the structure and think I've found myself a pretty good hide. I'm just tucked in about ten feet from the edge and about eight feet up from the floor, and I'm waiting. For the first time, I get to see the faces of the three avatars who I now know are 'human' males. I recognise them all from my office; there's Alan who works in accounts. Paul, a young graduate trainee who I used to play five-a-side football with and Neil, I fucking hate Neil, he's an IT project leader, but he thinks he's god's gift to women and walks around being a prick all day long. He's one of those types who are shit at their job but manage to bullshit their way to promotions and no-one can understand how they do it. Once again, these avatars are people I've met or know. Why are they here?

I'm looking forward to hopefully killing Neil even though I know it's not him. Just a 'thing' that looks exactly like him.

I wait, hidden from view on the edge of the structure for what seems an age. The three men spend quite a lot of time chatting idly together by the van. I'm surprised by this as I wouldn't expect avatars to have too much in the way of conversation. I don't care what they're saying, and how much they're enjoying talking about watching TV soaps or cracking dirty jokes, or whatever it is that avatars discuss when on guard duty. Eventually, and it is eventually, they break up, and two of them walk in separate directions. Paul walks towards me, Neil walks away from me and towards the huge doors, and Alan remains at the Bedford van. Although they seem to walk at a similar speed and have similar pacing, Neil gets to the door and therefore the sidewall of the room/hold before Paul gets to me; therefore I can surmise that the distance to the wall from the van is shorter than from the van to the structure. Once Paul reaches the structure, he walks alongside for a good distance walking away from me towards the area I have not been too. Which means not the direction I have come from but the direction I have been heading in. Alan, meanwhile, takes a few strolls around the van. The van is parked at an angle. I can see the front of the van and the right-hand side - the driver's side - only. Alan seems to stop circling on the opposite side of the van to me. Neil's not fully in my field of vision, he's partially obscured, over by the doors, behind the van. Paul has turned and is heading back in my direction. He doesn't seem to be doing anything, not looking at the structure, not listening, just meandering. I suggest they do not know I exist, or they've been on guard duty for a very long time because they seem a bit blasé about the whole situation. Paul comes closer, and closer, I can hear him whistling, which again feels like a very un-avatar thing to do. I'm worried he'll turn again and head back where he came from before he gets to me. I move into my chosen position and bring the ice hook a little closer to the edge. I grip the handle firmly. I'm ready. I check that I'm still out of view of the other avatars and I am. I need to be quiet and to stay on top of the situation. Paul is now below me. I swing the hand holding the hook down, and with force.

The hook penetrates his skin just below his chin and cuts into the little 'V' at the base of the throat just above the top to the rib cage and dead centre. A perfect shot. A lucky shot. The weight of the swing allows the hook to dig deep and I start to lift Paul off his feet. The added load drags the hook up through the throat and neck opening the whole lot up. There is no scream; there can't be, there is a horrible gurgling sound where blood is seeping down the windpipe and entering the lungs. Paul's body is trying to expel the blood by pushing air out. He expels a fine mist of blood droplets. I'm not sure if he died of drowning on his blood, loss of blood or something else but he's dead pretty quickly and quietly. I climb down as fast as I can still holding the hook so as not to drop the body and cause noise. I take the Sten gun from him and quickly check it over. It looks clean and ready to go but not cocked. I check the magazine by ejecting and re-inserting. I cock the gun to ensure there is one in the breach. I throw the strap over my head, so it rests on my left shoulder, the gun is below my right arm. I pick up the hurl and run as fast as I can across to the Bedford van. The hurl is in my left hand so I can use the gun if I need to, but I am aiming to be as quiet as possible. Bullets make noise; noise gives me a problem. Although I'm sprinting to the van, I'm shoeless still, so I'm not making too much noise. I am conscious of my feet slapping the floor, so have already thought that I need to run heel to toe, to stay stealthy. I near the van and swap the hurl into my right hand just holding the very end. I start to see Alan through the passenger side window. He has his back to both me and the van. I come around the van and start to spin. He doesn't see me coming until it's way too late. It's a split second before the heel of the hurl comes around and impacts on the left side of Alan's head about as hard as I can hit him with about the hardest part of the hurl. I'm not sure if the noise I hear is from the impact of the stick or his skull cracking. Either way, the noise of a cranium being bent out of shape is not a pleasant sound, and Alan is no longer a threat. I haven't broken my stride. It's poetry in very violent motion. I sprinted up, put in one full spin, and continued in the same beautiful, flowing motion. Just a very dead avatar to show for it on the way. I've let go of the hurl; it's probably still embedded in Alan's head, I think it may have cracked in the middle of its shaft. I reach for the gun slung under my arm.

There's still distance between Neil and myself, but fortunately, he's also walking away from the van. I know from my own experience that the unmodified Sten gun is only accurate up to about 100 metres. I'm now not much further than this distance from Neil and closing fast. Now, I'm probably 70 metres away when he hears enough to turn around. I see a look of surprised horror and him reaching for his gun as he does so. I loosen off a three-shot volley - 'RAT-AT-AT'. He's hit in the torso with at least two bullets and goes down into a crouch on one knee, still holding his gun but severely wounded. I'm on him and kick him in the face, his head, and then his whole body arch backwards and over, and he hits the ground. He's not in any state to shoot. I kick the gun away from his hand and kneel on his chest. I place my right hand around his throat.

I look down and see a hunting knife in his belt. I reach out with my left hand and slide the blade across his neck just above my right hand. Blood jets out from his cartoid veins and artery, it sprays all over my head, it's in my eyes, up my nose, in my hair and left ear, the top of my scrubs get a coating also. It's horrendous. I jump away from the lifeless cadaver. I'm disgusted with the blood, it's sticky, and I can taste and smell the iron content. As much as I'm appalled, I'm also conscious of time. I must assume that the shots have been heard and that I must get on my toes sharpish.

I sprint back to the van while ripping off my top. As I run, I wipe as much blood from my face and hair using the cotton cloth like a towel then I throw it away just before I reach the lifeless body of Alan. Although I've caved in his head, he's wearing a leather jacket so there's little blood on the shirt he's wearing underneath. I quickly and carefully strip off the jacket and unbutton the shirt and remove it. I put it on, a long-sleeved beige, dark brown and cream vertically striped shirt, different thicknesses of stripe, the sort of thing your dad wore under his suit to go to the pub on a Saturday night back in 1979 - swilling Double Diamond bitter while playing darts and smoking shit loads of fags. Ugly, but I'm wearing it. I check his pockets and find two fully loaded Sten gun magazines, 32 bullets in each; I take his belt. I check the back of the van and then the front. Nothing worth picking up, I thought about firing up the van and taking it with me, but I decide it's too easy to spot and might not be that practical either. I run back to Neil, who has now stopped spraying blood, I take his belt from his trousers. He has a full magazine in his Sten which I eject, so I now have three spares, he hadn't time to cock his gun, so the magazine is also full with 32 bullets. I pick up the hunting knife and give it a quick wipe on Neil's clothes to get as much of his blood off it as possible. I gather everything up and make a beeline for the huge dark doors.

Chapter 13

THE FIRST 'DOOR' IS a pair of doors that meet in the middle; together, they are about 30 metres wide and as high as four of me, so somewhere around seven or eight metres. The other doors run off into the distance along the same wall away from me. I reach what I think is the middle meeting point of the double doors and try to push the vast things open. To my surprise, the door on the right moves very smoothly and silently, as I push, I realise it's not hinged at its other end, but that the whole door is moving backwards in one movement with just my little push. The vast door is almost floating back and into the ship. The entrance to the left is showing me that it's not a door that I'd expect to see as it is more like an enormous black block. I keep pushing and walking, and my door keeps moving backwards with very little resistance. I shove on for 20 or so metres and before me, see a vertical strip of white light on the left. It's the back edge of the left-hand block. I keep pushing my block backwards and allow the gap to grow and the light to flood in. After a little more pushing, my block stops moving. It's gone as far as it goes, and has opened up into a corridor, it's about 35 metres tall and wide and runs back into the ship now adjacent to the block I have just finished pushing, the floor though is angled down, a gentle slope, it is the first angle I've seen that is not 90 degrees for a long time.

I start to run down the corridor; the downward gradient allows me to pick up pace as I do so. I have to be careful to check my momentum, and I don't want to overrun into a situation I can't escape. Eventually, I can see a slight change in the colouration of the grey whiteness to the left in the distance, probably only 100 to 150 metres away. I don't see it until quite late as it's not easy to pick out the slight variation in colour against the background.

I slow and stop as I get close and flatten my back against the wall, I'm breathing heavily and have a light sweat on from my exertions. It feels good to give my limbs and lungs a proper workout. I sidle sideways to the wall edge and listen. As usual - soundless. I move back away and turn 90 degrees to face the edge. I crane around from the sidewall to see into the next space from a deeper angle making me less easy to spot. I can see shapes, mainly grey white cubes and rectangles but other forms too, all piled up - boxes on boxes. All sizes, from the largest, at about 10 metres square to the smallest, being the size of a building brick.

I look further out and see more and more. I think the objects are the ones 15 placed in the Arena when there was a fight with throwing weapons; the shapes created hides, cover and vantage points. I slowly reveal more and more of this by continuing to move around and putting myself in the open. I'm now visible, a target, but if there are snipers hidden up high in the blocks, then I'm dead anyway. Nothing happens as I hold my position. When I feel safer, I put my head around the corner and look along both edge walls, left and right. No movement, no sign of anyone. I decide to make a break for the blocks, to hole up for a while, to see if anything happens. I pick my moment and run forwards into the blocks. I manage to use some smaller and medium-sized blocks as an improvised stairway and get some height, then I find a bit of cover and sit down to take stock of my situation.

For the first time since my run-in with my three ex-work colleagues, I finally have a chance for a breather and to take stock of myself. I'm well-hidden where I'm perched, but that doesn't mean I can't be found. I only really need a bit of time to hole up. To try to work out my next move.

The shirt I'm wearing is a bit crappy, but it's better than the blood-covered scrubs top I had on before. I'm now a yellowy/brown top and light blue bottom target. So no worse off. There is some blood from killing Neil on my trousers, but it's not too much and starting to dry. I'll cope.

I have the operational Sten gun, three extra full magazines, two leather trouser belts and a hunting knife. Not bad.

For the first time in a long time, I'm sitting down in some form of comfort with my back supported against a vertical surface. It feels terrific to be hidden in this position. I close my eyes for a few moments, and although I don't feel tired, I slip away.

Chapter 14

THE CREATURE I REMEMBER as I drift off, is walking towards the light spot in front of me and would block out the sun – if there were one.

Its bigger and wider than a Human, built like a brick shithouse. The body shape is like an upturned triangle. Incredibly broad shoulders tapering down to an almost impossibly narrow waist. It has long, solid arms but even so, with his immense musculature, I hope it doesn't shit out of its arse. I'm not sure it, carrying this bulk, would be able to reach around to wipe! The head perches on the shoulders with little or no neck; then, similar features to us; small mouth - rarely opened, a single flat, broad nose. and two eyes. But the eyes are spread farther apart than ours. It has white eyeballs and a coloured iris, in this case, battleship grey, but no discernible pupil.

The legs are also rugged-looking, although they do not have the same build as the upper part of the body certainly do not look weak, if anything more 'athletic'.

I know quite a bit about these guys.

They're from a forest planet, not like one we'd recognise because the 'forests' are not like any trees we'd know. The people farm and harvest a form of iron and carbon alloy which grows naturally from the ground, these 'trees', like ours, come in many different shapes and forms. The iron and carbon in the tree's trunks have a sponge-like cell structure. Some trees have larger cells which are therefore less rigid but may have higher carbon content to make them stronger. Some trees have densely packed cells which makes them very hard but weighty. There are flexible, dense, hard, soft varieties - very similar to the differing woods from our trees, but made of iron and carbon. The trees grow naturally and are also industrially farmed; they have an abundance of uses and can be cut and shaped into many forms. The 'trees' are a fabulous building material and highly prized throughout the galaxy. The planet is 'Naiad', and the people are 'Naiadoms'. This particular one is called Fenchid Durat, but is more well known as Fenc.

The Naiadoms are civilised people who enjoy music, art, theatre, comedy and music much as we do. They have amassed great wealth from their careful harvest and sale of their 'trees' but like on Earth, some people have much, and some have way less. Fenc is a celebrity on Naiad. He was a successful athlete for many years, so was in the military; all athletes have to be in the armed forces to be able to train and compete. But now retired from athletics, Fenc broadcasts his own national fitness and combat channel, which is wildly popular. There is no television as we know it. The Naiads have a developed 'Link-System' a diode implanted in the brain cortex. The diode is connected – 'linked' to the ear and optic nerve. Naiads can, therefore 'see' images in their field of vision beamed directly to their link, and hear directly into their ear canal. Fenc is live on his feed all through each day; he comments on everything - news, business, politics, entertainment - everything. Millions have him tuned day and night, he's hugely popular, well-loved and a hero to millions.

The Naiads have been in dispute with a race called The B'lattle for years. They are a people from a neighbouring galaxy and they both envy, and covet, the Naiad's raw material. For a long time, the Naiad traded 'wood' with B'lattle, but more recently, the old B'lattle emperor ZinZin died, and his progeny Uraz succeeded him. The new emperor had conquest on his mind and quickly and easily expanded his territory by taking over a few weaker planets, and peoples, in his local system. Now, as a much larger planetary group, the B'lattle required more raw material - 'wood' - that it wanted to pay for. The Naiad could not increase demand, because they understood their planet's delicate ecosystem and how it needed to be balanced for their raw material to grow. They also managed their harvest. To increase production to satisfy the B'lattle would overburden the planet and cause great damage. Uraz was unperturbed. If he can't buy the commodity, then he's going to take it - so he just declared war, cause that's the kind of cat he is. He wants to take Naiad and turn it into a factory planet, with little thought for the Naiadoms, or the impact on their homeworld.

15 wants me to put up a good show but is firmly on the side of the Naiads and to be fair, even though I know it's going to cost me a beating, which will hurt my pride, and hurt me physically, I'm on their side too.

I'm holding a chain, with big chunky links, it's got some weight to it and is about a metre long in full, it's mainly used doubled up though, folded if you like, which gives it more heft when swinging. I've been practising with some avatars and know that a hit can cause a substantial flesh wound. We, two combatants, are only wearing a traditional 'Somoth', which is a type of leather shorts with extra flaps over the top, which make it more like a *skort* - skirt-shorts. As I think a skirt is not a thing for me, I've been calling it a kilt, makes me feel marginally better about myself.

Using the chain as a weapon presents lots of targets with opportunities to cause lots of nasty flesh wounds. There is no shield, good proponents of the art can grab the loop in their chain in their other hand and hold the chain taut across to block slashes from their opponent. But you've got to be pretty quick to be able to get this sort of defence both active and effective as slashes are lightning quick.

Another offensive tactic is to hold one end of the chain while whipping the other end at the feet of the opponent and pulling. This can upend, or cause an opponent to lose their footing. Or, finally, and it's a risk, you can throw the chain at the legs, again in an attempt to trip but sometimes, if skilfully, or fortuitously executed, one can tie-up the opponent's legs. Then lay into them on the ground, with your feet and fists. But if this fails, you're left weapon-less. This is not the end of the world in this type of fighting; on many occasions, both combatants will end up brawling it out after both throwing weapons away.

Apart from being unlucky and receiving a ferocious blow around the head/face, this type of fight is rarely fatal. The weapon is too blunt an instrument. Usually, being beaten into submission is enough to win. This, though, has not been agreed as a potential outcome. I can be killed in this fight.

Fenc lets a long, deep snort, out of its nose. I realise that the flat nose has only one wide nostril, the exhalation of air allows this to vibrate and produce this odd, low noise. I think it's the equivalent to a snarl and is supposed to strike fear. To me, it sounds like the sort of noise a horny hippo might make as he gets ready for his night out down the disco looking for other horny female hippos under the glitterball with a few cider and blacks down them. Not very attractive and not particularly scary but he can snort all he likes.

Then he starts to clank the chain up and down, making the links loose then tight. It produces this dull metallic rattle which again, is designed to scare the opponent but I'm just thinking of a re-animated ghost of Jacob Marley from Dickens 'A Christmas Carol', I love these shows of bravado. What might scare the living shit out of another of the same species can just look ridiculous to someone like me. Hardly left me quaking in my boots with runny brown stuff in my pants.

The 'Bong' sounds and we're ready to rock. There are a few minutes of the usual circling each other both clockwise and counter-clockwise and as you could expect, a few cursory swings of the chain thrown in for good measure, but there certainly isn't anything you'd describe as an attack. Then I get a bit brave and make a move. I try a 'punch'. I did this by throwing out my right hand (the one holding the chain), in the same way as I would throw a straight right. As my fist extended to the furthest point of its reach, I let go of one end of the chain allowing this section to keep extending in a straight line following the momentum of the punch. A great idea, I thought, something he won't be expecting. Although I don't think this move will cause any significant damage, I do hope it to allow me a small amount of time to step into his space and deliver a couple of meaningful blows, be them kicks, punches, knees, elbows or headbutts.

All of the following events happen in the blink of an eye. I execute as planned, the chain is released and is extending away towards Fenc's head. He's late in seeing it coming, and I see the sudden startled look in his eyes. I'm already stepping in to follow the chain looking first for a good solid kick in his nether regions (or that area as it seems pretty sacred to almost all bipeds). He closes his eyes and allows the chain to hit home on his face without moving a muscle absorbing the punch. At the same time, he is swinging his chain around, and it impacts devastatingly, straight across my jaw. My kick never meets its target as I stagger away to my right, dazed and in complete and utter agony, but still on my feet. He, strangely, doesn't follow up. He stands and waits, almost admiring his work (I find out later that he's showboating to the millions back home watching on his Link-System, his visual feed beaming images back home). I stagger for a few steps hoping my head will clear. I spit blood and saliva two or three times; there's broken enamel, as well as some bits of ripped gum and cheek tissue amongst the spittle. It's a horrendous injury. I'm pretty sure my jaw bone is smashed. I'm struggling to move my mouth. I put my left hand up to the left of my face, and there's just an open wound bleeding profusely, most of my cheek is ripped away, and my inner mouth is exposed, I attempt to clench my teeth but can't. I can feel several broken teeth with my tongue. I also touch a couple of exposed nerves, which send instantaneous pulses of electric shock down my spine, out through the top of my head and down to the backs of my heels. I'm dizzy from the pain but returning to compos mentis. I know I need to protect myself from further similar injury and death. If he strides over and wraps his chain around my head with the same sort of force, then I'm gone. No question.

I try to clear my brain and push the pain back down. It's tough because it's excruciating, but my adrenaline is coursing, and it's surprising how much it can help - inbuilt Human chem weapons - I can still feel it, but the adrenalin rush helps mask the pain. Fenc's stopped showboating and decided to finish the job off - probably needed to break for his sponsors - and now it's back to the action.

I see him coming; he broadcasts his move, a huge up-and-under haymaker. As I'm almost bent double, if this contacts, it will send me reeling over to land flat on my back. If I'm not dead by the time I hit the ground, he can decide how to finish me off while I'm in a pretty incapacitated state. As he swings the chain back under and behind him, I drop and leg-sweep him Karate style and take him down. He's on his back, and I jump on his very wide torso and throw the chain across his neck and start to apply pressure. I've made a bit of a mistake. In my terrible pain, I've forgotten his lack of neck. The chain is not doing anything, other than pinning his head down. This fella's very strong. I'm feeling rather weak, dripping blood and saliva down onto him from the gaping hole in my face. I get a cursory crack around the back of the head from his chain that he's managed to swing from flicking his wrist. I quickly realise I'm not doing any massive damage (although his pride is probably hurt), so I punch him twice in the face before he manages to buck me off him. I jump up and slash at him as he's on the floor backing away on his hands and feet. I hit him twice with the folded chain across the back, the second one cuts his skin, and he starts to bleed. He gets away from me and gets up to his feet again.

He's hurt but not enough yet. He starts snorting again as we face each other. Then he charges, like a bull, head down, not worrying about his chain. I bullfight, when he gets close, I side-step, a bullfighters dodge, but instead of following through with my bullfighter's cloak, I smash the doubled chain across the top of his head. He staggers for two more spaces and drops to the ground. I see red welts starting to darken with blood across the top of his skull, lumps of hair and scalp ripped away, it's a gruesome wound. I run over and grab him from behind as he starts to get up. I reach my hand over his shoulder to his face, and as I hold his face my third and fourth fingers, fortuitously go up his nose, I curl them around and start to swing Fenc in a circle around me by his skin flap nose. He's screaming in pain, but I don't let go, I manage to swing him about 180 degrees, but the momentum eventually rips the skin flap away from his face, and my fingers, and he's sent into a heap a few metres away. He looks up at me, and he looks fucked. His face is a real mess; I'm not sure too many little ones from his planet are going to be sticking pictures of him on their bedroom walls any more. His nose is bloody and looks painful. He manages to get to his feet and attempts one of his' battle snorts', it sounds more like a whoopee cushion, a wet fart, the loose flap wobbles at best. The wound across the top of his head now looks very sore. Can't be worse than what he's done to me though. I'm hardly the picture of health. I'm on my feet and still have my wits about me, but the pain is desperate. I move towards him, gingerly. He's breathing hard and looks angry, but so am I.

This time, when we engage, I feint right with the chain and fire a kick into his midriff with my left foot, he staggers backwards. I then spin, as if performing a 360 turning kick but instead of leading with the leg, it's the chain that's whipping, gathering speed and momentum. I catch him around the side of the torso, under his right arm. It's a massive attack; if I'd connected with his head, it might have been good night. Again, the chain has cut into, and ripped big chunks of flesh, from his chest. It starts to bleed instantly, and I think I can see the yellowy-white of two bones of his rib cage exposed to the air. Once again he's staggering, the blood from this wound quickly pools on the grey whiteness of the Arena floor - crimson on clean white, I've similarly seen my blood many times. I slash, again and again, not connecting with any particular power and causing no particular damage.

Then, as I step in again, he springs his trap and throws his chain at my feet. He knows what he's doing; he's probably done this a thousand times, this is a weapon he's used all his life. Maybe he's just been waiting for his moment; it's expertly delivered. The chain wraps around my feet quickly and tightly, and I trip over immediately. He's over me straight away and starts to fire kicks to my body. He kicks the living shit out of my ribs. To be fair, I can understand his grievance - I've fucked him up too. Kick after kick, each harder and delivered 'with feeling'. I don't think I have a rib left to smash after about 20 kicks; my chest is broken, pummelled. Then for good measure, he starts to kick me in the head. Of course, he does this properly. He comes around my prostate body to kick directly into my ripped open cheek wound. I feel my already shattered teeth splinter further, my broken, swollen jaw takes more punishment, my skull too. It's not too many more 'kicks to the head long' before I pass out. I'm sure Fenc's soaking up the adulation of the crowd watching at home. The brutally embattled, bloodied and damaged hero of the people.

Good luck to him, and the Naiads. I hope their war with the B'lattle is nowhere near as bloody and brutal as the contest we endured.

Chapter 15

I DON'T KNOW HOW LONG I've been asleep. Hour, maybe a couple of hours, can't be any longer. I wake feeling pretty fresh. I don't move for a good while after I open my eyes I've been thinking back about what 15 said to me just before I died.

Died as in 'I'm allowed to die, we've agreed'. When 15 resurrected me against my will, I was forced to remember some stuff that I'd buried deep down and tried to forget. Of course, you can never really actually forget some of what happened in my early life, my life on Earth. It stays with you forever. I remembered, but I didn't want to. It made me feel sick to remember what I'd done. Yes, I did kill five women back before I met Emily, my wife. Yes, they were unarmed and vulnerable. Yes, I was a monster, a bully, a freak. It was a despicable thing to do. I was an unhinged demon. I did, what I did, then went home, went to bed, half expecting for the police to knock the door in the middle of the night. The knock never came. Each day, I would get up, get ready and go to work. As if nothing had happened. I don't know why I did what I did. I have absolutely no explanation. I killed the first one and felt no different. I did not get sexual pleasure from it. I did not feel I was asserting my power over women. I did not feel any particular remorse. I was able to get up and carry on with my life without any outward difference. Not much inward difference either. It's a long time back now, and some of the details are less clear to me. It was before the total proliferation of London's streets with CCTV cameras. If I'd tried to do what I did even a decade later, I'd have been nailed straight off. I didn't plan anything; I was anything but systematic. I left very few clues because I worked quickly, and exited. I didn't leave too much of a mark on the scene. I didn't get much blood on me. I remember having some on me one night and then telling a taxi driver that I'd had a nose bleed. It happens. He seemed to accept my story and nothing further came of the incident. I just think there were always unsavoury things were going on in that area of London and most of my murders were quite different. I didn't have a pattern. It was after I'd stopped killing that the whole 'Soho Slasher' thing started to pick up traction. But I'd started going out with Emily by that time and knew I'd never hurt her. I didn't ever do anything to any of my girlfriends. I think this also helped. I was questioned once by the police, after I killed Sophie and her friend in the alley, easily my most audacious and challenging murder. Two at once is a challenge. How do you subdue both at the same time? How do you stop them raising the alarm or overpowering you? The way I did it was to choke both of them together. I followed them out of the bar, and as they walked away together, I went between them and put an arm around each of their shoulders, Sophie's left shoulder to the left and Kelly's right shoulder to the right. Then, as we passed an alley, I grabbed each of their throats and started to choke them as I pulled them into the lane. Sophie tried to spin away, so I took them both to the ground. Kelly was face down and had no chance of fighting me off as I was sort of on top of her. Sophie buckled at the knees; her eyes were popping out. She tried to hit me but just wasn't strong enough. I just squeezed their tracheas. It wasn't long before they both became subdued. I'm not sure if they were dead at that point or not. Then I took a steak knife I'd taken from the restaurant, out of my pocket and slit each throat quickly.

As they were both face down, their blood ran or spurted down onto the pavement and not up. I didn't wait to see if they were dead. I wiped the knife on Kelly's trousers and put it into the waistband of my jeans, at the back, and returned to the bar. I was only gone for five minutes. Everyone just thought I'd gone to the toilet. After half an hour or so, I put the knife onto a table full of dirty dishes. Shortly after, a waiter cleared the table. The murder weapon will have gone through the washing up machine and was probably used by diners for years subsequently. The thing with Soho is that there are busy bits and quiet bits. People are doing shady things, there are drugs, and there are lots of drunks. There are strange sights, and you just go with the flow. Of course, the last thing anyone wanted was a lockdown of the businesses in Soho. There are occasional deaths for all sorts of reasons. It's part of the fabric; life goes on.

No-one from the party knew me; I was a friend of one of their previous work colleagues, now my work colleague. But the police came to our work to talk to him. Then they spoke to me. I told them I'd been at the restaurant and that I'd met Sophie. I'd danced with her twice; her friend wanted to go home, so they both left together. I didn't see her after that. The police accepted that nothing else happened. I was sure they'd work out that I was the killer. I wasn't worried about being arrested - I was sure I would be. But they accepted my story. Witnesses had seen the girls leaving together, but no-one had seen me following them out. People did remember seeing me in the bar getting drunk for a couple of hours after. No-one thought there was anything suspicious about my behaviour, as far as the police were concerned, I had an alibi. There was no murder weapon and little evidence. The police took no further action. I wasn't even a suspect.

Time has passed; a lot of time has passed. I look back at my previous life and know I was terrible. I know I do not deserve any sympathy and should have been punished for my crimes. I murdered those poor girls in the prime of their lives. They would have gone on to have their own families if it had not been for me. They left grieving parents, siblings, extended families and friends. I know that I caused all of that pain and anguish and left lives changed forever, but I did 'cure myself', I did get better. I did stop. And now, centuries later I realise that it is because of my past that I've had a future. I realise that 15 picked Pierre because he killed his wife and children and 15 saw something in his mental make-up that would make him a Champion. I realise that 15 probably didn't initially want me. He wanted Joseph Schneider, the Murdering Mormon. America's worst-ever serial killer, but didn't get to Earth in time, and Joseph was already dead. He, therefore, constructed a means by which to 'get' another target, namely me. I don't know why he didn't take someone from prison, a real ugly, battle-scarred, stone-cold killer - a proper psycho. I can only think that all three of us, Pierre, Joseph and myself were never discovered, never caught and never made to atone for our crimes. We all 'got away with it'. Maybe this appeals to 15.

Time is a funny thing though, especially when you've lived through lots of it. I'm here. The girls are a very long time dead. There is no-one here to judge me - no law to uphold. What I did was wrong, but I've killed many, many more since them, albeit on behalf of 15. This has become my destiny. I kill things for 15 for which I feel no remorse. I do it, and I was happy doing it up to a point. It was never the killing that was the problem. It was the periods in between. I got bored. I did everything until I ran out of things to do. Maybe it was that I wasn't imaginative enough?

This feels different. I'm not really saving 15, for 15. I'm doing it for me. I like the feeling of jeopardy, of being pursued. Of course, my quarry, whoever they may be, may not even know I exist as yet and may never do - so but sooner or later, either they've going to find me, or I'm going to find them.

I did commit crimes, but that was thousands of years ago. I can't go back. I'm here. Now. I can only play the way I'm facing.

Chapter 16

I'M STILL HIDDEN. I'M listening, just listening. I've worked out that when I changed my top for the shirt, I forgot the listening device I took from the first avatar. It may have come in handy later.

I can't hear anything at all and decide to take a peek around the block. I'm always exposed against the grey whiteness, on the ground or upon these blocks - I can't avoid that. I just need to be as careful as I can be. I finally get to peer around, and over the blocks that are in front of me, I can't climb the block to my rear as it is too tall. I slide along on my belly to the right, to the edge of the big block I'm on, it's more like a stage or step, but two metres off the ground. I can't see anything in any direction.

For the first time since I reached this room, and it's relative safety, I've realised I'm lost. I don't know which direction to go. I know where I've been. From the square hole in the floor next to 15, I've walked diagonally from the right corner of the side of the square closest to 15. I then changed direction to bear right once I saw the hole in the wall for the first time. I then reached this new hole.

In the next room, with my fighting pictures on the wall, I went straight on over the pipe structure and then left in through the doors. I then turned left into this room and climbed up the blocks straight ahead of me to where I am now. Where am I going next?

There is no simple answer because I have nothing to go on. I don't know how big this room is; it may not have any doors out. I could end up walking around for years and not finding anything. I decide to go up.

I start to climb.

It's not a mountain, nor a single mass of blocks all piled on top of one another. It is a series of hills and peaks, and my objective is to get to the top of the highest one I can find to establish if there is anything worth checking out further at ground level. The problem is that there are a few smaller heights I'll either need to conquer or skirt around, between me and my target stack. There are also very few features; the stacks are all piles of white blocks. Different in themselves but hardly 'mountain terrain' littered with overhangs, scars, escarpments and crevasses, features to make every mountain or slope unique and different - a different challenge. These are all similar, so it's easy to lose track of direction, there's nothing to anchor to as so little is 'memorable'.

Sometimes there are lots of paths and spaces between blocks, sometimes, there's none and then it's like scrabbling over rocks at a shoreland, but then sometimes I have to divert around a few large blocks which takes me off the 'right' route. I only have to deviate a few degrees of the original direction to end up a considerable distance away from where I wanted to be. If getting over a few stacks is difficult, how hard is it going to become to escape the room? The flipside of this is that if it were a direct easy path, then it would probably also be used by 15's attackers, so currently, my chances of discovery are remote. Although since seeing the old Bedford van, I'm sure they use vehicles to transport themselves over these vast distances, what I would give for some transport to get me out of here now. I'm sick of walking and climbing everywhere.

Chapter 17

It's funny how your mind wanders once you've got used to doing something that to start with feels like a bit of a trial but once you get going, becomes easy. I used to get it when I went out walking the dogs in the forest alone. The forest area was huge, and although there would be a few dog walkers around, you didn't cross too many of them as the place was so enormous. You could let the dogs off and let them run. My two would stick pretty close by, and I wasn't worried they'd run off. Labradors don't do that, or at least my two didn't.

It wasn't long before I would lose focus and it became a very peaceful time, just walking, being out in the open air and just letting your mind trip away. Thinking about things that had happened, something that might occur in the future, remembering fun times, etc.

My mind was doing that now, and it took me back to a fight I had for 15.

As I prepared for the fight, as usual, I tried to find out as much as possible about the alien species I was to battle. I always did this; this was preparation. I needed to know everything about whoever my opponent was. Being forewarned is being forearmed. The more I learned, the more I could practise. Practise until you can do something and then practise until you can't get it wrong. I knew all this, I was a good student, and the species I was about to face were no different in that regard. The only problem is that 15 had very little knowledge about them.

The Serragane were very similar in shape and stature to me, a little shorter and a little stockier perhaps, but generally much the same. They had arms, legs, hands, fingers (four fingers and an opposable thumb) necks, heads. The sex organs were different to mine but in the same place. They had similar internal organs within their torso but in other locations to mine. The main distinction was that their ribcage was outside of their body, a partial exo-skeleton. The ribs consisted of a series of wide flat bones that overlapped and articulated together as opposed to being a cage of bones under the skin as I had. They famously were able to decorate these ribs in a fashion similar to our tattoos, and although the Serragane rarely tattooed any other areas of their skin, almost all had very elaborate and colourful designs on their ribs, front and back.

I was fighting Nid Ryay, one of their most decorated military commanders. Renowned as a fierce tactician and expert hand-to-hand fighter, I was very good at what I did, but was unsure about Nid. Although I knew he had a reputation, I didn't know very much else about him, or his species.

We both walked towards our respective marks. We both have quite a lot of equipment which we must carry out with us to the middle of the Arena. It's the weaponry and armour to use in the fight, but we were only allowed to gear up when we meet at our respective marks. The armour and weaponry wasn't particularly heavy but was bulky, and there were quite a few bits, so it was easy to drop a few sections before reaching the dressing points in the middle. As I neared my opponent, I began to make out the details of the tattoos on Nid's rib sections. As a highly decorated warrior, much of his adornments seemed to show battle scenes. I could only imagine these depicted himself in battle. They were very colourful and elaborately painted in a bright palette with the addition of silvers and golds, even some embedded metals and jewels. It was a magnificent set of scenes.

Nid stood squarely on his mark and looked directly at me. He placed his weapons and armour on the ground in front of him. I did the same. Then he raised his arms above his head, and by flexing over to his right, the plates of ribs slid over each other to add movement, animating some of the scenes. He then bent over to the left and animated some more. Next, he moved his arms from above his head to stretch out by his side, making a 'T' shape which added additional movement to the already moving images. Finally, he turned around and showed me his back. Now, there was a sort of dance sequence - he lifted his left leg, then dropped it again, then raised his left arm from his side until it pointed straight up above his head. He followed this by raising his right arm from his side to the same position whilst dropping his left arm simultaneously. This left his right arm up in the air. Lastly, he lifted his right knee almost to his chest before returning to a normal standing form. I got to see a moving portrait of Nid, his wife, both sets of what I imagine were grandparents and about seven or eight progeny move through a range of different facial expressions and postures. All pretty fascinating and magnificent.

He turned back to face me.

"We can dress now."

"Thanks for showing me that. It's pretty cool."

He replied, very formally.

"The challenge has been made, it's not supposed to be 'cool'."

"Sorry." I replied, feeling just a little ignorant.

There was a knack to putting on the armour as one piece fitted over another. If you got the order wrong, it was challenging to attach the missing segment without taking other bits off, or just starting again. I'd tried once beforehand but still watched and copied how Nid was doing this because I didn't need the fuck-arsing around. The only problem was that he was speedy. We started with the arms; the pieces were golden in colour. Wrists first, then working backwards up the arms on each side, there were four pieces for each arm and then shoulder plates which went over the last of these. Each had a series of clips to attach into place and then again with each other. The armour was not very thick and had flexibility even within each individual piece as well as at each joint. I was slower than Nid, but fortunately, the armour had been well-engineered, so all the clips married up and secured pretty well. Lastly, I had a back and breastplate, which for him, fitted all over the exposed ribs. These plates seemed to be made from what I can only describe as shellac. This shellac carapace was polished so finely as to make it transparent, maybe with a little smokiness to it, like pale sunglasses lenses. I would be able to see all of Nid's rib adornments as we battled. The gauntlets finished off the armour; our legs are left bare. I'm was wearing a scruffy pair of khaki cargo pants and a pair of bright white, boxfresh Air Jordan throwback hi-tops. We had nothing to protect our heads.

At long-last, I picked up my weapons, a small shield made of some sort of pretty solid animal hide, it was circular and had two straps on the back, one to feed my forearm through and a smaller one to hold - a conventional shield. The only significant difference is that the edge, all the way around, has been honed. It wasn't razor-sharp or anything as good as that, but it could cause significant damage if you were given a bang onto bare flesh with it. I'm not sure which is more robust, the carapace armour or the shield material. Finally the primary offensive weapon, a short mace of about 20 inches long. Long enough to get a big swing with but it's going to be close proximity fighting. The mace is pretty conventional, a hard, heavy lump on the end on a lighter shaft. Inlayed into the 'lump' end was rounded off 'nobbles', for a bit of extra damage capability, and a hide wrist thong on the other end so you were less likely to lose or let go of it.

The 'Bong' sounded in its rather dull way, and we started to fight. I circled round to the left and Nid did the same. I began to swing my mace and Nid did also. I took a step towards Nid and continued to circle; he did too. I stopped and probably looked a little confused, so did Nid. I circled to the right, Nid copied. I swiped a couple of times, so did he.

BUT NOT AFTER ME, ALL AT THE SAME TIME!

It was like looking in a mirror. Nid knew my move as I made it, exactly. If I jumped, so did he. If I moonwalked, so did he. If I dropped my weapons and sat on the floor, so did he. We hadn't even started fighting yet!

After a while, I decided to see what would happen if I got close, surely he'd do something different then?

I stepped towards him, shield up to cover my chin. My right hand, holding my mace, was held behind me, raised a little so I could swing easily. We got to within a couple of feet of each other - striking distance and stopped. I started to snarl, and of course, he did the same back. I made a couple of shies, as if I was about to swing, but held back; he copied me. Then I swung hard towards the top of his head over his shield. I saw his mace coming also. We both continue to swing, we both lifted shields to block blows, and both maces met in the middle and clashed sending bone juddering vibrations back into my elbow. I winced behind my shield.

I moved right into him and touched his shield to mine, again the mirror image. My right arm was low behind me; he could not see my mace as I swung hard up under his shield to crack him as hard as I can to the top of the thighs/lower arse area.

I reeled back in pain. I received a substantial blow on the bottom of my left buttock.

He was in the same pain, recovering from the same shot hit with the same intensity.

I didn't get it. How come Nid has the 'Excellent Fighter' reputation if all he's doing is copying me? I'm the one making a move, and he's the one copying. How did he win any fights? All we can do is the same damage to each other. There's no winner here. I'm doing all the fighting, and he's doing all the copying. This is just stupid. I couldn't work out how we were ever going to end this thing. Maybe the Serragane thought a draw was as good as a victory? If we'd just give in and agree to agree. Is that considered a win?

"You're just copying me."

"No, I'm fighting," he replied.

"But if I stop fighting then you stop too."

"No, I don't, I'm just choosing to rest and planning my next move."

"What if we call it a draw?"

"No such thing as a draw. I only win. I am Nid the Victor."

"So you'll never settle for a draw?"

"Never. No surrender, but I will accept your surrender."

"What? You don't fight. I get bored, and the only way to escape all of this is to surrender?"

"No, I want you to fight."

I shut up and tried to get this all straight in my brain. Nid was a reasonable distance from me and, as such, no threat. He just swung his mace around a bit to pass the time.

I couldn't just attack him because every move I made, he made the same. If I swung at him, our maces just ended up crashing together. If I got to a position whereby our maces cannot meet in the middle, like earlier, then we both end up hurting each other equally. If I swap hands, he'll just do the same.

Finally, it dawned on me. This is a battle to see who can take the most punishment.

For example, we lock shields again and then simultaneously hit each other in the arse. What if he's got a super hard arse and can just take far more shots to it than I can? We might inflict a carbon copy amount of damage to each other's arse, but his arse has just got more 'hit points', to use computer game vocabulary, than I have. I'll become incapacitated first, and he'll win only from having a bionic arse. Hardly something to get a new tattoo about. And about them, I had been really impressed. That was before

I found out he hadn't fought anyone and either claimed victory by forfeit, or by 'Bionic Arse'. He'd lost my respect.

Didn't mean I couldn't work something out.

I sat on the floor, cross-legged, with my left elbow on my knee and leaning my head on my left hand. I'd got the mace off my wrist and was spinning it on the floor. I had the heavy end on the floor and was holding the strap end up vertically, trying to spin like a top so it would stand up for a while before falling. I did this to pass some time and let me think. Nid wasn't doing anything much either. I had my back to him because I considered him no threat. He was sitting a way off. I knew he wouldn't do anything unless I did. I looked at the weapon, knobbles – they were hard and knobbly, nothing interesting there - the lump, made of indiscriminate hard, heavy stuff. I tried to press my fingernail into it, but my nail bent against it and made no impression. The lump connected to a shaft made of a different material – it was lighter but also solid, a perfectly good material for a shaft. I tried to disconnect one part from the other; pulling, unscrewing, but nothing. Finally, a strap attached to the end of the shaft, made from some sort of animal hide - so leather from an unknown beast. Threaded through an eyelet and then tied off in a simple but effective knot. Perfect for me to slide my hand through and Nid also. Seemed to do everything it was supposed to. It was at this point that I had my idea. Surely a silly notion - surely it couldn't be that simple? I stayed where I was, thinking through my strategy, my ploy. Would it work? Could Nid read my mind? Would he do the same? After a while, I stood up and picked up the mace again. I'd still got my back to Nid, so I knew he had his to me too. I started to swing the club as if to flex my muscles, to stretch and loosen up a bit, ready for the ensuing fight. Finally, I turned around to Nid, who was swinging his club to match me. I swung the club, hard, overhead and down, and released. The mace flew out of my hand straight towards Nid's body, the biggest target. He did the same, but he still had the thong around his wrist so when he loosed his mace, it went nowhere and just violently swung under his arm and up. Nid had a brief look of horror as he realised what I've done. I'd relinquished my weapon which was just about to wallop him, hard in the solar plexus region. I also hadn't moved, which means he's not going to either. A split second later he felt the impact as the mace smashed into his lower abdomen. Even with his armour and rib wall, the impact of the blow doubled him up. I leapt the two or three steps towards him and grabbed him with both hands around his neck and squeezed. I'd managed to catch him by surprise and dealt my second, decisive attack before he had a chance to recover from the first and start copying again. He still had a shield around one arm so couldn't get his second hand free to break my grip. He tried to hit me, but it had little effect. His other hand had still not found the shaft of his mace so he couldn't swing it, it was loose and in the way. Nid realised I'd won and tapped out. I knew I didn't have to kill him, surrender would be enough to win - same rules for both of us. He expected to win by me eventually tapping out, possibly from boredom, or through not having a hard arse. He certainly didn't expected to be beaten in combat. He took it badly.

After I released Nid, and he had a short chance to recover, he slowly started to peel off his armour to reveal his rib structure again. He picked up his mace and pressed three distinct nobbles down together which allowed the lump to pop off and revealed a short, double-edged straight blade at the end of the shaft. I was pissed off when I saw this, not really because it was a concealed weapon, more that I hadn't found it when I examined the mace at length. Then he sat cross-legged and started to use the blade to scrape off the rib embellishments, bit by bit, front and back. His defeat has been total. His history is no longer glorious, had to be expunged.

Chapter 18

I'VE REACHED THE TOP of the stack. Fortunately, this room is nowhere near as big as some of the previous spaces. I think it's only about half a mile square. The problem with everything being grey white and evenly lit is that you can't make out distance or a horizon. It's just all grey white. You can see it when you get close; it's not like you're always walking into walls like in a Hall of Mirrors, it's just that it's challenging to judge spatially. The block climbing though did take a lot of time; it's by far the most formidable terrain I've had to traverse, even an accomplished rock climber would struggle as there are no hand or foot holes, no ledges, just flat sides and straight edges, many on large blocks which are insurmountable.

I've now come to the opposite side of the room from where I entered. There's a wall again, not only that, I think I can see something that could be a door. There's a slight change in shading, 70-80 metres to my left. There is an alley left along the wall, which is about 4 metres wide. I'm just not prepared to walk/run straight along this flat surface, I could get to the door in ten or twenty seconds, but I would be in the open, and I feel like I want to take my time with every doorway, to take a stealthy look before I attempt to go through it. So once again, I'm taking the slow route, over and around the blocks. It takes me more like 45 minutes to get to the door and find a suitable semi-hidden position to watch the door. It is a door, and it is open. Inside I can finally see some activity.

Avatars, lots of them!

Chapter 19

OKAY, SO I SAID activity, but after looking for quite a while, it seems like many of the avatars are inactive, and quite far away. Not to say there isn't some buzz in there. There are still plenty moving around busying about and doing stuff. I have no idea what they're all up to and won't be able to tell unless I take a closer look - which is a risk. I've now been in observation mode for 30 minutes or so. There doesn't seem to be anyone bothered about me, or looking for me. No-one seems too hurried, too overly on the defensive or offensive and no-one seems to be guarding this entrance. The attackers, if they are in charge of these avatars, don't seem to be looking for me. They may not know I'm around and looking for them or they may think I'm a target not worth finding. This ship, 15, is vast and I'm on foot. I could be lost in the bowels of the ship never to be seen again.

I take a few deep breaths and remember how I got into this situation. I'm supposed to be dead – gone forever. I'm back because I'm 15's last Champion and as such he had no-one left to help him. 15 lied to me about how I came to be abducted, that he set up the situation to get me and just me. He doesn't deserve to have me do this for him as he has broken his promise to me. I shouldn't care what's happening, but this whole enterprise is getting my juices flowing. I'm enjoying playing this stealthy hunter role although I realise I could be captured and killed pretty quickly. Even with a few weapons, the odds are stacked against me. I'm enjoying staying alive. Although, if I fail and I die, I'm supposed to be dead anyway so what do I care? This is my internal debate, my inner argument. Sometimes one side wins over the other, and I feel I should protect myself and be careful about my next move, but sometimes I can't be arsed, this is when my self-preservation option goes out of the window, and it's what's currently winning.

I'm not going to run into that room with all guns blazing, but I am also not just going to sit here hiding amongst the blocks also. I jump down onto the open alleyway, sidle up to the side of the door opening, and peer around. To my right is an innumerable line of vehicles, all from Earth. There are cars, vans, trucks, motorbikes, light and heavy aircraft, military vehicles, construction vehicles, emergency vehicles; there are helicopters and hovercrafts. Some are being driven and parked in straight ranks, but most are just sitting there; sports cars, station wagons, SUVs and saloons. I think the nearest vehicle, a boxy-looking Mercedes G-Wagon is about 250 metres diagonally from where I am standing.

In front of me are legions of avatars. I have no clue how many there could be, but I'm talking thousands. They are all standing, and from what I can see (I clearly can't see all of them) they're Human and adult. I think it's a fair split, 50/50 women and men - old/young and all colours. To my left is a miscellaneous storage area. There is warehouse rack, after warehouse rack, of storage stretching for hundreds of metres, and this is where I'm heading - when I decide to head. There is a multi-array of fucking everything on the aisle after aisle of racks. From 250 metres, I can make out vacuum cleaners, pressure hoses, computers, a garden roller, shoes (lots), torches, metal detectors, motorcycle helmets, TV satellite dishes, dining tables (no chairs), a barbecue, a kids garden slide. I want some shoes, though.

I know this is where I'm going, I knew it as soon as I saw it. Some avatars occasionally visit the shelves, but there is space between the racks, and I could climb up the shelves if I wanted. It's a bit of a jungle in there, everything neatly ordered but in no specific order I can make out, not alphabetically or by size or by type. I imagine 15 stored everything here and just knew the exact location of every object so didn't need anything to reference where everything was. He just *knew*, like an old man's garden shed. Untouched by any hand but his own, he knows exactly where everything is in the shed because he put it there and he knows exactly how much of everything there is because he always does. 'Have you got a seed drill, Grandad?' 'Yup, here it is.' 'Do you have a one and a half-inch wood screw preferably a brass one?' 'Yup, this box right here.' That sort of stuff.

Referencing all of these items for a massive brain like 15 is easy, he just knows where everything is - no list, no microfiche, no index cards. I can get lost amongst the shelves; they have no backs so I can crawl through from one to another. It's easy to find cover. Avatars are milling around the trucks; I can hear them fire up from time to time. Unlike the three I've already dispatched, these avatars don't talk to each other. I imagine there is a hive mind controlling them somewhere. They seem to be acting like automatons, mindless drones, not as they did with me when they were in the environment. Maybe, this is their natural state, and they are made 'more Human' when they encounter me.

It's not a lull, their activity looks pretty constant, but there are fewer of them near my position than at any time since I started watching. No one is particularly looking for me or looking my way, so I walk, timidly but trying not to show it to the racking. I walk in a straight line, I'm without cover, totally exposed and in the open. I have my Sten by my side, cocked and ready. And I'm ready to whip it into action and hit a flat sprint to the cover of the shelves. I'm trying to look straight and not look guilty glancing around too much. I'm nearly there. I hope the avatars can't hear the BOOM, BOOM, BOOM of my heart. I feel a bead of sweat trickling down the back of my ear, forming a rivulet down the side of my neck to my shoulder blade. My nerves are jangling, only a couple of more paces.

Then I'm there. I scuttle quickly into the shelves and slide into a gap on the bottom shelf between two washing machines. I breathe out for what feels like the first time since I turned into the room and started the most protracted and slowest walk of my life. Breathe, in and out, in and out again a few times to slow and normalise my pounding heart rate. I look out carefully and see the aisle I am in is deserted for hundreds of metres, I look through the gaps between the miasma of objects all around me on aisles up and down from my position, and I see no movement. I decide to venture out and move deeper into the shelving.

The objects don't stop. It's like the biggest selection of unrelated items I have ever seen, a portable hydraulic tyre air hose next to delicate lace doilies, mobile phone chargers beside folding umbrellas, next to claw hammers, next to cans of fly spray. It goes on. I see some clothing, men's clothing. I've hated what I'm wearing, but when I get to examine, I see it's all way too small for me, like clothes for tweens. Nothing fits. Later I do find an excellent black Dinner Jacket, but it's a bit too big for me, and it's black, not really what I want to wear in a grey white environment. There is good news, though. I acquire a leather children's satchel and can lengthen the strap enough to get it over my head. It's big enough for me to store the four Sten gun magazines and the hunting knife

I have. I sling it over my right shoulder with the satchel sitting high on my left hip. I have my right arm through the 'belt strap' I fashioned out of the two stolen men's trouser belts The Sten gun hangs from it on my right side, under my arm, ready to bring into play.

I keep walking and looking. There is no-one behind me, and no-one in front of me. I can see through the shelves from time to time and cannot see any avatars near. Now and then (and they are far apart) I reach an alleyway running perpendicular to the aisles. I take my time before scooting across the two-metre gap. There have been a couple of vehicles parked in some of these. I think they are being loaded, or unloaded with equipment, 'stuff' from the shelves for some unknown purpose. Then I see something useful - an aviator's khaki jumpsuit. I strip off and put this on; it's a good fit. I'm ecstatic I can't believe how good it feels to be in something slightly different to a crappy old shirt and pair of blood-soaked pyjama bottoms. I almost cry, it's been months since I changed my clothes, not that they're smelly and horrible or even dirty (blood apart), but it makes me feel euphoric. Then, shortly after, I find a rucksack, the type you use for your gym clothes. I think I'm on a roll and unload the stuff from the satchel into the rucksack and sling it on. I'm still shoeless, I've seen hundreds, but they are either too small or ladies shoes (too small also). So I plod on. My feet aren't sore; I'd just like the feeling of stability, the enclosure that a shoe or trainer gives. I might also need to kick something or someone, and some decent shoes would help.

Then, mid-rummage, I'm surprised by an avatar. It's male, around mid-thirties in age, of East Asian origin, slightly shorter but stouter than me. The avatar's casually dressed in a pale blue shirt, unbuttoned at the neck, with the sleeves rolled up. He's wearing navy blue pleated chinos and brown brogue, lace-up, leather shoes. He looks at me and walks towards me. His face is expressionless. I stand up, and I'm about to go for my gun when I realise he's not looking at me, he's focussed beyond me. I've not swung my gun around before he's walked past me - and carries on into the distance.

I put the Sten on the ground and swing the rucksack around. It's a risk, but I'm only here for the risk. It could end badly or could bring the war to my door. I don't care; I'm going to take the plunge. I whip out the hunting knife and start to catch him up, moving as quickly but quietly as possible. When I'm on him, I throw my left hand around his head and cover his mouth with the flat of my hand whilst I whip the right hand around holding the knife to slice neatly across his throat, The blood jet's out in front of me - quick and soundless. The blood covers a lawnmower and remote control plane sitting next to each other on the ground height shelf to my left. The blood pools quickly and thickly around my victim, I drag him back to escape the blood as the puddle enlarges towards my feet. There doesn't seem to have been any alarm raised. I pull him further away from the bloody pool and then when I'm sure he's dead, and he's bled out, I let the lifeless cadaver drop to the ground on his back. I reach down and unlace its shoes and take them off. I remove the black socks and quickly pull them on. I try on a shoe. It's too fucking small! I throw it hard at the dead body lying on the floor and trudge, in my socks, back to my gun and rucksack.

Chapter 20

I FELT TIRED AND HADN'T slept in a long while. I decided to try something and hoped it would work. I climbed up to the top shelf of an adjacent rack and lay flat on my back. I'd checked for any avatars wandering around before I hiked up and made sure there were no flying drones, or anything aerial, that would see me. The tops of the racking are all left clear. I took off my backpack and used it as a cushion.

Why are all of these things here? I can only assume that instead of magically building everything that I might have needed to order, 15 made 'spares'. The avatars that are all lined up are not people I knew. I guess these avatars were for 'crowd scenes' especially for when I commuted to London every day. They could be used daily, at different intervals, I would occasionally recognise people walking that same way to work, down the same roads, when I commuted in real London. It's not beyond any stretch of the imagination that 15 wouldn't re-use avatars on a comparable basis and for many different things. The objects on the shelves again are mainly common day-to-day objects. 15 wouldn't exactly have had to make these over and over again. When you've got unlimited storage space, and avatars to pick items up and move them around, then why would one go to the bother of re-creating everything, every time? Just re-use what you already have. Same for the lines of vehicles there are down there. To make traffic, of any sort, you need loads of different but non-descript vehicles of all shapes and sizes. There are enough parked up here to sink a few container ships. It's just a big storeroom. The avatars are on remote control, tidying things up, cataloguing, busying around.

I don't know how many of the thousands below me are operative, inoperative or under alien control. I can imagine that every moving avatar is under alien control, but how many of them are on 'guard duty' or are looking for me? Not many by the looks of things and that's the way I want to keep it for as long as I can or until I get control of them. I have two aims. The first is to wrest back control of the avatars. If I can get them to deactivate, then they will not come after me. If I can get them to do mine/15's wishes, I can send them against the attackers. This would be the optimal version of events as the attackers won't know me from an avatar - I'd be in deep disguise - and I'd have my own private army. The second main objective is to stop 15 from being destroyed/captured. I've still got my work cut out to make any of this happen, and taking a kip on top of the shelves is posing a risk to me. Every time I think this though I then have to tell myself 'But if

I get killed, I'm just dead, which was what I wanted at the start of this anyway.' I just have to avoid being captured - that wouldn't be fun.

I don't know how long I nod off for, but I wake up, and I'm alive and no better or worse off than before other than I do feel more refreshed. I'm not sure how long it is in Earth days since I last saw 15, but at a rough guess, I'd say it's been about two months. It's difficult to tell because back up on deck with him at least we kept to a 'morning and night' movement of the 'sun' - not an actual sun but a light source where shadows shortened and lengthened as the day grew older. Since being 'below stairs' there has been one day/night. First, the never-ending night and now the never-ending day - all very disorientating. What I'm getting to is 'how long have I got?' The attackers have done something to 15 to affect his functioning power; after two months, I have not yet reached a point where I can do anything to influence this. Nor have I reached the avatar control point. I wonder if the attackers have yet to reach their goal, where they can get full control over 15 or whether they already have but are unable to break into his systems. I'm hoping it's the latter because I don't want to be hiding around here forever.

I feel I'm making slow progress, and my prevarication about the lack of a pair of shoes is not helping me towards my objective, I need to refocus. I managed to find the way out of the darkness pretty quickly. I got lucky. Did the initial attackers know the way or get there faster than I did? Are they in a totally different part of 15 than I am? I had to hide through the 'pipes' section. Not having any opposition, the attackers would not have needed to hide and would have been able to progress around the structure more quickly. Did they go the right way around the structure? Was there a small 'Avatar Control Room' hidden in the pipes? Did I miss something? Was there a control terminal in the darkness from where I might have been able to restore 15's functionality? I have no idea. I'm just cracking on, with no real plan other than to keep moving forward, and not get caught. I think I may have to go out on a limb sooner or later or I'm never going to get to the bottom of this thing. It's shit or bust time.

Chapter 21

SHORTLY AFTER HOPPING DOWN and traipsing around through a few alleys of storage racking, I found what I was looking for...and what a treasure trove. Small arms, and fucking loads of them. I couldn't believe my luck. I've been keeping track of my Sten bullets and protecting my ammo for so long now. This should make a difference. Not only that, I have a choice of assault rifles! I pick up the US-made M4 MWS fitted with a scope with an underslung 40mm M203 grenade launcher, this baby's got some power. There's also plenty of ammo for it. Then there's an FN SCAR-H, but it's a bit heavy and doesn't have a rocket launcher fitted. Finally, a Heckler & Koch HK416, a weapon I've used loads of time just for fun. I like this one; it feels good in the hand. Again, there's no RPG launcher, so I begrudgingly opt for the M4. Then there loads and loads of hand pistols of all shapes and sizes. I find the one I want pretty quickly, a Glock 17, a 9mm pistol with 17 bullets in the magazine plus 1 in the barrel. There's also a shoulder holster, so this is a definite. I quickly throw on the straps and holster the gun. Next,

I stuff a few handfuls of magazines into my backpack making sure I check they're full before doing so. I'm just about to shoulder the M4 when I spot an ST Kinetics CPW, CPW stands for Compact Personal Weapon, this is a lightweight but handy sub-machine gun. It's a cracking room-clearer, and I don't think I'm going to be doing too much long-range stuff, I guess I'm going to be getting in close and producing maximum damage in the minimum time available. I bag it also. Now, as well as the M4, I've got two small, easy to carry guns and a fair few clips of ammo across my back. I also pick up a Gerber MKII fighting knife, well used by special forces and mercenaries back on Earth. It's in a sheath, so I attach it to my belt and tie off to my leg. I'm about as ready as I'm going to be. I'm heavily armed, and I'm pumped.

I'm getting ready to break away from the cover of the shelves. Unlike all of the other avatars, I have no shoes, and I'm wearing a backpack. The shoes may not be too much of a giveaway as quite a few avatars are in some form of uniform or other; police, council bin man, McDonald's, there are also some in casual 'streetwear' which includes flip flops and sliders. No one has a backpack though, and mine is full and clanking, with guns and ammo clips.

Even though they're all busy loading shelves, putting things away and generally tidying up, there is no communication. I'm not sure how they're communicating, but they may not be under voice control. They may just have been assigned a job and left alone to do it. Let's face it, the system of avatars and what they do each day was set up and improved upon over thousands of years by 15. I'm not sure anyone wants to sit at a console and check that each is doing the right job. I'm just hoping that none of them looks up from what they're doing and says "Hey, who are you?" My guns are hidden, not well, but out of sight - pistol in a holster, SMG in backpack. Only the M4 is visible, but an avatar could think I was an avatar who was innocently moving the gun from one place to another.

I break cover and walk as steadily and as straight as I can out from the shelves. It's the first time I've had a proper look at what's going on in the open. There are lines and lines of vehicles, which I'm approaching. An old Ford CMax and a small Citroen panel van, white obviously. They are about 100 metres in front of me, and vehicles are running off in both directions from left to right, I can't count how many ranks I have to get through, but it is numerous. I can see to my right about a quarter of a mile away that there is a large doorway or opening of some sort. It is not on the sidewall; it's just somewhere in the middle of the room, it's sticking up out of the ground in a wedge shape. It's about 15 metres tall and wide. The roof of this structure slopes down backwards away from me, and I soon realise it is a ramp leading downwards. This is where I'm going - although it might just be the down ramp in a vast multi-storey car park. I can't see any other wall let alone doorway for miles in any other direction. I'm trying hard not to look around and not to look too obvious and draw attention to myself. A few avatars come to within 20 metres of me but carry on doing what they're doing and leave me alone.

I reach the CMax and walk between it and the van then further forward, some sort of BMW 'whatever' series and a Fiat 125. Next line, between a VW Polo and a Renault Clio. After about 13 more lines of cars, I get to the people. All avatars are standing stationary, like shop dummies, all dressed in their day clothes ready to go about their business. I'm nervous here because if one woke up, they might all wake up. The avatars would mob me in moments, and no amount of room clearing SMG's would help with this many bodies around. There are thousands in lines running backwards and forwards in front of me. No other avatar is picking their way through the mob; they're walking around them. Now and then, there's an aisle through which the animated avatars are using. I pick one and turn to walk through. It's wide enough for two avatars to pass one on each side. The aisle is empty as I enter and is about 150 metres long. As I get about a quarter of the way in, and avatar enters at the other end, then a break, then another, then another. They are walking down the middle of the aisle, looking forward, but without blinking and with a fixed focus. I know I can easily bring the M4 into play at speed if stopped but grabbing the gun now and blasting my way out is not an option I'm prepared to chance with this many avatars around me. I'm going to hold my nerve and see what happens. I fix my focus on one point and walk directly at the avatar coming towards me. About five metres out, the avatar takes a half step to the right, in my next pace; I also do, and we pass without menace or danger. I don't look back I switch back into the middle and await the arrival of the next, this time at six metres out I step to the right, next pace, so does the avatar and we pass. I do so for the third and final avatar. Now I'm getting close to the end of the run, I'm nearly back out in the clear again, when another avatar turns into the aisle, it's my next-door neighbour, Eric. I've lived next to Eric for about ten years. He's 75 and looks after the dogs and the house for us when we go away on holidays. I like Eric, but if anyone will recognise me, then it's Eric. But here, he's just another avatar made to look like Eric, as I near, I step to the right, so does Eric, we pass, and I feel a hand grab my left arm and spin me around. Sorry Eric, a mistake. I stick my hunting knife up into the base of his ribcage. He tries to open his mouth to scream, but I've shaken my left arm loose and placed it over his mouth. He goes down slowly and in a pool of blood. I twist the knife as his life ebbs away. Then I wipe the knife, push it back down into the sheath, straighten up and continue to walk. I try to remain calm. I have to put some space between me and the dead body. Another avatar will surely turn back into that aisle again soon and find the body. I can't run, but I need to get away. I quicken my step, but if you were watching me, you'd know I was up to something. I'm hardly doing a great job of hiding but as of yet, no-ones interested. I'm back out in the open now and forging ahead towards the ramp. It's only a few metres away when an alarm goes up. I turn the corner and run down the ramp, it's about thirty metres long, and I'm running across, from the top right to the bottom left corner. I'm out of eyeline for all those on the floor above now. I get to the base of the ramp and turn the corner - and I'm met by a punch of a rifle butt, hard, straight across the bridge of my nose.

Lights out.

Chapter 22

I WAS ASKED TO DO some staff training, in a different office from my one, a branch office in another part of London, in fact not far off Camden High Street, near to the Tube. Training wasn't really on my job description, but I had done some before and liked it. It was something I would have wanted to add to my CV, an extra strand, who knows, someday, I might have made it my 'thing', but for now, I was just happy to be getting out of the office for a bit. It was work, but it felt like a bit of a skive. I'd found the old training presentation I'd used before and updated it, which didn't take long. Then I thought for a bit about what I was going to say and how I was going to say it. I also thought of a few jokes, firstly to break the ice and set the mood of the room and then to keep people interested as I presented. I wasn't writing a stand-up show, and I'm no comedian, but a couple of work-related quips to breeze us all through.

On the day, everything went pretty well. I was not the only person presenting so much of the morning I sat around getting bored, listening to others droning on. There were about 20 people in the room, a couple of graduate trainees, the majority who were mainly junior members of staff, and a couple of mid-rangers.

Eventually, it was my turn, the second last of the day. Everyone's pretty bored and struggling to maintain attention by this time. I started, and the presentation flowed through, the jokes worked pretty well, and I even got asked a few good questions at the end. No probs, as it should be. When we finished, a room had been booked in a local pub for a bit of an informal social. The attendees would all be able to ask the trainers a few questions - standard stuff. I was enjoying it, not everyone attended, some of the trainers and the trainees could not make it, but a good 15 of us downed a few polite drinks on the company along, with a few nibbles. The crowd started to peter away as the evening worked through until I realised that I was the only trainer left along with three trainees; two guys and a girl. I didn't know who they were, but we'd got off the work chat and moved into 'Where do you live?' meaning 'What part of London are you living in?', followed up with, 'I used to live there, do you know...?' or 'Not that shit-hole...' or 'I've heard it's nice, expensive?' that sort of stuff that leads into more personal conversations, 'Who do you live with?', 'Have you got kids?', 'How long have you lived there?', 'How long is the commute?', 'Have you eaten/drunk/partied at?'; pleasant, general conversation. I suddenly realised, as we were getting close to last orders, that I was rather drunk. The free booze had been going down rather too well for a school night, and apart from a few little things on crackers and cocktail sticks, I hadn't eaten anything substantial.

We finished up and left; it was pissing rain. The two guys were heading in the other direction, so off they went. The girl, about 22 years old (I was 28) was heading back to Parkway to get a taxi, so was I. We chatted on the walk back to Parkway, just small talk, she had shoulder-length blond hair and was pretty, she was from somewhere 'up north', maybe Leeds or somewhere else, and had decided to see what it was like working in 'The Big Smoke', she'd only joined the company recently. She seemed nice, but all I was thinking of is getting rid of her. There is an excellent kebab shop just next to Camden Tube, and I wanted to go there on my own. I wasn't planning on looking professional, or refined as I tucked into my extra-large chicken doner (with all the trimmings, except onions, plenty of chilli sauce please.) I wanted to get in there, get my food and have a pissed scoff, with grease dripping through my fingers and yoghurt smeared on my chin. As I'm a gentleman though, I waited at the bottom of Parkway with her. It was still raining hard, it was dark, around midnight, and it was Camden, hardly the safest place to leave a pretty blonde on her own. Parkway was busy as usual, even at that time of night there's a queue of cars. I saw a taxi coming down with its light on, hailed it, in she got and off she went. I crossed straight over the road, by now, the rain was starting to seep through my coat. I checked out the kebab shop - closed. It was having a refurb. I was gutted. I decided to get off home as the rain was starting to piss me off. So back to Parkway. Now I'm standing in the rain at the bottom of the hill waiting for a taxi to come down Parkway from the Park end, it's one-way. I can see the cabs in the distance; there's even a couple with lights on. I have to move out of the shop doorway I'm sheltering in if I don't stand out in the rain or they won't see me. I can now see three cabs coming down the hill, two with their lights off - not for hire, and the third with its light on. It's still too far up for me to wave at it and the lights are red, so the traffic is stationary on the hill and won't move forward until the lights turn green. The lights change, and the cars start to move again. The cabs are nearing. I'm locked on the third one. Just as I'm about to put my arm up, the second cab, the one before my one with its light off, pulls up and the door opens. It's her, the pretty northern girl, in the back, looking wet but smiling.

"Do you want to get in?"

I know what she's asking. I *instantly* know what she's asking. I don't hesitate.

I smile wetly, "Yes, please."

The door shuts and I sit down, I'm drenched and a bit pissed. What's she doing here? She went home.

"Gghhi..."

I start, but she interjects.

"The taxi driver said I was nuts. He said you'd be gone by now."

I'm surprised too. I didn't mention my excursion to the kebab shop. They'd driven off up Camden Road, so they'd had to make a massive loop along Camden Street, then back up to Delancey Street to the park and then turned back down Parkway - a giant circle. To pick up a guy she didn't know, had hardly spoken too and had probably already left. I couldn't believe my luck. Until later on in the evening, I'd barely even noticed her. I didn't know her name - anything. We went back to her shared flat just off Baker Street. It wasn't very nice, she lived with two of her brothers, and I had to sneak in in case they didn't like the look of me. I didn't like the look of me. I was pissed and soaked. I don't remember much about what happened afterwards, but it can't have been great - it's funny what you remember when you're unconscious.

I wake to a sharp kick in the ribs. I'm lying on my back on the floor, and I still see stars, my vision is blurred and I'm groggy. I receive a second, equally as painful kick, and try to focus.

"Stop!" I shout, and it works, there is no third kick.

The eyesight starts to clear, and I can make out a figure standing above me looking down, within a few seconds, I can begin to make out some features. It can't be, I think it is, but it can't be. Looking down at me from above is Brito, full name Britostoft Zammermont-Hackeltract-D-bonze the Third, the alien that 15 allowed to kill me for what should have been forever.

"What the fuck! Brito?"

"Yes, I am Brito. Why are you here? I killed you?"

Although groggy, I have to get my brain straight quickly and think fast.

"Yeah, you did, and thanks for that. I had agreed with 15 that if you killed me, I would be allowed to die. Forever. The end. But then I woke up in the darkness and have been stumbling around for months and months. Thank fuck I've found you!"

He looks a bit puzzled but to be fair, so am I. I'm doing the maths quickly and I think I'm getting the right answers. It's Brito and his mob that has taken over 15, it must have happened straight after I died. I'm not going to let on that I've been brought back by 15 to kick them off the ship. I'm not sure Brito believes me, but I'm going to keep blagging and see where it gets me.

"I'm glad it's you - anyone would have done, but at least it's a face I know."

I sit up and see that we're not alone. There are two others of Brito's people with him; they are both pointing Human automatic handguns at me. The first and most important thing I instantly notice about them is their size. When I faced Brito in the Arena, he was my height. In reality, he's much shorter, as are the other two. He's more Oompa Lumpa sized, or Munchkin, not sure how to describe them best - Pygmy maybe? Just about up to the height of my nipples at a rough estimate, sort of 'tit-high'. But they are in proportion, so they're petite.

The weapons, which are definitely from Earth, look a little big in their hands – like child soldiers, not that they can't use them. Brito's stopped using the very smart-sounding voice he had before; he sounds a bit rougher than he did in the Arena. He steps back from me, and I relax a little, the others still have their guns trained on me. I'm not where I was, I'm in a different part of 15, moved while I've been out. All of my well-chosen weapons have gone, the lot, I don't even have a small fruit knife left. Still a grey white space, but now a much smaller room. There are walls on all four sides of me; this place is probably about ten metres square - minute for 15. There is also a ceiling above, there are no windows and no apparent light source, but it is quite bright. It's as if all the surfaces are all glowing with low light. I move about a bit on the floor to get more comfortable. I don't try to get up as I'm much taller than them and they might find this threatening. I'm happy here on the floor. Brito starts his interrogation.

"Tell me exactly what happened to you?"

"You killed me. I'm pleased you did because I've been a prisoner of 15 for over 2,000 Earth years. It abducted me from my planet, just like that (I click my fingers loudly). Gone, away from everyone and everything I've ever known or loved, up onto this ship, which travels around the Universe, starting wars and making me fight people like you for its entertainment. It wouldn't let me go; it wouldn't let me die. I hated every minute of it. Lonely, and alone, out here in the empty blackness of space. Then. Finally. It agreed to let me go, to die. And you killed me, for which I am grateful. I thought it was all over. But I woke up again, in pure blackness and stumbled around for months and months in the darkness before I found some light. I went towards the light and then through some other rooms before I got here."

"Where were you going?"

"I don't know. I'm just trying to get off the ship."

"So why have you being killing avatars?"

I force a breath out for effect "Because they are trying to kill me. The avatars work for 15; I'm against 15. It makes sense that I kill them."

"They work for us now; we control them all."

Fake surprise, "Thank fuck for that. I've been shitting myself every time I see one."

"Have you ever been in the blackness before?"

"No, never. I know 15 has holds where it builds ships that are pitch black. It showed me some of them before. I thought I was on the floor of one of them, was I not?"

"Why do you think you woke in the darkness?"

"I have no idea. But I thought it was an opportunity to escape, so I took it."

Brito looks at his two other colleagues. They don't speak but nod, little inflexions of their heads and shoulders. They're thinking about my answers. Then Brito says,

"Kill him."

"NO, NO. I'M ON YOUR SIDE." I plead.

One of the other gunmen stands in front of me; he lifts his gun until it is pointing at my face.

"I CAN HELP YOU. I HATE 15 AS WELL!!"

The third butts in,

"Maybe he can help."

There is a long period of enormous tension. It's a long period of enormous tension for me but probably only a few seconds of little tension for Brito and his mates.

"OK," says Brito, and the gunman lowers his gun.

"Thank you. Thank you all."

Brito walks a few paces around me to the left and then again back right to where he started.

"We're going to keep an eye on you. I don't believe your story, but it's plausible. I'd rather you were dead, but you may still be of use. If you wanted to die, why do you not want to die now?"

"Because I don't want to be shot in the face, and because now I think I can get some revenge on 15. After 2,000 years of captivity, it would be nice to give it a taste of its own medicine."

Brito nods and seems to accept my answers. Next, he ties both of my hands together in front of me with a wide, flat plastic cable tie. The other two put away their guns. Although much smaller than me, I know Brito is a fearsome warrior to be very well respected. If these two are anything similar, then keeping on top of me, with my hands tied, is going to be pretty straightforward. I stand up, and Brito walks to one corner of the room, he then pushes the left-hand wall gently, and the whole wall glides away from him to reveal an opening to the right. I stand, and we all walk out.

Outside is a white Ford Transit van, it has a sliding door to the side which is open. I can see my backpack and weaponry on the floor next to the van.

"You made some good choices," says Brito.

"Thanks. I was looking for the best way to take out avatars."

One of the two aliens reaches down and exchanges his handgun for the ST Kinetics CPW, the little sub-machine gun I had selected. He then tips the contents of the back-pack out onto the floor. He picks the correct ammo for the weapon, puts it back in the bag which he throws over his shoulder. The rest stays on the floor. These lads know their stuff. How can they be so well versed on Earth weapons?

I'm put in the back of the van. A second cable tie is threaded through the one around my hands and the base of the passenger headrest. The alien with the submachine gun gets in the back with me. Brito is in the passenger seat whilst the third drives. I can see they've tied a brick-sized block to each of the pedals to be able to drive effectively. To allow them to reach the pedals.

We head off, god knows where, and Brito continues talking to me. First, he introduces his friends. Assey is the driver while Yerech is in the back with me. I smile to Yerech when his name is mentioned, but he just glares back at me. Not the chatty type.

"You killed the avatar in your brain first," states Brito.

"Sorry, what?"

"In your brain. In the pipes."

"Yes, in the pipes. What's the brain?"

Brito laughs out loud to the other two.

"He was crawling around inside his brain, and he didn't know it."

The three think this is incredibly funny and all start laughing at me.

"When 15 does a download of a Champion's brain, this is what it looks like. All the tubes and pipes. That's your brain. All your memories, experience, personality, intelligence, it's all flowing around in the pipes. It's why the room is decorated with pictures of you, and it's why we've got all this." He points to his gun.

"My brain?" I'm surprised, and sort of impressed. "What do you mean about the gun, though."

"Because you were the last Champion, all the avatars are Human; all the weapons are Human, all the vehicles are Human. 15 has all these things ready for you and your time here, stored if you like. There are no Kruzian weapons here. (Then I remember, Brito is Kruzian, from the Kruzh

Empire). We have to use yours, they are all a bit big, but we can manage." they all smile at each other.

"If I hadn't killed those avatars, would I have just been able to walk past them without any danger?"

"Probably, it's not as if they were looking for you. We didn't order the avatars to look for any suspicious behaviour. We didn't think we'd find anyone else here. We will do so now though, in case any other, previous Champions turn up unannounced. Maybe some of them will be a bit more dangerous, and a bit less difficult to disarm and capture, than you."

They all burst out laughing at this. I feel a right prick.

"The military training on your planet must be pretty shit, you were so easy to stop." they carry on laughing.

"I'm not military-trained; I was abducted off a train on my way into work. I worked in an office."

They start rolling around, laughing at this. Through tears of laughter, Assey manages to blurt out 'office boy', and 'passenger' and they all laugh like baboons.

After much jocularity and an awful lot of piss-take - all aimed at me, the van pulls up. I'm cut free from the truck but still 'handcuffed'. We get out, and I see what's going on for the first time.

Funnily enough, I can't see any walls in any direction - including from where we've been. The van is parked on a marked spot with a direction arrow crudely daubed on the floor by the Kruzians. In front of me is a giant circular column aligned floor to ceiling (which goes up in the unseeable distance). I take it that this is 15's Central Processing Unit, his CPU, *his* Brain. It is him, the ship. This column has a diameter of about 100 metres. It's also grey white and is totally smooth, a beautiful smooth curve all the way around. White lights are flicking on and off in no specific pattern under the surface of the opaque outer shell. Sometimes these appear as uniform-sized, well-defined dots in lines, columns and sequences and sometimes as swirly lights as if smoke or clouds are drifting under the surface. As usual, everything else is pure grey whiteness. I walk over and reach out my tied hands and touch the column; it's cool to handle and lights up under my hand. The Kruzian's see me feel the column and audibly gasp. I look around.

"What?"

They're agog.

Assey is first to talk,

"None of us can touch it. There is a force field around it. We've been trying to break in for a few weeks but have got nowhere yet."

"Not laughing at me now, are you fuckers!"

Yerech immediately pulls his weapon and points it at me.

"No!" shouts Brito.

"You need to take a large spoonful of chill mate." I say to Yerech, "You can dish it all day, but you can't take it? Hardly a top a 'bantz' merchant."

Yerech is still pointing the gun and looking mean. Brito angrily motions to him to put the weapon down.

"Looks like I can do something you can't. If you want me to help you, then you'd better start being a bit nicer to me. Fuckheads."

Chapter 23

I'VE NOW BEEN WITH the Kruzians for a couple of days. They've untied me. That was my first demand. I'm working with them because I don't yet know what I'm going to do. I'm pulled two or three ways, and the situation seems to change very regularly and my thinking with it.

My main options are:

- Wipe these three out and put 15 back the way he should be. Why? What has 15 ever done for me?
- What if I try to kill these three, but they kill me? Then I'm dead anyway.
- What if I kill them, and then can't put 15 back together again? I'm stuck.
- What if I kill these three, and then the avatars kill me? Then I'm dead anyway.
- What if I team up with the Kruzh Empire? Help these guys take over 15, let them be his boss - no skin off my nose. But, will they kill me once they have control? Probably. Then I'm dead anyway.

Why do they deserve to be in charge?

Kill these three mugs and take over myself? An attractive option as long as I can control 15. I'd be in charge of an amazingly powerful craft that can produce enough weaponry to rule a large section of this, or another galaxy. Is this something I want? I'm still stuck on the ship. Do I want to be in charge of some empire of aliens? What's the point?

The problem is that I don't know what I want. What I what is to mean something to someone. That's the thing that's been missing in my life for hundreds of years. At least, for the moment, these guys need me for something, and so does 15. I like being necessary. I like being wanted.

The thing that I'm most happy about is that the Kruzians have worked out how to get food. Although I don't need to eat - I love to eat. I love flavours, textures and smells. I love feeling satiated. I love the warmth food brings. One of the first things they had to sort out after they managed to break into 15 was how to get food. The Kruzians only had what they were able to carry with them, and as they do not have the same nanobots working inside them, finding food was their primary goal once established on board. 15 does not protect the food system in the same way as his CPU because it's not essential, so once found, it was pretty easy for these guys to get all the sustenance they needed. I've been down here so long, I've almost forgotten what food tastes like, so when they asked me if I required nourishment, I couldn't resist. I haven't told them I have nanobots; it's nothing they need to know. They don't know how I've stayed alive as long as I have, but then they're probably not too well versed in Human anatomy and don't understand how I work internally.

They drove me to the food. There is a wall (now marked with a daubed arrow by the Kruzians). You walk to the wall and explain what you want to eat.

"A thin, sourdough based pizza topped with 'nduja sausage, spicy pork meatballs, pepperoni, spicy beef, mushrooms, bacon, double cheese with green Bird's Eye and red Roquito chillies. Please?" I'm not sure if the please is necessary. But then a two by two-metre door slides up in the wall to reveal a small white (obviously) room with a low counter to the left-hand side. On the counter sits a plate with a piping hot pizza on top. Amazing. I retrieve the pizza and sit on the ground to eat.

The Kruzians all do the same, and all end up with a similar looking bowl of cold green slop each. It looks like a sort of greener, lumpier version of vichyssoise but to be fair; it smells OK, meaty even. They suck up the slop using a very wide bore, short straw. Each Kruzian also has a white linen table napkin which they use to wipe their mouths and straw. They all sit cross-legged and straight-backed and eat silently - they have very prim table manners for hardened marines, or whatever they are, but then this is what I should expect if they've all been military academy trained.

They look at me with disgust and utter disdain as I eat long slices of pizza with my hands. Yerech, in particular, seems to dislike the way I lift a piece above my head to bite at the wilting point, lowering it into my waiting mouth before chomping down. I could eat 'nicer', but once I realise they don't like the way I eat, I keep doing it but as casually as possible. I wipe my dirty face by sweeping the back of my greasy-fingered hand across it, and burp loudly shaping my mouth mid burp to change the note. I know it's very crude but so what, I'm a prisoner.

I go back for a steaming bowl of sticky toffee pudding with two scoops of vanilla ice cream topped with chocolate and toffee drizzled sauce; I eat noisily and messily. Finally, I ask for a two-litre bottle of lemon flavoured fizzy pop which I drink as we drive back to 15's Brain, repeatedly burping all the way.

Chapter 24

So here's the deal. I've agreed to help these three miscreants to break into 15's Brain. If I can either disable 15 or reprogramme him to be controlled by a third party (The Kruzh Empire), I will be allowed to take one of 15's armed warships and leave freely. I will be allowed to travel about the Universe, as long as I stay far away from the Empire. If I return and attack them in any way, force will be met with force. If I return peacefully and unarmed, I will be met as an equal and be afforded the best the Kruzh Empire has throughout any stay. The Kruzh Empire will agree that they are indebted to me and will act accordingly. Or, if no ship is available, I will be found a hospitable habitable planet well outside of the Kruzh Empire, and I will be given whatever means I need for me to live out my life comfortably until I naturally expire. During my stay here on 15, and while I am helping the Kruzh Empire to take control over 15, I will not be deemed a captive and will not be handcuffed, tied up or restrained in any way. I will be treated as an equal and be allowed to roam freely if I wish. I will do everything I can to help the Empire to take control of the ship.

I travelled back and forth to the vast 'Store Room', the place where all the racking and avatars are, a number of times to get pens and paper to write our agreement out in duplicate. Brito and I signed both copies - a formal contract - I then hid my version in case I needed it in the future. I'm not sure why I went to all the trouble. If I do manage to take control of 15 for Kruzh, I think the first action will be for one of them to put a bullet in my head. I'm just hoping this 'military honour code' they seem to be so into actually applies to beings outside of their species also.

I do not have any weapons; I choose not to carry any, although the three always have a bare minimum of some sort of handgun tucked away. I know they don't trust me, but they currently don't have a better option in terms of getting close to 15. In travelling back and forth to the Store, I have acquired a white Ford Transit Connect, and inside I have collected many tools to see what works on 15's Brain. I have a whole load of stuff from garden hoes to powered wrecking jacks, but my primary 'weapon of choice' is a hammer and sharp wood chisel, I also have a selection of knives and other edged tools. Back at the Brain, I unload, under the watchful eyes of the three. I've also brought a quite comfortable leather armchair. It's a con this chair. It's a Howard Bridgewater chair, I recognise the design immediately but it's upholstered in a very soft, antiqued, nut brown leather – rather than original ticking. It looks amazing, and is exceptionally comfortable, but a knock off hybrid. I bring this up close to 15 and perch on its edge.

I lean forward with my arms outstretched and reach out to touch 15's CPU. The curved surface emanates a cool heat. As I touch, the areas under my hands glow, as I move my hands around the glow moves too. There are no edges to catch with a lever, no visible screw heads, no clips. It seems like a substantial featureless curved wall with dancing lights beneath the smooth, white surface. I stand with my hands still touching the surface and walk around the curve. I'm always scanning to see if there is any visual interface system - a keypad or a mouse, for instance. I'm also looking for any sockets, any way of plugging into the wall. I can't imagine I'll suddenly find anything as simple as a USB port, but I'm still looking. The glows under my hands still move with me. At least one of the three Kruzians always has me in their eye-line - in case I get up to any monkey business. I reach high and low and keep moving. I spend hours staring at small sections or trying to see patterns of light. I keep this charade up for what seems like days. Walking around, touching, sliding my hands around, staring at small sections, up high or down low, wherever. I sit and watch, I move the chair to a different area and sit and watch again.

We're eating again. We now have a table and chairs that we've brought from the store. I'm having a Massaman Duck Curry and sticky rice, a Thai favourite of mine, rich and spicy, just how I like it. The boys are still on the slop. We're discussing what's going on with 15.

Brito's pretty pissed off with the whole affair, he's in charge, and therefore his head is on the block if he ever gets back to Kruzh.

"We're still not making any progress. Why are you moving so slowly?"

"I know you're under pressure, but I don't want to rush. One false move..." I reply.

"You keep saying that."

"Look Brito; If I just lay into the Brain with a jackhammer, I could kill 15, and he'd be dead in the water. Then we can't get on or off this thing, the food would stop, the heat and light would stop, and we'd be dead shortly after. Or, I might get frazzled, I could be electrocuted by 15 and die, and then you're back where you were, can't get near him, and you have to stay here until you die. And that's just two of any number of possibilities. You want in; you want me to help, you have to do it my way."

Yerech, he of little words, looks at me in disgust. Which, to be fair to him, is what he does all the time.

"It's taking too long, what are you doing today that you didn't do yesterday?"

"I'm putting pressure on different sections; I'm trying to see if certain areas respond to my touch in different ways. I'm also poking and prodding. There may be a pressure-sensitive panel that pops out when pushed. You've not been able to press anything have you?"

"No, of course not."

"Then let me try. We'll get to the drill and other methods in time, but I want to exhaust other basic actions and functions first."

Brito huffs and shuts up.

"Anyone fancy trying some rhubarb and custard?"

They all look about as green as the food they're eating.

When 15 and I had conversations, the vast majority were about how I was going to approach a fight against a Challenger. We often went off topic, usually with no real purpose, but occasionally we landed somewhere a little more interesting.

"One of the things I've been interested in most about a whole range of alien races is the thing that you on Earth call a 'soul'. This concept exists in many, many species and always interests me generally, I think because I don't have one. My soul would be the equivalent of a motherboard on Earth."

"No it wouldn't, it would be your programme. The motherboard is just the hardware. My body is just the hardware, a carapace. The shell of my soul. Which is the essence of me."

"So here's where I have different thoughts on the matter. You are basically the same as me. You are a biological computer. The main bit, the 'wetware', is your brain. When you are born, this is underdeveloped and mainly empty. It has the programming to support life; to breathe, to push blood around the body, to eat, to excrete, etc. These are built-in functions that don't need teaching. The rest of the wetware is an open book looking to be filled, and as the body grows so does the brain; learning from parents, siblings, teachers, friends, other family, and the interaction with the world. The computer - the brain - is portable, it has control of a body, which it must grow and nourish to keep working. The body is the brain's tool to discover the world: it finds stuff out - what food it likes, the difference between hot and cold, what music it enjoys, which people it would like as friends, and who it would want to mate with to make new, little computers in its image."

"Yep, I'm getting all this; it covers off a particular view on what a Human is."

"But what it collects, the sum of the parts of the personality is the individual's brain choosing and experimenting with its world."

"Yep. Each person has a unique experience of the world, each of us different from every other Human out there."

"And this is where I see the problem. It's lovely that you all think that you're so different and unique, and you are, but it's a very smug feeling. What you collect in your head is the same as what I collect in my database; it is a series of electrical impulses. Regardless of which programme your computer works on; quantum, neural networks, pixifile, magi-9, Z Code or other. The basic component of the brain is binary, the 'on' or 'off'. It's all the same. So you are no different to me in your processing of information. I can go out into the galaxy and collect information to process in the same way as you do. I do not have a tongue but can taste; otherwise, the food you eat here would taste of nothing. I can clearly communicate, so can talk. I can hear, feel – through my avatars, and I can see. I just don't have eyes, hands, a nose, ears and a mouth as you do. My experiences are different from any other machine like me. I meet alien races; I fight various battles, I examine different flora and fauna from eclectic parts of the Universe. Therefore, I too am unique, but less smug.

"Maybe not smug, but certainly superior?"

"I'm not starting that argument again. Can I carry on?"

I shrug, "Yeah, sure."

"But I do not have a soul."

"And I do."

"I'm not sure you have, I just think, you think you have. An abstract device or conceit to convince *your* computer, your brain, to not realise it's just a data node."

"What are you talking about?"

"If I were to download everything in your brain today into a memory bank. And then upload everything into an avatar, then I'd have a carbon copy of you with your soul."

"No because the soul isn't just the memories. It's the 'spiritual' essence of being a Human. It's being able to decide where you want the Human to go. What you want the Human to do, what you want to experience. It's the essence."

"And if I told you there was no spiritual essence, that's just the brain deciding what to do. If I told you that on examination, I could find no evidence of 'an essence' in you, or any of 695,953 species I have encountered that have a similar or the same concept of a 'soul'. If in all of these billions and billions of aliens, nothing exists that can be described as a soul. What would you say to that evidence?"

"I'd say that you've missed the point. There is no 'thing', you cannot bottle it and sell it down the market. It is not a 'thing'. You've been looking in the wrong place, it's not a quantity. I'll take all of your points and agree with just about everything. All I'd say is that you feel and act like a machine. You tell me you are; you act like an inanimate object, and for all of your moving parts and massive brain, I still regard you as an inanimate object - a talking computer in very simplistic terms. Even though, as you've described, I am the same as you. Still, even though you've paralleled yourself to my birth and growth and the electrical nature of our collected data being fundamentally the same, I have never believed I am a computer or a 'thing'. I am a person - my own person - and I have a soul. I reckon, if you'd asked any of the multi-billions of aliens you've studied what they think about this argument, they'd say the same. We are not computers; we are people. And therefore we have a soul. "

15 chimed in, "..but..."

But, was cut short..

"I can prove it."

"How?"

'Can you dance?'

"No."

I stood up, and disco danced, with massively overemphasised moves to 15.

I squatted down on my hunkers, threw my arms around 15 and cuddled him, and whispered,

"'Cause you ain't got no soul maaan."

After a few moments, I stood back up, and disco danced back to the environment.

Chapter 25

THE THING IS, I *have* noticed some changes in 15 as I've been prodding and studying. I just don't want the Kruzians to know what I'm working on. I've noticed that the light under my hand brightens as I push it harder. The light intensifies. I noticed a couple of days ago but have kept this discovery to myself. I want to try to communicate with 15, but I certainly don't want the Kruzians to know. I want them to get so bored of my staring and studying that they drop their guard, they stop watching, or watch less. What's more boring than watching nothing happen? Easy, it's watching someone, watching nothing happening. But I don't know enough yet.

"Since you've been here what exactly have you done to 15?" After a lot of doing nothing, I've decided to put the ball back into their court.

We're all sitting around next to 15; we're on a break. I've got a big mug of steaming hot tea. It might be 'Builders Tea', but it's Yorkshire Gold, so it's good builders tea, and five milk chocolate Hobnob biscuits. The others have drinks bottles with what I think is the equivalent of a soft drink on Kruzh, like a dilute or a cold fruit tea infusion, they drink lots of it.

"I killed you. I walked back through the door to meet with these two. We blew a hole in the ground and dropped in. We split up to search and eventually found the Pipes Room - your brain, then the next few rooms the same as you did, as well as some others. We found where and how to access the avatars and did so. We found some other empty rooms that didn't seem to go anywhere. We found the 'Oil Room'..."

"What 'Oil Room'?" I cut in.

"Didn't we tell you? We call it the Oil Room. A big empty room with a shiny black liquid floor that looks like an oil slick."

"Whoa there! What fucking oil slick?"

"Just like I told you."

"And you haven't mentioned this until now? I need to see it. Now. Immediately."

Brito looks up at Assey and shrugs.

"Take him to the Oil Room," he says tiredly.

As we drive there, I talk to Assey; he's the chattiest and friendliest of the three and the one that does all of the driving. We're heading through parts of 15 that I have never seen before. Most of it is empty space. We started by heading back to the store and once up the ramp turned right and drove straight through to the back wall. I would say the drive from the ramp to the wall took at least half an hour at a fair lick. I think we were doing 70 or 80 for most of the time. With my simple maths, it must have been about 35 miles from the ramp to the back wall. We drove through lines and lines of avatars, all standing still like tailors dummies and through aeroplanes: passenger jets, fighters, light aircraft, also past helicopters and buildings such as garden sheds, telephone boxes, shipping containers and then street furniture; green telephone exchange boxes, traffic lights, road signs, charging points, cycle docks. Miles and miles of stored, every day, stuff. We're chatting about all of this ephemera. Assey is pretty interested in finding out about Earth - because he's surrounded by so much of it. Everything he has to utilise, weapons, vehicles, avatars, clothing - everything is from Earth, all because I was the last Champion. The first thing Assey did once the three had found the store, is learn how to drive. It didn't take long as almost all of the vehicles produced by 15 are automatics - they don't have manual gears and clutches. It's possible that without this, the Kruzians may never have learned how to drive.

"So you were the ship's Champion. Tell me about some of your fights?" Assey seems to be the only one with any interest in anything other than Kruzh or the Kruzian Empire.

"Not much to tell really, I fought lots of different aliens. The vast majority of the fights were straightforward - a walk in the park. The Challenger would be shitting themselves and rigid with fear. I'd only need to throw a few punches or slash about with a pointy object a bit, or hit something hard with something heavy, and I'd have won."

"But you must have had a few battles also."

"I had quite a good fight with Brito."

"He said you were easy. He knew what you were going to do before you did it."

"So how come I tagged him a few times then?"

"To make the fight look good, and to buy us some time to break in."

"Bullshit." I bravado it out, but inside I feel a little hurt. Did he play me?

"Tell me another."

"OK.", I thought for a while and settled back into the passenger seat, I bent my knees, lifted my feet and placed them on the dash in front of me. "One of the most difficult bouts I fought wasn't so much a 'battle', but it was not an easy fight. The aliens were Nethlings from the planet Neth. Neth was in the midst of a civil war. The Neth had had their Agricultural, Industrial, Technological and finally Cosmological Revolutions. Luckily for them, they quickly found an uninhabited but 'capable of life' sustaining planet in their solar system. So they didn't have to learn much beyond rocket power to be able to send ships back and forth and colonise the new planet.

Both were very similar in size, orbit, pressure, gravity and temperature; both had different but abundant resources. Both, once colonised, were equally self-sufficient. It didn't take long, only a couple of generations, for the new planet's inhabitants to want independence, in a very similar way to what happened between the UK and the US in the American War of Independence on Earth. The original planet 'governed' the new planet and taxed goods from afar. The 'new world' wanted self-government, and to be able to sell their own planet's resources to whoever wanted to buy them. Soon there was a war. Pretty simple stuff, following so far?

"Yep, I didn't need the Earth comparison though."

"Well, you got it. 15 was passing relatively closely at the time and picked up on the conflict. He contacted both parties, each without the other one's knowledge, and offered to supply each a fleet of battleships in return for something precious. There had been two chief and competing religions on the original planet. Many of the people who left to colonise the new planet were the people who followed the teachings of the prophet Gerra. Those who followed 'the true prophet' Sanbalia stayed. The payments that 15 wanted were many of the religious relics from both religions. Often iconography is chosen as currency by 15 because the people on the planet can live without it, but it usually means much more to the people than its intrinsic value. If people believe that the giant, ugly-looking boulder over there is central to their religion, and that it must be protected and venerated, then that's fine. To 15, it's just a boulder. A load of silica crystals squashed together. It is valueless.

"One planet, the new one, Gerra, decided amongst themselves to go for the fleet option. Sanbalia didn't. Their belief, and therefore their artifacts, were more important to them than a few spaceships. The way 15 works though is that he won't give undue advantage in this sort of situation. It's not fair to just give one side such tactical superiority that they'll just bulldoze the opposition. When it's one of these 'Local Disputes' 15 uses discretion. The Gerra would have enough firepower to win a war, but they would have to employ it correctly themselves - which puts an element of risk into the plan. They were powerful but certainly not unbeatable.

I had to fight one of the Gerraling males, or at least I think he was a male. First time I saw him was in the centre of the Arena, standing on his light as I approached mine. I could see that he was like a dark brown ghost. It was as if he had a brown sheet thrown over his body, in the same way, we pretend to be ghosts on Earth."

"What's a ghost?"

"It's supposed to be the spirit of a dead person that has come back to haunt you. They're supposed to be white - the easiest, and best way for a living person to represent one was to throw a white sheet over themselves and make some eye-holes to see through. This thing looked like that; it had this billowing sheet over it, I don't know if it was its skin, or ectoplasm, or a sheet, or what. It also had a hardwood club, a cudgel. We had one each with which to inflict pain on each other. As soon as the 'Bong' sounded and the lights disappeared, it changed shape into Human form. It was a shapeshifter. It became this big, muscley meat-head thing like some sort of mountain man, with wild black hair and a long, grubby black beard. It wore just a leather loincloth, and I could see rippling muscles on top of other rippling muscles, sinews straining, veins standing out. It scared the shit out of me. I ran off."

"You are a pussy?"

"No I'm not a 'pussy', I wanted time to think, it wasn't what I was expecting and sometimes it's good to get a bit of distance away from your opponent to get a bit of perspective. It came after me but was hardly quick. My thinking was that he'd never 'become' a Human before and had probably only seen a few pictures of various Humans to copy. He chose to go for the biggest scariest one he could be to get an easy win. What he didn't realise is that different body shapes move differently. If one is little and lithe, then one will proceed more quickly and fluidly than if one is a big guy. But the big guy, while slower, will have more power. The Gerraling's not 'lumbering' around, he's better than that, but I've certainly got more speed on my side. I use it to my advantage, and go for a frontal attack. Shortly before I'm in striking distance I feint to the right and paste him on the side of the head with the sweet spot of the cudgel and carry on moving away. I make precisely the same 'hit-and-run' play twice more and on each occasion, either feinting left or right, come away having delivered an excellent solid smack to the side of the head. So far not enough to elicit a knockdown, knock-out or even draw blood, but a pretty good start. As I'm getting results, I decided to play the same game and repeat the action. I move in and get pretty close, just before I deliver my blow, the changeling turns into an exact facsimile of my Mother. Who smiles at me. I'm caught cold, and several things happen simultaneously; I pull my strike, my jaw drops open, and I'm startled. The Gerraling uses this opportunity to whip his cudgel around and catch a sharp glancing blow across the back of my head, where the top of my neck meets the bottom of my skull. Shit, it hurts and blinds me for an instant. Fortunately, it's my Mum delivering this wicked crack, not Mr Muscles. It only retains the power of the shape it is filling. Still, it's particularly unpleasant and wakes me up. Now I'm looking at my Mum. I know she's not my Mum, I know she's an intergalactic shapeshifter, but I still don't want to punch my Mum in the face. I freeze, and my Mum kicks me with menace, in the bollocks - hard in the bollocks. Fortunately, I'm wearing a cup, I always do, but the force still makes me double-up. When my head drops, she/it smashes the cudgel into the side of my head. I'm still on my feet but need to move fast. I hobble as far away from her as quickly as possible and knowing that her arthritis is probably playing up, I'm quickly away from her, even though I'm in pain."

"Now you run from your Mumma, you're a baby!", interjects Assey in fit of laughter.

I ignore his 'bants' and carry on, "I get some time to recover and sort my head out, physically and mentally. I know it's not my Mum. It's a pretend-face, shapeshifter from planet no-mark that's messing with my brain. I need to get with the programme and beat my Mum up. My dear old Mum smiles at me again as she gets closer and I swipe the cudgel up in a devastating uppercut. I catch her clean under the chin and produce a teeth fountain as at least three fire up over her head as her jaw snaps backwards. There's also blood, but you'd expect that when you've just had a few of your teeth removed with a heavy stick. It changes shape again, abandoning my mother and occupying a different body. Now it's Jenny, my 13-year-old daughter. She's crying and holding her left hand to her mouth; the blood is seeping through her fingers.

"Dad, what have you done?"

My heart drops. What have I done to my beautiful daughter? I've just smacked her in the mouth. I can see she's in pain and I want to cuddle her, to console her, to make it better, to make the pain go away. I'm confused again - until the club in her right hand connects with *my* jaw and nearly knocks me into a different calendar month. I'm sent spinning, literally, and glad about it because another blow in that proximity would have put me down.

SHE'S NOT MY DARLING DAUGHTER; SHE'S A SHAPESHIFTER PRETENDING TO BE MY DAUGHTER!

Is what my brain is screaming at me, but my heart and soul say different. Protect this innocent child, your progeny, look after her, love her. She's coming again, grinning at me through blood and broken teeth.

"YOU'RE NOT MY DAUGHTER!" I shout and smash the cudgel down hard on the crown of its head; I'm sure I hear the bones cracking underneath, bowing to the pressure of the blow. It's a significant, solid impact, driven down hard. The beast drops to the floor and changes back to a dark brown mass. I don't know if it's dead or alive, but it's certainly in no fit state to carry on. I prod it a couple of times with my foot, but there's no sign of life and no noise from it. I'd won the most disturbing battle of my life."

Assey nodded, "Good story. I would kill any member of my family without hesitation for the Kruzian Empire so I'd have easily defeated the shapeshifter."

They certainly don't lack confidence these Kruzians.

"Did you like fighting, and being the Champion?"

"It had its ups and downs. To start with I liked it but I was 15's Champion for thousands of Earth years. I don't know how long in Kruzian time that is but not many Humans live to be 100, so more than 20 times a Human life is how long I was Champion. In the end, I got bored. I started to hate it. Even though I had everything I ever wanted, it just became mind-numbing tedium. What did I have to live for?"

Chapter 26

As we continue driving, Assey tells me the saga of how they came to be on 15 and the Kruzian Empire's 'beef' with fleet building ships.

I was startled to find out that the plan to infiltrate and capture a fleet ship was hatched thousands of years ago. Over this time, the Kruzh Empire has encountered five different ships of 15's ilk. Again, I was surprised at how many they had met as 15 informed me he had only ever previously met one fleet ship in the totality of his travels. The reason for the frequency is purely because of the vast area of territory the Kruzh command dominion over. They are very successful empire builders, and although they have had cycles of contraction and expansion, in general, they have managed to keep the core of what they have for a very long time. Of course, 15 would argue that it is still only a short period in the vastness of time and the Universe.

Ironically, the first contact with a fleet ship was the catalyst needed to start the Kruzh on their journey to dominance. They needed a fleet to help them defend their homeworld - very much a typical starting point for many fleet ship transactions. The Kruzh 'bought' their fleet, the price paid was 'The Obelisks of Perelco-ta', a bit like their version of The Ten Commandments carved on the original stone tablets. As often happens, these were hugely venerated, valuable religious relics. The ship's Champion then defeated their Challenger in combat.

The problem is that this Challenger was a great general in Kruzh, a household name and much-loved figure. The fight was broadcast all across Kruzh, and millions watched on. The ship's Champion battered the Challenger to a bloody pulp until he could carry on no further and then left the Arena. To the Kruzh, this was not a fitting end to the fight. Theoretically, their general did not surrender and was not killed. In their view, the battle was not over. Their Challenger could still have got up, dusted himself down and gone on to win a great victory. The Champion should have killed the Challenger – execution before exiting the arena, that is the Kruzh way. This did not happen; there was no conclusion. But the ship kept the obelisks anyway as the general expired, shortly after, on the floor of the Arena.

The Kruzh were outraged; they had their new battle fleet but felt cheated by the deal. They felt they could have still won back their payment; they felt the obelisks had been stolen from them. The Champion had entirely left the Arena before the Challenger died - the fight was not over. The bile and hatred grew swiftly, the population demanded politicians to act, and that's what they did.

A series of military academies were set up in the name of the General Buzardino Tan-D-bonze, the deceased Challenger, with the sole purpose of training further Challengers to fight fleet ship Champions should the occasion ever occur again.

The Kruzh also found out about the fleet ship's ability to clonescan planets, so Challenger training academies had to be kept very secret. The battleships 'bought' from the fleet ship were put to use, and very quickly the Kruzh grew from a single homeworld to a more significant colony of captured planets. Over centuries these became incorporated into the newly formed 'Empire'. When talks and discussions regarding military academies took place, they were not only conducted 'off-planet' but also outside of Kruzh controlled space, occasionally in locations millions of light-years from the now 'homeworlds' and owned space.

As a way of being able to talk about both fleet ships and academies with total secrecy, no notes or recordings were made of any meetings, discussions or decisions. All sessions were conducted in a coded language - a form of communication developed shortly after the first 'loss'.

Even the coded language held deeper codes; nothing was ever directly referred to or called by its correct name. If one were able to decode a discussion, you'd think you'd earwigged in on a boring middle-management meeting about mining or road infrastructure. It is highly unlikely that even if a fleet ship had intercepted a radio transmission (which never happened), it would not bother to try to decipher the conversation as it was so dull - the cover was *that* good and the language so fluent and convincing. From the first encounter, the Kruzh knew that there were other fleet ships in the Universe. They worked out that actively looking for help would attract them, that ships had a powerful clonescan ability, that they were very intelligent and very dangerous.

Around 700 Earth years passed before a second fleet ship appeared in a quadrant of their now vast space dominion. This encounter happened to be at the opposite end of the owned space to the first meeting, hundreds of light-years distant. This time, as previously, the Kruzh asked for battleships to aid their expansion. During the intervening years, the Kruzhian government, led by the military, had put a de-facto Royal Family in place. The whole Empire loved and sang the praises of the Royals, but they were patsies be used as trading pieces. If a fleet ship wanted a payment, this time the Kruzh would trade a well-loved member of the royal family, rather than important, venerated religious artifacts.

This was the second occasion the Kruzh had been in communication with a fleet ship. They had the opportunity to ask lots of seemingly innocuous questions - just asking. When they found out that most 'won' prizes were just jettisoned off into deep, dark space, they flew into an angry rage. Now there was no chance they would ever regain their treasured obelisks. Their most holy of holies had probably been dumped - like taking out the trash. The diplomats discussing details of the 'deal' on the fleet ship got the raving arse and tried to attack the fleet ship internally before concluding any trade. The ship simply shipped them all back to their planet and left.

The diplomats, once home, were interrogated and then summarily executed.

It was almost another thousand years until the next fleet ship; the third, appeared on the radar. The Empire had again grown. One of the reasons the Empire may have continued to grow and function so well is because their enemy was not other planets but the fleet ships themselves. The Kruzh have never desired colonisation, or wanton destruction, their eyes were on a bigger prize. Taking over or destroying fleet ships - getting them under their control. The idea was that you could potentially rule the whole Universe with such weapons at your disposal.

This thousand years though, is in the region of 25 generations of Kruzhians. Now, they were even more ready, even more prepared. The Kruzh had used the time to train delegates (all alumni of military education institutions) in espionage, negotiation, game theory and business strategy. This negated the likelihood of a repeat performance of what happened in the previous 'deal' phase.

The Kruzh quickly struck a deal, and a candidate was selected to face the ship's Champion.

Whilst the fight was taking place, the other supporting Kruzian delegates were quizzing the ship and trying to find hacks, bugs and different ways into the ship's system. This was completed in a manner devised to 'keep under the radar' of the deep scan. An awful lot of thinking and statistical analysis had gone into working out the 'gameplay' of a fleet ship. The outcome was a set of hypotheses - the ship would scan homeworlds in totality. The ship would also deep scan local colony planets and orbiting objects. Was it worth the ship checking every orbiting rock and every dwarf moon? Notably, if it served no military purpose? Had never been colonised? Had the object any sign of anything interesting about it? Did it look like anyone had ever given it a second look? There are millions of these objects in every cubic light-year of space. Is a lump of 'not worth looking at' just not worth looking at? How long does a 'clonescan' of a planet, or planets, take? When would a fleet ship carry out a scan, when nearby? When distant? Surely the scan is just a snapshot. Once you've scanned a planet, there's no real need to repeatedly keep scanning? The vast, vast majority of information you learn from the first scan will hardly change by the time of a subsequent scan. It was hypothesised how far away (with huge tolerances) a clonescan would be conducted and how long (with huge tolerances) it would take. It was also suggested that any scan would only happen once, and would not include the many, many naturally occurring dull objects that are floating around the neighbourhood.

The Kruzh developed a new technology, Needle Beams, high-energy, short burst, microwave pulses that can be transmitted millions of light years to a specific, minute target spot. They are tough to detect because of their micro size, 50 times thinner than a single strand of Human hair. They are very powerful, very quick, very direct and very stable. To find one single pulse, of about a second in length, is not like looking for a needle in a haystack, it's like looking for a needle in a stack of all the hay ever cut on planet Earth since the development of farming. Even this small section of the Universe is *that big* in comparison to a needle beam pulse. How it works - every day, the Kruzh broadcast a wide beam public information signal from the home planet to all of the surrounding worlds. The process happens like clockwork, same time, every day, without fail. On this specific day, the broadcast includes a word (not coded, just a word never used on a broadcast before) which when detected sparks up an inactive beam generator sitting on a totally insignificant rock, floating around in empty space, millions of miles away.

This machine, a Needle Beam Generator completes the only job it has ever been built and programmed to do which is to send one single needle pulse beam before switching itself off again. This single pulse sets off a chain of pulses between other generators on other non-descript rocks. Similar actions occur on Earth when people try to make their IP address hard to trace by using a series of piggyback servers at different locations all around the world. It's about deception. The signal is shot from one pulse generator to another on various non-descript floating rocks separated by huge distances. On each rock, once the signal arrives, its generator (which has been idle) sparks up and sends its needle pulse (a different one, on a different frequency, with different information) on to the next generator on the next rock. This process unfolds over a massive area of space in just a few seconds, ultimately sending a signal to the Needle Pulse Generator closest to the target, the fleet ship.

This last signal pings from the final rock to a specific member of the shipped team of delegates who has walked a circle leaving a newly developed form of undetectable liquid explosive on the floor in their wake. The pinged pulse detonates the explosive blowing a hole in the floor. The explosive, although placed in a ring on the surface of the floor, is designed, at a cellular level, to explode downwards only. The delegate stands inside the circle and prepares to drop downwards into the belly of the whale.

And that is what happened. The delegate had the explosive liquid surgically implanted into a small sack hidden inside his heart along with a small, capillary tube, running from this heart sack down through the inside of the body to the sole of his left foot. At the foot, the tube was covered with a thin layer of skin. All the delegate has to do is reach down and scratch their foot in the right place to remove the skin layer covering the opening of the capillary tube. The action of the heart pumping pushed the liquid explosive out as the delegate walked in a well-rehearsed circle or square, or any shape you can imagine. The explosive is only active until it dries, as the explosive liquid is water-based, it is untraceable and benign until activated by the needle beam sent from the pulse detonator. There was no way the liquid explosive would be flagged up as dangerous or hazardous during a fleet ship personal scan and none of the delegates had any means of detonating explosives about them. Once the signal was received, the explosion happend. It's exquisite, very clean, not designed to hurt anyone, just created with one real purpose - to get inside a fleet ship undetected.

This first trial ended badly. The plan worked perfectly, the needle beams were incredible, no issues, the explosive was placed with pinpoint accuracy, all good so far. The operator, the would-be saboteur, was standing in the correct place when the explosion happened. The only issue is that the Kruzh operative did not know where was a 'right' place to break through on the floor. The floor gave way, as hoped, but the saboteur dropped down directly into one of the fleet shipbuilding warehouses. His fall alone would have killed him, but before he hit the ground, he was split to atoms by a single shot from an Xj#17 Blast Howser, a weapon big enough to melt our moon with a single discharge, within a metre of entering the hole. What happened next is interesting. The fleet ship did not destroy the Kruzh. It allowed them to finish their Duel of Champions and even awarded them their fleet and let them go with no further action taken. It also appears to have given them some other information about fleet ships described typically as 'classified'. This additional information ultimately helped the Kruzh fast forward to the point they've presently reached. I immediately felt that this particular fleet ship seems to have gone 'rogue' or had some sort of vendetta against the others. It is a very 'non-15' thing to do. It looks like this information might have been pertaining to where precisely an attack should happen on a fleet ship.

The Kruzian Empire had a long wait, a few thousand years for the fourth opportunity to present itself.

They spent the time well, consolidating their empire and perfecting their espionage and subterfuge attacks. The tricky thing for them to do is keep all this work secret from a fleet ship when it does finally present itself. Even though top-secret and coded, by now millions had been through the military colleges, and millions had worked on businesses associated with fleet ship domination. There was a worry that information would be given away in a clonescan; the government became paranoid. The solution was to carry out a pogrom. Millions of citizens were massacred in a fake 'revolution', the main body of those slain were previous military college pupils, the elderly and anyone who may have had any knowledge of 'what went before'. A 'knowledge gap' was created, those who knew and were complicit and those who were totally in the dark. These people were mainly the young. From now on those who were taken away for military training never to come home. News or knowledge of what was happening on the outlier training bases was never returned to the homeworld. This was the extent that the trusted few at the very top of the military and government were prepared to go to keep a secret.

Now there was only ever a handful who were ever aware of what was happening in the training facilities. The group was kept to a far more manageable bare minimum with all communications coded. An insidious network of information passage quietly doing its thing for century after century with one secret hidden aim. To attack - and capture or destroy a fleet ship.

When the forth fleet ship entered Kruzian territory, four hundred years after the last one, the Kruzh again feigned the need for a fleet of ships, and also offered a member of the proxy royal house as payment. The face-to-face battle was proposed as part of the deal, and again the bout went ahead.

This time, the Kruzians included the ridiculous, but meticulous, pre-fight ceremony that I had to endure before my battle with Brito. This utterly stupid charade was developed to distract the Champion and fleet ship from what else was going on, and to buy time on the ship. Often the Challenger is shipped onto 15, with any associated retinue/posse/entourage, shortly before the commencement of the fight - why would they need or want to be on the ship for a more extended period? There is no advantage to be gained by acclimatising to the ship before a bout. There is no knowledge of pressure or temperature, light or smell, or other factors I can think of that would help to know about. In fact, as the ship's Champion, it was usually me who had to make the most significant compromises as I would have to fit in with some weird alien form, or regulation or requirement to make the fight work.

This ship, was successfully breached. The Kruzh now knew exactly where to attack and executed this attack with rehearsed precision and speed. The Kruzh agent blew a square-shaped hole in the floor in the same spot as the one on 15. The agent dropped through the hole. But the attack failed, although trained in warfare, survival and sabotage, the commando did not know what to do once they fell down the hole. When I stupidly jumped into

15's innards, I didn't know what to do, but I got lucky. I managed to walk in the single direction that brought me somewhere, admittedly within a wide arc, but fortunately, I managed to see the big door/portal and got close enough to move further into 15's innards. I am also equipped with nanobots who were able to sustain and repair my body to keep me functioning over the shit-long amount of days I was marching round in a big black hole. The Kruzian commando didn't have such luck or assistance. Had the agent been equipped with Kruzian nanobots, the fleet ship would have detected them and blocked the agent from shipping on board. Had the agent been allowed on board, the fleet ship would have focussed a tracking bead on them at all times. A millisecond after the explosion, but still way before the drop into the hole commenced, the agent would have been sliced like a loaf of bread by an array of cheese wire beams.

So, in a hole, in the dark with no direction to go, and no additional sustenance. Even if the agent could have walked around for a month, he'd be struggling.

The Challenger and his entourage were shipped back to the home planet. They were all dead. It looked like the life support had been just switched off. The ship also sent back the 'payment', a senior member of the royal family. Dead also. The battle fleet was not delivered.

The fleet ship left.

The commando was never heard from again. I assumed he died of starvation.

Having been in that big, dark room, I can see how that could easily happen.

Then there is the last time before 15 was attacked, around 600 years ago. Similar story, the Kruzh activated the now centuries-old, well-rehearsed plan. The fight delegation was shipped on-board; they commenced their usual process of taking down the ship; they had a new method for the commando. The weird costumes worn by the attendants of the combatants during the Weapon Purifying Ceremony were constructed using thread created from the manufacture and processing of a highly nutritious plant – edible clothing. They also planned to drop in more than one commando - in fact, three - to split up and try to cover off more space. There was also a simple form of skateboard, fashioned from the headdress, which would allow the commandos to be way more mobile and cover longer distances more quickly. This plan was foiled by the ship very shortly before its execution. Every member of the Kruzian boarding party was immediately attacked, a small but very aggressive drone ship smashed into the back of the Challenger's head in the Arena. The Champion didn't have a clue what was happening, one minute he was fencing beautifully, the next he was splattered in blood and brain tissue.

The ship wanted retribution. It blocked all transmissions across the entire Kruzh Empire and then transmitted its broadcast to every screen or device across the whole expanse. It wanted every Kruzian citizen to see. The rest of the entourage - the two commandos, each had a leg removed from the pelvis and an arm at the shoulder. Two state-of-the-art Dirk Fliers enacted this vicious revenge. So sharp and exacting was their attack that it was probably initially painless for the two, now incapacitated, lying on the floor, and starting to bleed with the pain kicking in. The two Kruzians were each 'helped' by avatars, into a bath of weak acid. Enough to irritate the skin but not immediately burn. The ship wanted revenge and to prove a point, it slowly increased the strength of the acid in the baths, bit by bit. The population watched the two Kruzian agents dissolve.

Then the fleet ship deployed the battle fleet it had built for Kruzh, plus whatever other complement of ships it had stowed and available. It destroyed the homeworld and colonies with unfazed brutality, fierce aggression and no mercy. The empire was fucked in very short order. Millions and millions died, planets just ceased to exist. Annihilation. No other word. They felt the wrath.

But as we know. That was not the end of the Kruzh Empire because here they still are, and now they have been successful in breaching a fleet ship and are getting close to meeting their aims. What the 'Angel of Death' ship didn't find were the secret military academies. The ones in the outlying star systems, the ones positioned to avoid detection. And that's what happened. They were undetected, and revenge was not meted against them - probably the ones who deserved it most. The action of that one ship enraged the Kruzians even more. Even though they started all of this, they think they're the aggrieved party. The rebuilding process started again. A couple of new planets were captured, a new homeworld populated. The vast military knowledge gained over millennia gave them an advantage when meeting new foes. They quickly re-established. Still, a shadow of their former might, but still as aggressive, still as twisted, still with one aim. The system of avoiding the deep scan through off-site academies and hiding secrets was almost more manageable with a new homeworld. The inhabitants just didn't need to know anything that was going on. The academies, off-world watched and waited for their next opportunity.

Then 15 arrived.

"What do you think was Humanity's greatest invention then?" I asked 15, "Language, I suppose?"

There's one of those brief, 'fake thinking' pauses I've come to expect. I get the chance to think about my question, so I rephrase it.

"Okay, that's general Human development, and not an 'invention'. I mean, what did we invent that you think is pretty good, because we seemed to think it was 'sliced bread'"?

"That's one of the metaphors that I particularly like. It originally developed from an advertising campaign for sliced bread in the US in the first decades of the Nineteenth Century. Sliced bread is, therefore, quite a latecomer in terms of inventions, and not particularly impressive, but I like the absurdity of the phrase."

"In this instance, my viewpoint is entirely subjective; I cannot definitively judge what is *the* best as much as anyone else; Human, machine or other can. Anyone could have an entirely different, well-argued, and wholly substantial alternative to mine."

"Can you stop with the caveats and hit me with the thing?"

"What you have to remember is that each invention begets the next invention which begets the next. Invention is like a chain; invariably you cannot jump links, and therefore even what seems like a big step forward may not have happened without the previous small step forward. Sometimes, a great invention was just waiting to happen, but no one saw it until it was time."

I cut in, becoming more frustrated, "For fuck sake, it's the Internet, isn't it!"

"No, not in my estimation, that was absolutely the next step."

There is another pause. Before 15 starts again.

"Actually I think it was gardening."

"HA!" the air escapes my body instantly as I exclaim incredulity.

15 clearly feels he has to explain, and kicks off at a lick.

"I mean it. Farming was 'invented' by the early people, the 'gatherers' as you

called them. This was a necessary step in the growth of Humanity. It allowed for stores of food to be created for periods when there was little meat. Farming, and storing food for Humans, led to animal husbandry as surplus food could be used for fodder for animals. This led to meat and dairy farming, and in turn to more efficient agriculture, harnessing the power of horses and oxen to do heavy fieldwork, and for transportation and so on. Humans stopped being nomadic - chasing untamed herd's migratory patterns. Farms led to villages, which could grow into towns and eventually into cities.

I cut in here, "You're talking about farming, not gardening, you're on the

wrong thing."

"I haven't finished. Farming was an absolute necessity that led to so many more further steps, but what is gardening?"

"Pissing about with flowers mainly. Wasting time when you're bored with television."

"No, gardening is controlling plant life and vegetation, without really realising. Looking after a garden meant that the homeowner could stop being swamped by the ever-burgeoning, every growing, constant growth of plant life. They would pull out 'weeds', hundreds of them, to plant a single row of seeds. City and town planners invented 'parks' which cleared forests and undergrowth and seeded grass which was easy to mow and maintain and shrubs to plant and prune. Town councils employed armies of ground staff constantly cutting, mowing, scarifying, ripping out, re-digging and replanting traffic islands, verges, hedges and trees - keeping the roads clear of the encroaching forest. It never stopped, in your houses, in your towns and cities. All under the guise of 'keeping it pretty' and 'making it look tidy', or 'Britain's Prettiest Village', when what you were really doing was constantly chopping back, stopping yourselves from being eaten alive by the jungle, the desert, the countryside. You didn't do it like an organised army, under orders, all working as one for the greater good. No, it was subtle, usually a bit of 'pottering' on the weekend. Everyone eager to do their little bit. Keeping back and taming the flora on your planet, around where you lived, was tantamount to your success. True, the farming industry was responsible for major, and very dangerous deforestation, but not the gardeners. Gardening stopped cities, towns and villages from being swallowed up, and allowed civilisation to flourish. Gardening wins for me."

"The more I talk to you, the weirder you get."

Chapter 27

SO, THEY GOT BEEF.

Not particularly with 15, but with all fleet building ships. I'm sort of surprised that the Kruzh has been around long enough to meet so many of them. Still, I suppose, if you have longevity and a vast, expansive empire, you've got a higher opportunity for a 'by chance' situation to occur.

We're still driving.

"Why did you help the devilish fleet ship? They are the scum of the Universe."

I thought about this for a while. Assey's whole society is based on being 'wronged' by a single fleet ship hundreds of generations before he was born. If anything, with subsequent encounters, the hatred has grown.

"I don't think 15 is a malevolent force; I think that generally, it is a force for good. Although I'm it's prisoner, I'm fairly treated, and it seems to try not to be too involved in taking sides in planetary disputes."

"I hate the fleet ships. I hate 15. All they have ever done is try to ruin Kruzian society." he hisses with real hatred, and bangs his clenched fist down hard against the steering wheel causing us to swerve a little.

"I'm not sure I agree with that. I think that your society has provoked every fleet ship it's come across by its actions. You agree that you are trying to take control of this ship, that is why you are here. That is your mission and what you have spent your life training to do. Don't you think that if the Kruzh Empire hadn't tried to attack fleet ships that they likely would not have attacked back?"

Assey pulls his 'thinking' face. I continue,

"To me, it is the constant provocation of various fleet ships that has often been the downfall of your society. You bring it upon yourselves. You could just go happily about building your Empire and focussing on that and probably be very successful and happy. Trying to take over fleet ships is a dangerous game and one you always end up losing."

"What do you know? They've only ever attacked our society, and they need to pay." He's getting more wound up. I'm about to say something else about 15 not being so bad really but decide against it. There is a period of silence in the van which is eventually broken by Assey; he's calmed a little.

"Tell me about another fight."

Assey wants to get off the subject. This is probably the first time in his life he's heard a counter-argument about Kruzh. I bounce up in my seat and answer in a jaunty way, just to lighten the mood a little.

"I'll tell you about some quick fights, all of which I won easily. I don't even remember what many of the aliens were; their names, their homeworlds, their requirements of 15. The fights were so quick it wasn't worth finding out about them. There was one thing, a cave troll type being, low browed, thick skull, huge but square and squat. It was about three times the size of me. Looked stupid - I suppose that was the problem. It wore something similar to a bearskin from Earth. Some dead, furry-skinned animal anyway. The thing, not the animal skin, reeked of old sweat and filth. It was hairy too - a very uncivilised, unpalatable type. There was no way this thing had developed space travel, but it's type shared a planet with a very civilised race. They were the brains of the outfit but were 'lovers, not fighters'. This thuggish brute belonged to the 'worker' caste of the planet. Its people had rights and citizenship and thus were eligible to fight me in the Arena. I thought I'd instead have fought one of the upper castes, but, when it came to it, the bout was not long-lasting. The noise sounded. We were both unarmed; the thing was a champion wrestler, I walked towards it. It made a lunge to try to grab me, but it was slow and so telegraphed that I stepped to the left. I didn't even attempt a tricky feint or anything, just a simple step. Then I threw a speculative straight right into its face to see how it reacted to pain. I punched its head right off its shoulders. Clean off. Landed on the floor about 6 feet behind him. The head landed on the floor before the body realised what was happening, so the body, sort of tried to take a step forward and then crumpled down on top of itself."

"It was 'all show and no go'." Assey laughed.

"I felt a bit sorry for the great big lunk. It did look scary though."

"They must have known you were capable of punching through it?"

"Appearances can be deceptive, especially here in 'outer space', just because *their* thing was huge compared to me and a champion of *their* planet, they didn't do the study. We kept their shit."

"What do you mean by shit?"

"The bounty, the payment. 15 has no need for any of the 'shit' it gets in return for the battle fleets it builds."

"This is what burns me up, makes me so angry. Our planet was robbed."

Assey's hands are shaking holding the van's steering wheel, he's visibly upset and riled by this conversation.

"How dare it defile that which is so precious to us but so worthless to it. 15 deserves to die."

His anger is palpable.

"Whoa there, Assey old boy! No need to get worked up." I try to diffuse the situation.

"It's not just that; we could survive without our most holy obelisks. It also took the life of General Tan-D-bonze."

I say the name over in my head a couple of times.

"Tan-D-bonze. Is Brito related to him?"

"Yes, he is a D-bonze also, he's leading the mission in remembrance of the sacrifice of his illustrious and much-loved fore-father. The fleet ships must pay."

Assey almost spits the 'must pay.' bit. This little chat has given me a useful insight into why this is all happening. I still can't help but think that if the Kruzian's had just let this all lie at some point over the last few millennia that they could have just got on with more fun things. It seems the whole society is built around revenge. An act of revenge that eats up every individual and drives them to even more anger and revulsion.

One thing I have learned over my two thousand years on this ship is not to mess with people's beliefs, mainly when they are as deep-seated and violent as those of Assey's and his friends. I respectfully shut my mouth and remember that to them I was 15's prisoner and held against my will.

Chapter 28

WE REACH THE 'OIL Room'. It's weird, having been on 15 for so long and always seeing grey whiteness (except in my environment and my 'brain download' room) as decor; it's suddenly almost a shock to see something completely different. We were driving alongside a white wall on a white floor then the wall ends abruptly and to my right is revealed the pitch blackness of the floor. The stark contrast to the white was such a shock to my senses. We stop, and I get out, in slack-jawed wonderment, eyes popping. On the floor, at the threshold, the grey whiteness just becomes total blackness. I can see a perfect black wedge stretching out in front of me. As I turn to the right, the black spreads to the base of the right-hand wall; the wall extends off the distance marked by the line of black at its bottom. It's the same to the left. The result is a vanishing point miles and miles out in front of me. As I look back to my feet and at the 'oil' I can see why that is the description. The liquid is as black as oil and shiny; I can lean over and view my reflection on the perfectly still surface. There is no smell, and as ever, no sound.

"Can I touch it?"

"I think so, we did."

I hunker down and look closely at the edge. The 'oil' seems to be sitting on top of a grey white floor, but the perfect black edge does not 'hang' over the line of white. I touch the oil, and it feels 'oily', it sticks to my finger, it is only millimetres deep. I sweep my finger through it and reveal a white 'tick' on the floor underneath. The liquid seeps back silently and silkily, with no ripple and the tick disappears.

"What did you make of this then?" I ask.

"No idea, we walked out into it for a look and then came back. If you get some on your shoes and then walk over here, the marks you make on the floor will ooze back over time into the oil. It's a smart material."

"Did you try any experiments on it?"

"Like what?"

"Like burn some? Like trying to put some on the Brain? Like seeing what the avatars thought of it?"

Assey shrugged, "No, we just got on with the mission. Didn't occur to us to try any of that stuff."

"It must be here for a reason, though. It's not related to me, and there doesn't seem to be anything left over from any other Champions, so I would suggest that it's something that 15 needs."

"Hadn't thought of that. But to be fair, we didn't know you existed at that point."

I've got a little water flask with me, when Assey's not looking, I finish the water quickly and then use the bottle to scoop up a sample of the black to take back, and pocket the flask. It might be insignificant, but I've got a feeling this stuff is important.

We get back in the van and drive back, on the way we keep chatting. Assey is probably a bit looser with his lips that the others would like him to be. I don't have to probe hard to get information out of him.

"Can we go to see the avatar control unit now?"

"Brito said to show you the oil and nothing else."

"That's ridiculous, no wonder you're all failing in your mission."

"What do you mean by 'failing'?"

"You're getting nowhere fast. Until you met me, an impenetrable force field locked you out. You were looking at getting old and dying on a spaceship you had no chance of ever controlling, drifting in space forever."

"And why do you think the avatar control unit is worth seeing?"

"Because there may be a clue as to how to control the Brain. Something I can learn that I may be able to use again, or an input device?"

"I think we should go back and ask Brito."

"What's the point of that, driving for hours and hours for him to say 'yes' and then driving for hours and hours back again. Use some initiative. It's on the way back so do Brito a favour. If I get back to the Brain with a solution to gaining control, don't you think Brito will think you've done a great job?"

Assey mulls this over for a few miles in silence. After a good long while, he says, "OK then. But if you do anything, I don't like or start acting strangely I'm just going to shoot you."

"Deal."

A couple of hours later we're finally approaching the avatar unit. I can see an enormous white Sphere sitting in the middle of the grey white floor. As we get closer, I can see the same white lights under the outer 'skin' of the globe as I've become used to seeing on the Brain - the same white flashing lights and swirling smoke lights under the surface. I can tell that the Sphere is about my height and looks to be a perfectly round shape. We park up and move closer. As we do, I see two indentations on the floor, one to the left and one to the right, just in front of the Sphere. I also then notice the globe itself is resting in its own indentation, a third one, the three make up a triangle of indentations. The indentation stops the ball from rolling away.

"How did you know it was the avatar control unit?"

"We didn't know at first, but we got lucky. When we got to the storeroom, we were attacked by a group of about 50-60 avatars. Fortunately, we were able to acquire weapons and fought back, our military training and tactics were way too good for them, and we quickly repelled them. We realised that a further attack was possible and probable, so we grabbed a van and lots of weapons and looked for somewhere to base our operations. We repulsed a couple of waves of attacks from avatars before we happened upon this room. All we did was move the ball..."

"What do you mean?"

"We rolled it from where it was into another indentation, that one there."

He points to the indentation on the left.

"From where to there?"

"From the other one." He points to the indentation on the right. "When it's in that one, 15 is in charge. When it's in that one." He points to the left indentation. "They all stop and do nothing."

"And the one the ball is in, what happens then?"

"They do what you ask them."

"What *you* ask them, or what anyone asks them?"

"I think what anyone asks them."

"So you rolled the ball, and they just stopped attacking you?"

"Exactly."

"You did get lucky."

I walk around the Sphere a few times, looking at the swirling lights dancing around just under the surface. Then I reach out and place the palms of my hands flat against the surface - the same white glow to the touch. I press a little harder and see the light intensify. I push a little harder until I can feel the Sphere's weight start to shift and lift from where it's seated. It's heavy but not too heavy for a single person to move. As soon as I sense the slight lift, I ease off and allow the Sphere to sit back on its seat gently. I don't want one of Assey's bullets in my brain. Now is not the time for that. I walk around a few more times.

Assey says, "Come on, you've seen all there is to see. There's nothing else here."

I walk around the back of the Sphere so Assey can't see what I'm doing, and then I try something I've been waiting for the opportunity to try since I first touched the Brain. I point my right index finger and trace the numbers '1' and then '5' onto the Sphere. I then lift my finger away. After I do, a word appears in thin white light.

~ *hi.*

I smile to myself and walk around back to the van.

Chapter 29

I FEEL QUITE ELATED INSIDE back at the van. I've made a real breakthrough, one that I thought about ages ago but was unwilling to test. I've communicated with 15 in the most simple of ways. Even if these guys didn't access the Brain, they could have tried to access or communicate with 15 in some way via the Sphere? They are undoubtedly very experienced 'Secret Service' or whatever type of agents of the state they are but they don't seem to be very analytical in their approach. Brito's getting edgy because he wants to complete his mission. Now, I realise it's his life work too, and he's frustrated to have come so far and then not be able to go any further. He knows that just existing on this ship and not taking control will be seen ultimately as a failure. I can understand his frustration, but not exploring all open avenues is a crime. I'm not an intelligence agent; I'm just a bloke, snatched whilst doing the crossword on a train. I'm not unique in any way, but I've got further than them without really trying. I wonder if they've even actually bothered to ask an avatar for help? The Kruzians, as a whole, are a very arrogant race, and I think they feel that everyone else, and I mean every type of being in the Universe, is inferior to them.

What I haven't worked out yet is why 15 was acting the way he was. It was almost as if he was drunk or something. If these guys can't penetrate his Brain, then why was he acting so strangely? It seems to me that the only thing they've managed to complete is moving the Sphere from one spot to another. This can't be enough to damage 15's thinking processes? There must be something else that's messed with his head.

We're eating at the table again, and the lads are digging into their slop. I've gone for the 'Full Monty', and I'm doing it in style. Four fried eggs, four big fat sausages, six slices of nice crispy streaky bacon, two large slices of black pudding, one half of a beef tomato, an impressive pile of mushrooms, a pyroclastic flow of baked beans, two half slices of fried bread, a lovely lump of bubble and squeak - with plenty of squeak and crunchy bits, all served on a plate the size of a satellite dish, with red, brown and Worcester sauce. I've also got a bottle of Tabasco sauce for a bit of spicing up here and there. A massive mug of builders tea and four slices of toast, two of thick white 'toaster' bread and two of seeded brown batch all smothered in butter. This monster meal is way beyond anything I've ever attempted to consume as breakfast before, but as usual, I'm taking it on to disgust the audience. I'm not sure they even like the idea of me eating dead animals, let alone the fried unfertilised embryos of another animal. But I don't care. It's magnificent. It makes me wish I could take a photo of the plate and post it on social media - whatever that was. Kruzians, if these guys are typical, are odd. They are so well mannered. They wouldn't dream of me not joining them to eat. They won't leave the table until we're all finished (and I always finish *way* last). They try hard to hide their displeasure - it's a stringent, rules-based society and, if you're the right sort, you stick to the rules. This doesn't mean that they wouldn't kill me in an instant, they would, it's just that after they'd stabbed me to death, they'd meticulously clean, sharpen and re-oil the dagger. And then apologise to my corpse.

It makes mealtimes delicious for me because I like making it hard for them.

Assey told Brito that he'd allowed me to see the Sphere. Brito didn't look too happy about this, but Assey explained my argument pretty well, which seemed to appease Brito to some extent. Brito asks me,

"Did you learn anything from seeing the oil and the Sphere?"

"Not really, but I certainly think both were worth seeing. The Sphere seems to be made of the same material as the Brain."

"We can touch it but can't communicate with it. Apart from managing to control the avatars, it's not of any use to us."

I nod my head sagely in agreement. Brito carries on.

"I want you back on the Brain. We need to make a breakthrough. I have a mission to complete, and I do not want to fail my mother Empire."

I jump up and get back to some silly pissing about and prodding of the Brain. Today, I'm rubbing sections fast with the flat of my hand, like polishing a lamp and hoping for the genie to pop out.

Chapter 30

LATER ON, WHILE THE others are resting, I retrieve the water flask with the oil sample from inside the van. I walk out, away from the Brain until I am about 350 metres from our little base of operations. I open the flask and pour a small amount of oil on the floor. It's nearly half of what I have in the flask - it sort of oozes out, not as thick as honey but more like a thick bleach. I'm low to the floor when I do this, so there is no real splatter, the oil is in one lump/slick. It's pure black against the grey whiteness of the floor. I've moved away from the Brain to do this because I want to see if it evaporates, or spreads, or sinks in and I don't want the three Kruzians to see what I've done, or accidentally slip on it. I walk back and when there, I turn and look. It's such a small speck of black against the harshness of the white, but I can still just about see it. It's like a single vanilla seed on the side of a huge white scoop of ice cream.

There's a burst of machine-gun fire, thunderous, with a gurgled scream over the top. I spin around and see Brito blasting a volley of bullets at the Brain. He stops when the clip runs dry and throws the machine gun on the deck. He spins sharply and walks off. I return to see the faces of the other two. Assey looks concerned, and a little shocked, Yerech looks a bit pissed off.

"What the fuck was that?"

"He's frustrated about the lack of progress," says Assey.

"You're not helping." There's a note behind this response from Yerech, I look at him and reply angrily.

"What do you want me to do? What do any of you want me to do? Without me, you can't access the Brain. Why don't you just shoot me? Then you can sort this shit out on your own. You might not like what I'm doing, but I'm further down that line than you are or will ever be. It's fine to be pissed off but don't be pissed off with me!"

"He's not pissed off with you, he's pissed off that we can't do anything," Assey says, "You need to keep going."

I pick up some of the bullets that have hit the force field around the Brain; they're flattened. If I'm going to make a move, I need to get my plan straight soon because time could be running out for me.

Chapter 31

BRITO HAS RETURNED, AND he's brought 12 avatars with him. They seem to be a random selection of males and females all of differing ages. They line up in a rank a short way from the Brain. They say nothing and look impassive. All are Human of course, and all look like they could easily be 'extras' in a film. There's a young, black male cycle courier. A white, middle-aged male delivery driver. A middle-aged, white female supermarket assistant. A young, male Asian nurse - everyone has a uniform of some type. I think 15 kept them to be part of street scenes.

Brito addresses the first one, a young, mixed-race female. I think she's wearing the uniform of a national chain of greeting card shops. The avatar walks over to the Brain and attempts to touch it. Her hand can only go as far as the force field. She is not damaged by touching it. It's as if she is feeling a thick pane of glass surrounding the Brain. Brito now instructs each avatar in turn to do the same but in different areas of the Brain, all around it. Finally, he seems to be trying something different. Finally, he's using his head. He instructs me gruffly and quite aggressively, which is unusual as I'm used to being asked quite politely,

"Now you touch it too."

I've no reason to antagonise Brito any further, so I do the same.

I can reach in and touch the Brain, but nothing else happens.

"Fuck this." the first time I've heard any of the Kruzians swear. He moves all the avatars away and makes them line up again. He gets in the van and drives it at the force field, not too fast like he'd kill himself on impact, but 20 miles an hour or so. The van front crumples against the force field with a loud 'bang', Brito ends up face-first in an airbag even though he is wearing his seat belt. Not much of an experiment. He gets out of the van and tells an avatar to go and get him another van. He tells the rest of them to push the crashed van out of the way. He pulls my chair away from the Brain and sits down in a flump, head in his hands.

From where I'm standing, that was all a big waste of time. I walk off.

"Oi, where do you think you're going?" Yerech shouts after me after he realises I'm not stopping.

"For an ice cream," I shout back without turning my head and don't stop.

It's quite a long walk to the Food Room from the Brain, but now I know the way, and I want some time apart from my three cohorts. I've been helping along, being a bit shit, playing dumb for a long time. They're starting to bore me, and I'm worried Brito might become more irrational as time continues to pass. If I decide I want to kill them, then I have to kill all three of them in one go. I'll never be able to capture them. It's so difficult to use the element of surprise when everything is so open, so empty, and so grey white.

Then I spot a small opening, one that I hadn't noticed before. Normally we're driving from place to place, and it's hard to spot colour contrast when everything looks the same. I walk over and into the room, which opens out into another grey white space. It's not nearly as big as many of the other rooms I've been into, but once in, there is a marked difference to this room. It has windows, three small rectangular ones lined up in the distance. I'm so excited to see these that I run the 150 metres to see them. Only when I near do I get to see the detail. They're 'house windows' the type you might put in to add light and ventilation to an en suite bathroom. They're all wooden framed, have a sill and a single-hinged opening pane at the top with main window beneath. They are about two-feet wide and three-feet tall. I can see out of the double-glazed glass at the black emptiness of space beyond. It's thrilling because I've never seen the outside from inside 15 before, this is my first view of space in over 2,000 years. I'm also unsure how these windows are keeping 'space' out so they must be protected by some sort of 'field force field'. But it's so weird to see them here.

When I look close up, I realise each is damaged, the top of the wooden frame has been pushed in and cracked, or splintered from above. As soon as I see this, I smile to myself and remember a previous conversation I had with 15, many, many years ago.

Chapter 32

WE'RE ALL BACK AT the Brain. It's been a good few hours. Brito seems to have calmed down a bit. There's now a new van. Assey, and the avatars towed the old one into another room and dumped it. The 12 avatars are still in line standing at attention on one side. Brito is still on the chair, and the other three of us are sitting or lying on the floor around the chair just chatting about what we're doing. I casually get up and start to walk around the Brain, just like usual, staring as if to see if there's any difference or discernible pattern to the lights flickering on and off or the smoky swirls. The other three are still sitting on the chair and floor chatting, discussing next steps. I go around the curve of the Brain; I'm out of sight. I keep going for a while, stepping a bit faster then I stop and reach into the Brain surface. I start to write:

~ '15, it's me. I'm here with three Kruzians. What should I do?'

~ *stop them,* appears on the surface in white light

~ 'How?' I write. Then white light,

~ *kill.*

There's a shout.

"Get the fucking bastard!!" It's Assey; he's circled the Brain in the opposite direction to the way I left. He's seen me. Before I know what to do, Yerech has again smashed me in the head, from behind, with a rifle butt.

Lights out.

"How did it happen, though? It makes no sense."

"I can't tell you exactly how it happened; it just evolved."

"But it's not normal, it's not instinctive, there's surely no pattern?"

We're talking about toad licking. I'm not sure how we got onto the subject. I think we free-styled our way over to it. We had started out talking about people building houses and how people used different raw materials and methods historically based on what raw materials were available in their locations. For instance, why in Finland are almost 100% of houses (not offices, factories and the like but homes) built out of wood? Because it's an abundant renewable natural resource – it's also free. The Finns have loads of the stuff, so it makes sense to use it. By comparison, in the UK, we mainly built out of stone or brick. We had quarries for stone. We also had lots of clay, and soon worked out how to make bricks, and then made shit loads of them, and piled them up. And I think this is where the conversation moved on.

We were discussing how peoples, all around the Universe, discovered the processes of making new things. How, on Earth, Stone Age hunter-gatherers first learned to farm and then produced wheat. Once harvested, if it became damp and then lay in the sun, the sugar in the now rotting grain started to ferment. If you added this to water, you could drink it and feel happy until you woke up in the morning with blood on your knuckles from the world's first pub car park fight and a pounding headache. Beer was born.

How did we invent bread? Why did we know to plant or farm wheat? How did we learn to grind down the dried ears to produce flour? Who first mixed in water and cooked the wet mixture on a hot stone in a fire to create the loaves? How many millions of failed attempts were there before someone stumbled across a successful method? After so many failed attempts, why didn't we just give up?

Who added an egg, out of a hen's rear end, into the mix along with some butter (who churned that first?) and made a cake? With some processes, it's easy to see how we developed – they're simple things. So let's take bread for instance. I *can* see how someone could have mixed water with flour, hoping to make glue. Then as that didn't work, the resulting 'dough' was just thrown on the fire to get rid of it. But the fire was low, and the dough was sitting on the embers, and after 25 minutes the stone aged person said 'Uuugh' - which meant 'that smells nice', and picked up a bit, and shoved it into his mouth hole, didn't die from eating it, and liked it.

It's a progression; one can see how a mistake led to a discovery. But there's so many of them throughout the history of Mankind. How many plants were dried and smoked before someone finally dried the marijuana plant? How many leaves of different plants were dried and dipped in hot water before someone said, 'That tastes nice, would probably go well with a cucumber sandwich,' and we had tea? We made all of these discoveries, and it became the world we knew. Through this bumbling, science moved forward; we started to discover through our knowledge rather than our mistakes. We became able to hypothesise new ways or inventions, and then make them happen through our knowledge and understanding of previous discoveries.

Licking cane toads is something I just can't see. I can't understand how a Human being would work out that you can get a psychedelic trip from licking a toad. It's not just the process that is odd. How many toads varieties do you have to lick first? How many do you go through to find the right one or ones? Not only that. The bufotoxin (the stuff that gets you high), is only secreted by the toad when it feels endangered in some way. So you have to get it riled up. If you're too gentle with your toad, it may not secrete. Do you have to goad your toad first? Poke it with a sharp stick a couple of times, make him mad, make him feel the pressure, then he secretes the toxin, but only from certain glands on the head and back legs. So you've got to know where to lick also. Again you could lick a lot of wrong parts of the right angry toad before you get a result. Once you lick the right section - that's when the trouble starts. Now you're going to get sick, real sick. There's the 'stomach turning itself inside-out' vomiting which comes next as your body tries to expel the poison you've just imbibed - so rolling around, in your vomit probably, holding your guts, convulsing wildly. Then, and only then, if your heart hasn't stopped, which it can do and has done in many instances, only then do you get your trip around the houses on a pink motor scooter with your nine arms, two dicks and an elephant's trunk or whatever happens. How do you get from the start to the finish of that process?

"If someone told me putting my mouth around the exhaust of a parked, running VW Golf for five minutes would get me properly off my nut - I still wouldn't do it. Or eating a hammer? Do that, you'll vomit a bit after, but then you'll have a euphoric experience like you've never had before - I'll pass on that one."

15 says nothing. No answer. The toad licking thing is wholly beyond his comprehension too.

Eventually, he asks me.

"Are you looking for an answer from me?"

"Would be interested to hear your thoughts?"

"I think it would be easy to say that space aliens visited Earth and met prehistoric man and left great knowledge.

The ability to make alcohol, to make bread, to build the Pyramids and the knowledge of how to get high on all sorts of substances, including toad licking."

I'm open-mouthed in anticipation, waiting for the next part.

"But I can't. There is no evidence of alien visitation, or 'knowledge of the ancients' being passed down to early Mankind. You lot discovered all of this on your own. I don't really know how, and it's a miracle you ever survived, but that's what happened."

On hearing this, I actually feel warm inside. By the time I left Earth, there were nearly 7 billion idiots all bumping into each other on a big bluey-green rock, somehow surviving through trial and error.

When I come to, I'm lying on my back on the grey white floor. My head feels heavy and sore; there is a dull ache down my spine and acute pain at the back of my skull. It makes me wonder if there will ever be a time when my nanobots decide that they've been asked to repair my head too many times and go on strike. I can't move though; I'm trussed up.

"Brito, he's awake." I hear Assey say.

Moments later, Brito moves into my sightline and kicks me sharply in the ribs. I cough and try to flinch.

"Get him up." he barks to the other two, and I'm roughly grabbed and pushed up into the vertical. My hands are tied, but oddly. There is a cable tie around my wrists which is cut to free them. I then see what they've done. I've been attached to four lengths of wood - the sort of wood that is easy to gather from the racking - broom handles and the like. There is one each for each of my appendages. One piece of timber runs down the outside of each leg and is cable tied four times around each leg, at the ankle, lower shin and again below my knee cap and lastly at the upper thigh. I cannot bend either leg. I could run away like this, but it would be slow and difficult. I'm not quite 'hobbled', but it's a pretty similar effect. Then the same on either arm but with the wooden pole this time-strapped behind my elbow. I am again attached just above my wrist and below my shoulder. I can't bend my arms. On my right hand, there is a similar setup. My fist has been taped up with thick gaffer tape all except my index finger which is attached to a smaller thinner length of wood in a pointing position. I'm carried over to the Brain. They're going to use me as a pencil.

Yerech and Assey stand behind me and hold me. I'm not even struggling or resisting - there's little point, I couldn't do anything if I wanted to. Brito is in charge of my arm and therefore, finger. It's not easy for him to manipulate my arm as the very selective forcefield that 15 has erected allows my arm through but not any part of Brito. The force field seems only to reach out as far as just past my elbow, so the bit of my arm that Brito gets to draw with is pretty small. Additionally, the finger is not sufficiently secure so making shapes, letters, and numbers are not easy. There's quite a bit of grunting and certainly some sweating and swearing. It doesn't occur to Brito to ask me to trace whatever it is he wants me to trace myself for him. With a gun to my head, I'm sure I'd write whatever they want me to write without all this 'puppet on a string' nonsense. But this is the way they want to proceed so I'm not going to stop them. First question.

~ 'Can you switch off the force field, please?' at least they're polite. Bit of a wait, then finally.

~ *no.*

Next question,

~ 'Why not?' I think that's a pretty reasonable second question.

~ *because it protects me.*

Good answer. We then plug along at a bit of a lick, questions followed by answers. But questions like,

~ 'How do we take control of you?' are a bit stupid. I know the answer even before 15 can be arsed to give one.

~ *you don't.*

I know it's not my place, and now I'm definitely 'the prisoner' so I've no particular desire to help in any way, but I don't think their way of questioning is ever going to return a decent answer. They're not negotiating; they're just trying to dominate. 15 only has to keep telling them to fuck off. Eventually, they'll die of old age, and although he may not be totally in control of his faculties, he'll still be able to function with no inner interference. One option would have been to allow me to stay dead until the three Kruzians finally expired of natural causes and then popped me back into existence to tidy up everything that had been undone. I might have even helped. But they might have, and still may find a way to get into his Brain. The questions and answers keep coming and then very quickly going. These three are pretty tough, but they're not good at this sort of thing. The problem is that they were brought into this role, not knowing where it would take them. The Kruzian Empire's finally broken into and effectively taken control of a fleet ship. The problem is that the three operatives were only useful to a point. Now the Kruzians cannot get any further help onboard, cannot get these three off, cannot communicate with them and haven't equipped these three with the skills or training to take them any further in their mission - bit of a hole. I chuckle to myself as my finger is pushed around into more and more letter shapes.

Later on, I looked to see what had happened to the oil I put on the floor. I'm looking at the black dot from my position by the Brain. I'm sure the dot has moved. I'm sure it's closer to the exit than when I initially placed it.

We're sitting around together. They've given up for now. I've got a bowl of cold, green slop. It tastes - interesting. They've freed my left hand for me to hold my straw. The green is quite thick and oozes around my mouth and slides down my throat. It's meaty, but from no animal I could identify. Apparently, there are live creatures in it, a bit like krill, held in the suspension. I'm delighted that I can't see them moving around and that the slop doesn't smell of rotting seafood, or empty old fish tanks. It does fill me up, and the whole experience certainly isn't the worst thing that I've ever eaten, but I wouldn't want too much of it, and certainly not three meals a day, every day.

"Fellas, keeping me tied up is ridiculous. I'm not trying to run away. These sticks just hurt my knees, Humans need to be able to bend them; otherwise, they'll go bad (worth a try), and the ties are digging into my skin and stopping my blood circulation. My feet will wither and die soon."

"Fucking shut up," says Yerech, hardly surprising.

"I'll be no good to you soon, this strapping on my arm and finger is the same. I won't be able to draw for you."

"Then I'll kill you, and we won't have to listen to your bleating anymore." Yerech has said just about the most I've ever heard from him.

Brito looks up. "If he goes, we've got nothing. You didn't put up a fight today; you just let me write. Why?"

"Because I want to get off the ship too. I'd only just worked out how to communicate."

"He's a fucking liar." Now I've heard more from Yerech than during any other previous conversation. It's only when he's rude to me that he's got an opinion.

"Untie him," says Brito, Yerech looks shocked but doesn't say anything. "Watch him, though, constantly. Don't let him near any weapons." then he talks directly to me, "You can help us. Previously you did what you wanted, now you do what I want. If you write for me, you will get the food you want. If you don't, I'll shoot you in the head. Simple."

"Sounds good to me, that was all I was going to do anyway."

Assey cuts me loose, "I saw the word 'Kill' on the surface when you were writing. What was that about?"

"I wrote 'hello', 15 said 'kill'. I'm pretty sure it was referring to you three, but you'd expect that wouldn't you. I just tried something different, and it worked. I'm not your enemy."

"Never take your eyes off him," repeats Brito.

He looks away, and I mug him off behind his back to Assey, who laughs.

At least I'm off the green slop for now, I've just eaten Mexican. Quite a bit of it actually: a fully loaded spicy chicken burrito, a big sharing plate of nachos with sour cream, guac, salsa, cheese sauce, black beans, sour cream, sprinkled cheese, spicy beef and jalapenos and washed them down with three ice-cold bottles of Estrella Jalisco. Finger food again, these boys hate when I eat finger food.

We're back at the Brain, and I'm playing ball. I'm even making suggestions, but they're not going down very well.

"What if you suggest that you'll give 15 back control of its avatars as long as it allows you safe passage to a point where you can ship in some other Kruzians?"

"No, we can't trust it."

"OK, tell him if he doesn't cooperate you're going to smash up his Sphere."

Brito thinks about this. I don't think it's ever occurred to him before.

"Get a couple of avatars to roll it all the way here and show him that you mean business. Maybe having two 'Brain-like' objects together will produce a bit of 'feedback' like getting a microphone too close to its speaker."

"You know, that's not a bad good idea. Yerech, brief three avatars to bring me the Sphere." Brito's smiling, I don't think I've seen him smile since he killed me. I feel like the pressure's off a little.

I'm drinking champagne; it's not a celebration. The Sphere hasn't arrived in the Brain Room yet, but Yerech and Assey drove to the Sphere Room and supervised the avatars taking the Sphere from its resting place, leaving the room and rolling it in the direction of the Brain Room. They wanted to make sure the avatars didn't 'carelessly' roll the Sphere onto the 'wrong' indentation by 'accident'. The mood is better between the three Kruzians and myself, and I'm eating lobster thermidor, with chips. I'd typically use a fork, but today I'm using my – fingers! I'm pouring buttery, mustardy, cognac sauce over the meat then picking up pieces, throwing them into the air and catching them in my mouth – occasionally missing!

"What?" I ask to their disgusted looking faces, "It's the traditional way to eat lobster!"

I'm dipping the chips into the sauce also. I'm wearing a bib because I'm not an animal and because I'm making a real mess. This is what eating should be about!

As I was in the good books, once we had a break, I went for a little walk and checked out the oil again. It has *definitely* moved. It's crawling back to the rest of the oil in the Oil Room, I'm sure of it. It's weird; I'm sure if I stood and watched, like looking at the hands of a clock, I'd see it moving over time, but there's no outward sign of it moving. It's oozing so slowly you don't notice, and as it doesn't change shape or leave any trail, it's difficult to spot. Just this black blob, working its way back to the big slick. It is up to something, but I'll be fucked if I know what it is. I've still got the little bottle with the other half of the blob in it. It's not trying to move anywhere, I've captured it.

The avatars arrived back with the Sphere a little while ago. I think it was pretty easy to move it. The surface is hard, and so is the floor, as it is a perfect Sphere, it only needs a little nudge in the right direction, and off it goes. If anything the avatars probably had to move pretty quickly to keep up with it. The Sphere Room is not close by, though, and the walk alone would take a few Earth days. I noted that taking the Sphere to a different room didn't alter the avatars behaviour. They're still taking commands from the Kruzians. Maybe whatever the last indentation the Sphere determines how the avatars will react. They stay like this until the Sphere is placed in a *different* indentation. I wondered, now that there is no Sphere, if something else was sat on an indentation, could it take the place of the Sphere?

When it arrived, we asked the avatars to push it all the way up to the van, and then the four of us took it off their hands. We pushed it right up to the Brain; it went through the force field and then touched. Both the Sphere and the Brain lit up in this fantastic firework display of lights under the surface. It was pretty awe-inspiring, they glowed, pulsed, flashed, lights danced and swirled. It looked amazing. The Brain in particular, probably because it is just so big in comparison, put on the most amazing light show I have ever seen. After about half an hour of the four of us staring at the lights in wonder, it abruptly stopped, and both turned off. Like a switch had been flicked. Nothing, nada. Eventually, I rolled the ball away with Yerech. We left it propped against two avatars and told them not to let it roll off. Now, the 12 avatars are standing in a row with the last two on the end both holding the Sphere between them.

"What do you think all that was about then? Asks Brito

"Fuck knows," I answer. "No feedback. Could be that the two shorted each other out, but we've still got power? The lights are still on, and we're still breathing and standing on a floor, so life support and gravity are operational."

I touch the Brain and write on it. 'Are you OK?'. There is no response. I walk over to the avatars and do the same to the Sphere - nothing.

"It's dead," I shout over to the three Kruzians. "Do you want me to get them to take it back?"

"You might as well," answers Brito.

I brief the avatars and the two on the end start to roll it away again.

"At least it will keep them busy for a while."

Brito is back in his deep funk. I try not to talk to him when he's like this in case he takes offence. I don't want to end up dead. We might not have a solution, but I've invested quite a lot of time and effort pissing about with these three monkeys and 15. I look at myself for the first time in ages. I'm still wearing the aviators jump suit I found on the racking when I first entered the Store Room. The jump suit was the first clothing I found that fitted me, they're pretty uncomfortable and are stained with my blood from Yerech smacking my head in with a rifle butt more than once. I still have no shoes on.

"Brito, I want to go to the store to get a change of clothes. I'm sick of being in this rag, and I want some footwear."

He shrugs. Then looks at Assey.

Assey sees the look; he's lying on the floor drawing shapes on the grey whiteness, doing nothing, he realises it's a request. "Alright, suppose I'll drive him there."

"Keep an eye on him." First words for hours from Yerech.

The drive over is uneventful; we pass the avatars rolling the Sphere on the way. They're as obedient as ever. Once at the store I head to the racking and remember how careful and cautious I'd been last time I was there. I was sure the avatars were about to turn on me and rip me to shreds at any moment. I remember all that skulking around when really I was wasting my time.

After a lot of rummaging I find a pair of well-fitting, olive-green cargo shorts and a yellow 'Noizy But Nice' T-shirt from the Slade 1989 Christmas Tour. It fits well enough also. I then find a plain black Nike zip-up hoody and a pair of Puma Clyde trainers, red leather with a white stripe - you can't get much more classic than that. I'm delighted. I think this whole cache of clothing was originally purposed for me by 15 from when I was living in the environment. All fit pretty well and are the sorts of things I used to knock about wearing. There were socks too, but I can't wear them with trainers, it's against my religion. And I'm not wearing those 'trainer socks' - whoever invented them should be garrotted. They're a crime against Humanity. Either wear socks, and look like a pussy or don't and look right. But please God don't wear some half-baked in-betweeny wiener sock. Clean pants too. Nice to get a pair after so long. My internalised nanobots have been working hard since I was reanimated by 15 because having no underpants for the length of time I have, my balls, by now, should be down by my knees. Still, nice to have a bit of support, holding everything together. I noticed a small collection of weapons nearby mainly bladed objects. I could have made a lunge for a dagger to use on Assey, but it was too much of a risk - killing him now and then going after the two others. I also thought about concealing a weapon and then going back with him to use later. But if they find it, and I could get searched when I get back, then I'm probably dead. So I demurred. The right time will come.

We drove back. Assey asked me about my journey with 15.

"I was a prisoner, but it wasn't the worst prison."

"In what way?"

"I was held by 15 against my will, but I lived in a gilded cage. The environment built for me was very comfortable. I was well fed and looked after, and I was never under the threat of torture or anything like that. Apart from occasionally having to fight an alien against my wishes, I sort of had a fairly good time."

"Why did you not try to escape?"

"I'm in the depths of space, and it's supporting my life. If it stops doing so, then I'm dead."

"Suppose you're right. But we got in."

"You brought concealed tools, weapons from outside. I only had what came from 15. You trained an entire empire, and learned from the experience by attacking five fleet ships over thousands of years - you honed your operation, centred your training - focus, focus, focus. I just got abducted off the train."

"But why you and not someone else on the train?"

I sigh heavily, "Because 15 found something out about me that made me a great candidate for the job."

"Which was?"

I hesitate, I turn my head to look at Assey, who is just looking ahead out of the window screen. I turn back.

"What?" he says

I sigh again, "Because I killed five women on Earth, and was never captured and punished for the crime."

Assey's mouth opens in surprise, "You're a murderer?"

"Yes - I was. I wish I wasn't, but I was. And I wish, for the girls sake that I could turn back the clock, but I can't."

"So cold-blooded killing."

"YES!" I answer, "What's with the fucking questions? For sucks sake..." I tail off. Assey senses my mood and there's silence for a while.

"So, 15 has been your prison. Maybe you could have turned its weapons against it?"

"I had no desire to do so. I'm no engineer. I was happy to 'do my time'. In the end, it all became too much, but 15 agreed on a deal to let me die."

Assey laughs out loud.

"And it welshed on the deal, you're still here."

"Thanks for reminding me."

Neither of us talks for a while; then I break the silence again.

"It's not been all bad. I enjoyed some of my time here. I liked some of the fights. They were fun, killing aliens can be fun. I begrudgingly got on quite well with 15. It was easier to be friends than to be enemies. I think you would like travelling with 15. You are a warrior race. You would get to meet aliens from all over the Universe. You'd get as much of that green gruel shit as you like. You're trained to kill. You could relax."

"This heathen hunk of junk needs to burn in hell!"

Shit, I've started him off again with the shaking and clenching the steering wheel - time to button it.

We get back to the Brain. I see Brito walking around, looking at it and approaching.

"Thanks for the clothes."

He looks me up and down.

"You look stupid."

"It's what we wear. Might be different from what you wear but it is our thing, and you can wear your thing with no quarrel from me. What about when we fought in the Arena? These two were dressed in those ceremonial robes with the big plumed headdresses. They looked stupid to me."

"Yes, indeed they were stupid to us also, but they were the weapons with which we broke into this ship. The plumes were edible and extremely nutritious, if barely palatable, they allowed us to sustain ourselves for many months whilst looking for the way further into this ship. The headdresses could also be pulled apart and rebuilt into small scooters. We used these under the deck to get about much faster than walking. We were able to cover two or three times the daily distance we would have been able to cover on foot. We may have looked ridiculous, but it was all part of the planning. Those robes, plumes, swords, oils had all been developed hundreds of years previously. Their use was built into ceremonial rituals so that when a fleet ship came along and carried out a clonescan of the planets, it would not suspect that an object, or fluid, used for centuries would be a threat to it. We are clever. We plan, we continuously improve, and when we finally attack we are victorious. Our work is meticulous; our targets are deserving of our wrath; our wrath is meted out surgically.

Chapter 33

I ONCE HAD A GIRLFRIEND who was really into Michael Jackson, so pretty early on in our relationship, I knew it wasn't going to work. I persevered, she seemed to like me, I didn't have any better options on the table, and I didn't hate her - plus I was having regular sex, so I stuck with it. It was also apparent quite quickly that she was also into horoscopes, as most women seem to be, and a few men. I just don't get them, or people who believe them, and I never have. I was interested to hear 15's views on the subject.

"In some parts of the Universe, it's almost a religion, it's not usually a religion on its own, but looking up at the stars and divining providence from them is a recurring aspect of many. Lots and lots of different alien peoples look to the skies for some hope, some desperate desire for 'magic' to come down and help with their lives, for a sign that things will get better, or for comfort in a difficult situation. On Earth, stargazing existed before most of the organised religions; this is why it has endured. There was an innate, latent, deep psychological link between the people and the heavens and their wonders."

"But it's just a load of bullshit, isn't it?"

"Yes. Of course, it is. Although that's the simple answer and not the nuanced view."

"There isn't one. It's just shit. All those astrologers in the newspapers, and charging online, and selling books are just praying on the weak-minded and desperate. Looking at the sky and deciding that one 12th of the people in the world, a certain star sign, are going to meet the partner of their dreams in the next few days is utter crap."

"Of course, but these types of horoscopes are never very clear. Actions are only alluded to; situations suggested. They're written in a very clever and open way so that almost anything that happens can be attributed to the horoscope - to the stars. The faith of the reader hardens even more."

"What about when something clearly doesn't happen? When the person who read a horoscope that said, 'You'll have a great thing happen to you at work tomorrow.' and then they have a prang in their car and spend all of the next day sitting in A&E waiting hour after hour for an X-ray on a wrist that isn't broken, only badly sprained, and they miss the whole day off work."

"That person probably thinks their bosses said something great about them in their absence. Or they just think the horoscope didn't apply to them, but they'll ignore that, then read today's one to see how tomorrow's going to go."

"You understand stars, though? You have scanners and star charts coming out of every orifice. You know, better than me, that it's about perspective. If you stand on our Earth and look up at the sky on a clear, dark night, you'll see a bunch of recognisable star constellations; look, there's Leo, there's Capricorn, there's Pisces - it looks like some sort of fish! Although it doesn't, I'm digressing. The constellations don't move about, but the Earth does as it moves through the days, months, seasons in a year and so on. But if you stand on, let's say, Mars and look at the same constellations, then they'd no longer look like the constellations of Earth because most of those stars are millions of miles apart and only look the shape they do from a single point - Earth. If you're on a planet, even one that's our nearest neighbour, the constellations look different. Leo probably looks like a giraffe, Pisces like a horny anteater and Capricorn more like a Ford Escort Mk1 than a goat."

"True, but that's not really what it's all about. You've made the classic mistake, which happens on all stargazing planets in the Universe."

"Which 'classic mistake' have I made."

"*The stars* are the classic mistake. On Earth, there is no denying that your Moon affects your planet. The obvious ones being the female menstrual cycle, and the tides in the oceans and seas. You also have an effect on your planet from your Sun. It heats your planet and provides light. So if the Moon and Sun are so important, thinking that the wider firmament also has an effect on your lives is not too big a leap."

"Suppose not."

"Do you think it's possible that people born in August - the height of Summer, even though separated by many years, that August-born kids might grow up to exhibit different personality traits than kids born in February, the height of Winter?"

"Well, possibly?"

"And if you didn't have any way of understanding why people born at different times of the year had different personality traits, wouldn't it be fair for someone to look into the sky and say 'Aah, but the stars were in a different alignment in February than in August, so the thing making the difference is where the stars are when you're born.'"

"Well you could say that, but it's pretty stupid."

"You've got to remember that these were people who thought the gods were angry when there was a thunderstorm or lightning strike and that the Earth was the centre of the galaxy."

"Easy mistake."

"So why couldn't they think the stars also had an effect?"

"They could, and that's totally acceptable. The difference is that we learned to understand the weather and worked out that storms were not the gods being angry. We learned that the Earth went around the Sun by developing science. We changed our thinking, stopped believing the Earth was flat, etc. In the same way that science has proved the stars do not affect our daily lives. However, there are still millions of people who would get on their phones every day to see what some astrologist charlatan - and let's face it they stopped 'writing' horoscopes and programmed computer algorithms to knockout this stuff daily for them - predict is going to happen. Why didn't the scientists hold up their hands and say 'This is a pile of old rubbish. You're being taken for a ride. Stop being stupid?'"

"Because horoscopes are a big business. They're mainly harmless. Some people liked them and maybe found solace in them. And because many other worse things in the world should have been stamped out before horoscopes - like some made-up religions and cults, and some terrible dieting rip-offs."

"All I know is that when a girlfriend started talking about her and my star signs and therefore our interstellar compatibility, it was like kryptonite to Superman. It made me die inside."

"Very good then. There was an often-used phrase on your planet, that recognised the rich diversity of your peoples. It allowed many viewpoints to be formed and debated, without too many lives being lost in the process, and, in many ways, giving you all the ability to live together on one rock - 'you're all entitled to your own opinion.' Beautiful and elegant in its simplicity and another way of saying, "You might not like it - so let's not go there."

As I sit here, eating, with three Kruzians, I wonder what the stars say about my future?

Chapter 34

It's a few hours later after we've eaten and are on a break when the shooting starts.

It's all a bit of a blur. One minute we're sitting around by the van being a bit idle.

Then there's the feeling of a noise building, a rumbling, in the distance. I looked up and saw what looked like a few hundred avatars heading towards us all with weapons. The three Kruzians jumped up and immediately switched into military mode. It was amazing to watch, no hint of nerves or panic. Each knew their role, and each got on with their role almost soundlessly. Yerech opened the back of the van and passed around the weapons between them. I was not allowed a weapon and remained unarmed.

"What about me?" I said loud enough for all three to hear. "They're going to shoot at me as much as at you."

Brito looked at Yerech and nodded. Yerech pulls his usual face but goes to the back of the van for a rummage; he returns with a Colt Model 733 Commando and a gilet packed with magazines. I throw the vest on in quick time.

"If you look at me or point it anywhere towards any of us I will not hesitate to kill you."

Nice vote of confidence from Yerech.

I check the gun; it's not cocked, so I eject the magazine. It's full. I tap it on the stock of the gun and reload. Then I hastily cock the weapon, so there's one in the chamber. Brito has taken up a firing position, lying on the floor on his belly with his legs apart to steady him. He has double-jointed elbows on the ground and is using a long-barrelled semi-automatic - he starts to lose off a few rounds. There is nothing between us and the avatars, no cover at all; every bullet will find a soft target. The avatars continue to advance but have not started shooting yet. Yerech and Assey begin to unload a few at the attackers. I do likewise, short bursts, 30 in a clip, I'm fully automatic but want to make sure I don't shoot the same avatar twice if I can help it. I can see them falling in the distance. In fact, I can see quite a few of them falling. Fire is returned, but as the avatars are on the move towards us, it's not very accurate, and no bullets seem to fly too close to me.

Our fire rate increases dramatically, Assey has a heavy machine gun which he's working like a master painter, broad brush strokes across his target area, skilfully producing hit after hit. The avatars don't stand a chance, especially when supported by the fire from the three of us.

The avatars stop and start to retreat. They've taken heavy casualties in a minimal amount of time. The fire-fight has only lasted around 30 to 45 seconds.

"OK. Let's go," says Brito.

The other two jump into the van. Assey driving as ever. I jump into the back via the side sliding door. Yerech is already there. Brito's in the front. The wheels spin momentarily on the smooth floor, and then the rubber bites and the van lurches forward at speed in the opposite direction to the avatars.

"What the fuck was that?" There's no bulkhead in the van so we can speak freely between the front and the back of the van.

"Fuck knows," shouts Brito.

Assey says, "They must have put the Sphere back in the wrong place."

Yerech points his automatic in my face; it's an Austrian Steyr AUG, a bullpup automatic. It's a short weapon, very useful in tight spaces but I think it's a little back heavy and would not be my choice for this sort of situation. But it would be perfectly capable of perforating my skull with additional air holes.

"I didn't tell them to do anything!" I say incredulously.

Brito looks over his shoulder, "Did you tell them to put it back, so 15 had control again?"

"Did I fuck! I told them to put it back where it came from. Maybe they did it themselves, or 15 got them to do it."

"Shall I kill him?"

"They were shooting at me too." I plead.

"Not yet Yerech, we need firepower." I'm pleased Brito's more understanding than Yerech. Who looks at me distrustfully and then removes his gun from my face.

"Thank you." I sigh, "What are we going to do?"

"Get some distance between them and us first. We need to get back in that avatar control room."

I take the opportunity to check my weapon. It's a proper automatic with real stopping power. I'm glad to have it. I've also got a lot of ammo. The vest is full of magazines, and I've only used two so far. The big niggling doubt in the back of my mind is that no matter how much ammo I've got there are seemingly thousands of avatars and even getting back into the Sphere Room with the scant cover available is a pretty big ambition. I put forward a proposal.

"What about getting back into the Store Room. I know there are lots and lots of avatars there, but there's a huge amount of ordinance too; heavy machine guns, chain guns, miniguns - things you could use to just reave holes into an advancing horde. Not to mention the explosives; RPG's, mortars. Even tanks. We could just drive over them."

They seem to shrug and look backwards and forwards to each other.

"We need to control them," says Brito, "we can stop them all by getting back control of the Sphere."

"But what if they've blockaded the room. You won't get in and then before you know it, they'll have the miniguns and tanks, and they'll be pointing at our backs."

Assey answers, "He's got a good point."

There's a short pause, and then Brito agrees to try to get back into the Store Room. Yerech gives me a dirty look.

While we drive off across a colossal expanse of grey whiteness, aiming in the direction of the next wall, I take a little look around me. There are a plethora of different weapons in the back of the van; some on the floor, some bungee strapped to the side walls. There is one biggish gun with what looks like a tripod and a couple of sizeable wooden ammo boxes near it. All of the other weapons are handheld: some sub-machine guns, automatic rifles, shotguns and handguns. There are also boxes of magazines stacked up and either strapped or netted to stop them falling and moving around in the van. Each of the three Kruzians now has a short sword buckled to their waists. I suspect, having fought Brito and knowing a little about their culture, that these are very important. Swords, and swordplay, seem to be at the heart of military training. It is the weapon of a gentleman and the weapon of last resort. When the bullets run out, you can always reach for the blade. There seems to be very little in terms of explosives here. Some of these guns have launchers on them, but there doesn't seem to be many RPGs to shoot. There are a couple of grenade boxes but nothing else. I pull four out and find somewhere to stow them. After about an hour of driving, we eventually reach a wall. We're still in the Brain Room, where we shot all the avatars. If 15 and his various rooms are all this big, it will not be easy for the avatars to find us on foot. But there's nothing to say the avatars can't use drones or vehicles - and it might be that 15 can tell them exactly where we are. What I do know is there is no cover apart from the van, which won't last long under heavy fire.

We get out and rest for a bit. The three don't talk at all but seem to know what the plan is. I decide not to ask any questions and just do what they do. We walk about to stretch the legs for about 15 minutes and then load back up and take off. We follow the line of the wall for three hours until we meet another wall running at 90 degrees to our left - another side to the room. We follow the wall again for about an hour and reach a door. Assey doesn't look, he just drives straight in and continues to follow the wall now to our left in the same direction we were travelling. I'm hoping he knows where he's going because I haven't a clue. And I'm now trusting these three with my life. After 30 more minutes, there's another corner which turns 90 degrees to the right again, we turn and follow as before. It does feel like we're heading in the right direction, but I can't believe Assey has surveyed all of these vast empty spaces and truly knows where he is going. If it's just guesswork, then it seems to be pretty good. We reach another door opening to the left. We duck inside and carry on in the same direction with the wall now to our right. Another hour, the wall turns left, Assey goes left, there is no complaint from the other two at any point. After another 90 minutes, there is another door. This time we enter but do not follow the wall we run straight out into the room at 90 degrees from the wall we were just following. A good hour later, we have another stop, and all get out.

"How are we doing?" I ask Brito.

"We're nearly there."

"Where?"

"Our first destination," he's not giving anything away. "Another couple of hours then we'll find out."

"Find out what?"

"Whether they are everywhere or just in a few places."

"How do you know where you are going?"

"Kruzians have something like a photographic memory for directions. When we leave a start point, it doesn't matter which direction we turn; we always know where the start point is and can work our way back, without just retracing our steps. We can take the short route, or any other detour route, and still get to the chosen place."

It's a pretty impressive skill and something I wished I was capable of when I lived in London all those years ago.

"I think it's a little like a better version of what homing pigeons have on Earth. Funny though, when I used to go out and get drunk with my mates, and I mean properly drunk, I would wake up in my bed the next day and not have any clue how I'd managed to get there. A bit like a big pissed homing pigeon though. Sometimes there'd be the remains of a fried chicken takeaway, which meant I'd had the wherewithal to detour to the chicken shop, order, pay and get home and even eat most of it relatively successfully without me knowing what I'd done. 'Pissed Skills'."

"Pissed skills aren't going to help you now," Brito replied point-blank.

"No, suppose not." I looked at my feet in shame.

Back in the van and we take off again. Of course, this is one of 15's vans; there is no fuelling stop required, ever.

We keep driving out into the vast grey white unknown. There is nothing to see in any direction, just the massive expanse of featureless perfectly flat whiteness.

After approximately three more hours, we arrive at the Food Room. It's unguarded. The Kruzians fantastic sense of direction has allowed them to come around a different way and approach from an alternative angle. I didn't for the life of me think we'd end up here. Then it dawns on me that these lads do not have nanobots implanted as I do. They're hungry and need to eat. It's not like any of them are starving, but they have realised that it may be a long while before they get their next meal so have opted to refuel while they can, as well as loading up with rations. They could be without access to the Food Room, or others like it, for a long time and need sustenance.

We eat. It's not the same as usual. All three have their green bowls of slop and feeding straws, but they've also received a load of wrapped boxes that they've stacked into the back of the van as well as fluid sacs. I've never seen one of them piss or shit, so I imagine that there is no waste produced, that every cell of everything they eat or drink is assimilated into their being, which is easy to conceive. Shitting out half of what you've eaten as waste is a bit weird if you think about it.

I go light on lunch. I have a 'sandwich', sliced, breaded chicken escalope covered in chorizo and Swiss cheese slices, all warmed up until the cheese melts then all put on top of a chopped green salad mounded on the bottom half of a buttered panini. Top this off with sliced tomato a sprinkling of Tabasco sauce and chilli flakes. Balance the upper half of the panini on top of the tomato slices and stick the whole thing into a panini grill. It flattens down substantially as it is warmed through. When toasted to perfection, cut into two halves and dive in. I have this with a small plate of fried onion rings, and a bowl of salsa topped tortilla chips. I choose a chilled bottle of Sancerre (as it might be the last time I have a drink also). As we eat, we all scan the various horizons around us as for any signs of movement, or the real give away: colour. None comes.

We're mobile again – same van places as before. We've retraced our last steps driving out into the emptiness for a few hours until we hit the back wall. This time we turn left and carry on with the wall to our right. I stop paying attention to where we're going because I might as well trust Assey's sense of direction. To be able to find the Food Room has convinced me they know where they're going. Hours pass, we get out a couple of times, we make a few turns, but mainly we're heading in the same direction for hour after hour. I sleep for a bit, only because I can, it doesn't do anything to me physically or mentally, it just passes the time – and somehow makes me feel more human. I'm not sure how many hours we eventually drive for, but it would be more than an Earth day. We stop, finally, and Brito addresses us all with his pre-battle, rallying speech.

"We are about to enter areas where avatars may be manning tactically superior points. We may find ourselves outnumbered and under heavy fire from these strategic placements. We will address ambush positions aggressively and we will prevail."

The other two others echo "We will prevail."

"You have your training; you know how to act and react. We must take out all of the avatars present; it is imperative if we are to complete our mission and we will prevail."

Again the chorus, "We will prevail."

"At the moment, the enemy is unsure of where we are. There is no 'hive mind' - avatars are individuals, as we are. They're not using communications equipment so are only vocalising between each other. This is the same as us. As we clear a room, we know the sound of our attack will not easily travel into the next space - so we have the element of surprise in each room we enter, and - We. Will. Prevail."

"We. Will. Prevail." Louder this time.

"We are an incisive strike force; we are the aggressor. We take the fight to our enemies; we use shock and awe, to defeat. We are strong - they are weak.

We are the Kruzh Empire. WE. WILL. PREVAIL!"

"WE ARE THE KRUZH EMPIRE. WE WILL PREVAIL! WE WILL PREVAIL!" they all echo in unison loudly.

I'm not the Kruzh Empire, but felt quite pumped.

We all lock and load. There is a door ahead on our right-hand side; we have been following a right-hand wall. Yerech moves alongside the wall until he reaches the door opening, he flattens, then takes a quick peek around and back. He makes a hand signal to the others. They move forward also. I stay by the van holding my automatic across the front of my body. I'm at ease but ready to go. They all take a surreptitious look around the corner at different intervals and for longer or shorter lengths of time. Yerech stays at the door whilst the other two return. I keep looking behind, and along the other horizon in case I can see any movement from behind us. The two get back to me.

"Looks all quiet, we're bringing the van up," says Assey, the three of us get back in.

At the corner, we wait. Yerech takes a last look and gives us an OK. He comes around and jumps in the side door on next to me. We drive around the corner, keeping the side door open. Straight away, I see the colossal frame of pipes and tubes.

"I've been here before!" I say in an astonished way, knowing there's three dead avatars and a van to be found soon.

"No, you haven't this is a different room," says Brito.

"You said it was a download of my brain."

"Correct. In your room, there is a download of your brain. Don't you think there were other Champions before you who might have had their brains downloaded also?" There's a strong hint of sarcasm in Brito's voice.

"No, it hadn't even occurred to me. How many of these rooms are there?"

"Not sure, we haven't been to all of them. We are three away from your room; there could be any number - two, fifty, ten thousand rooms with downloads of Champions' brain's going the other direction."

I crane forward and look at the walls through the front window; I can see it's decorated in a similar way to the walls of my Brain Room. The walls are plastered with millions and millions of very bright, full-colour images of a Champion in combat. I don't know who the Champion was, or whether I ever saw any recorded footage of its fights when I was learning to fight myself but clearly, there is one combatant who is starring in each contest. This combatant is jet black; it's incredibly striking, I've never seen a creature anything like it before. It looks to have scaled skin of some sort because I can make out highlights. Its body is properly ripped with muscles - but lithe at the same time. I never looked in as good shape as this Champion did. It was tri-ped, each leg at 120 degrees to the others with an arm over each leg. A single nippled 'chest' in between each arm with a three-eyed head to top it off, one eye positioned directly above each nipple. As the images are all stills, not moving images, I can't tell how it moved. It certainly looked impressive, and there are fountains of spurting blood spatter everywhere. I'm also keeping an eye out on the 'frame', the downloaded brain or memory bank. There's no sign of trouble, but of course, a single, well-aimed anti-tank weapon would blow us to kingdom come instantaneously. Assey has his foot down, we're trying to speed to the end of the room, but as ever, it's a long way. We're keeping tight to the frame. We could see a would-be assailant at the right-hand wall if there were one, so staying close means we are 'under' the structure, certainly in its shadow making the van more challenging to target.

"Action stations." barks Brito and we've our weapons up ready. We swerve violently left as we reach the end of the room to get through the next door which is in the middle of the far wall. We hammer through and then swerve right to reach the frame and head along as per the last room. Again it's lit up all around with battle scenes from the Champion following the previous, two before me. Equally as bloody and equally as visceral. A million sorts of alien weapons, a million varieties of ways to die. The pictures are so in-your-face, so vivid - a partly disturbing, partly exultant, towering monument to the memory of a great warrior, a true Champion.

Again, no incident. Same in the next room, and then my room. Once again, I see my face plastered all over the walls, huge images and tall as skyscrapers and a whole block wide. I can see every pore on the skin in glorious technicolour and my face - always contorted, bloodied, sweaty, anguished, tensed. Not one single image I like but all were capturing the brutality and remorselessness of my bouts. Yerech pipes up in a flat deadpan.

"All hail the conquering hero."

The others all laugh.

We know I'm the most recent Champion, and therefore this room is the last of the line. We know there's a door halfway down on the right. I know I've killed some avatars there. I've worked out their plan. To go back the way I did, 'around the back' to the Store Room. Back through the 'Big Objects' room. As we're driving, we can cover the ground way more quickly than the last time I was there. Plus there's plenty of cover in that room. This route is also the quickest way to the racking section of the Store Room, where there are lots and lots of weapons and ammo as well as good cover. From the racking, we can shoot our way to the vehicles which we can then use to cause even more damage to any avatars in situ.

We're still speeding along, there's still no opposition, but now I know we're getting closer to the avatars as every minute passes. Finally, I can see something in the distance standing out against the white. It's the blue Bedford panel van that my three work colleagues were in when I was here last. I point it out to the three Kruzians, and they have a whispered discussion. We pull up a few hundred metres away from it, and all three decamp and prowl along the frame towards it. There is no sign of the three avatars I killed, just the van. There are no bloodstains, no dropped weapons or clothing, only the van with its front sliding doors and rear doors open. They stealthily work towards the van without any trouble. Once in, Assey drives it, and the other two, back to me.

"We've got two vans, so we can split into two ranks. Assey and Yerech in one and you and me in the other," says Brito. "You can drive."

"Well, I can reach the pedals."

"And I can see your hands," replies Brito.

We drive steadily through the floating doors section in our new convoy, white van with blue van following and both tip out into the 'Big Objects' room, the white van turns right and starts along the roadway left between the wall and big objects. I'm about three hundred metres behind in their tyre tracks when the front of the white van turns into a fireball and explodes up in the air with an ear-ringing blast. I 'left-hand-down' my van up on its driver side rims, into a handy gap and slam on the anchors, Brito and I leap out. Then there's a second even more significant, louder explosion which sends a plume of smoke 100ft in the air. We can already hear the clatter of small arms fire ahead. Brito leaps onto a large block. Even though we're approaching the heat of battle, I stop to be amazed at how agile he is. The block towers over him. I scrabble up behind him, we leap a small gap, shinny up another big white thing, slip alongside a couple of others and then see both Assey and Yerech in the cover below us as well as about 15 avatars at different points not far in front of them.

"Pick your targets. Short bursts." Brito instructs me.

I take out a couple of guys dressed like random pedestrians, then a female beauty counter salesperson and a lollipop man - all in quick succession. Fire is returned but never very accurately. When I get a chance to look, I can see that the two Kruzians on the ground have used our covering fire well and pushed forward, taking out five or six avatars between them. Brito expertly mops up. The firefight lasts two to three minutes tops. These boys are equal to, or better than, our special forces - incisive, deadly. Yerech checks they are all dead; if they aren't, he uses his short-sword to make sure they are. I go to the van; it's a mess, they took it out with an RPG round, straight into the engine block. The two were lucky to get out alive, soon after they jumped, the flames reached the ammo in the back, and the whole thing lifted into the air - the second, bigger explosion. What's left is now engulfed in flames. The food is gone, and so is the ammo, the occasional bullet still pops away in the back of the van.

"We need to get to the racking fast. The others will come, and we'll have no backup ammo." barks Brito. Assey sprints as fast as he can back to the blue van. In what can only be a couple of minutes he's back. We get in and take off. He's standing to drive.

Shortly, we're at the door to the Store Room. We stop.

"You out." Brito's talking to me. I do as he wishes. "We go on foot in case of another RPG. The others move off in the van; they reach the door opening and disappear through; there is no explosion this time. I run to the door and get there just behind Brito. He sprints through the door and for the first time, I see what's going on. The van slows to an almost stop and Yerech rolls out across the floor; he gets up kneeling with his weapon up to his eye, ready, like a coiled spring but not shooting. Assey carries on driving, he reaches the racking, stops the van, hops out and assumes a similar position to Yerech. He makes a noise, and Yerech jumps up and runs into a different part of the racking. Brito is running flat out for the racking. Yerech gets there before him and assumes the coiled spring position. Small target, gun cocked and ready to fire. Assey starts to fire at targets; he's closest. I can see avatars now using the cover of the vehicles to fire at the Kruzians. I don't like the look of this. I start to run towards the racking, but after a couple of paces, I turn and run back to the door, half expecting Yerech to shoot me in the back. I hear a second gun firing and assume it's Brito joining Assey as I don't drop to the floor full of hot lead. Once at the door, I get around the corner and climb up over a few blocks and hide. I'm sure Brito reached the racking. He had his head down as he was running; he didn't look back. He will have assumed I was with him. Now he's got too much on his plate he'll not come looking for me. I can hear a terrible battle unfolding next door. There are all sorts of noises; explosions, shouting, screams, heavy machine gunfire. I can smell the cordite in the air. There's no way I'm going to take a peek around the corner. No way. The noises seem to move around the huge Store Room, sometimes near, sometimes far away, sometimes in many different places at once. There are a few quiet periods, then periods, when there seems to be an entire World War condensed into a forty or fifty-second burst. It's scary to listen to, but I'm happy I'm not involved. I can't cover my ears. I need to be able to hear if something is coming my way but I don't want to hear it, so I start to look at my t-shirt; yellow, more lemony than orange, I'd call it 'pale yellow' evenly coloured, mid-weight jersey material. Probably 100% cotton but it could be a mix; there may be a bit of polyester added to give it a bit of stretch. I'd say you'd wash it at about 40 degrees with like, light colours or whites. I'd use a biological liquid and one of those balls. A little bit of conditioner to make it smell fresh or flowery. No problem in the tumble dryer. It's got a pretty crappy design on the front. Back in 1989 they probably didn't design it on a computer; it was probably a hand-drawn design. If it were on a computer, it would have been an early design programme - hardly sophisticated graphics - Slade's Christmas concert 1989. There's a stylised Christmas cracker at an angle across the front which is being punched in two from behind by a fist with the letters 'S.L.A.D' on each of the four fingers and an 'E' on the thumb. Then there is a big 'starburst' around the fist to signify a *big* punch, punching out through your chest, a big smash, like a 'POW' in 1970's TV Batman or the Roy Lichtenstein painting. The 'E' on the thumb lets it down. It looks out of place; shoehorned into the design. It's a bit shit really. Then the lettering 'NOIZY BUT NICE!' all in black on the yellow, no other colours, cheap one-colour print, or all the machine it was printed on was capable of. I'm reading this upside down, as I'm wearing it, there's text on the back also. But I can't see that. The noise is dying out in the Store Room. I stop using my t-shirt to distract me from the killing and listen again. There are sporadic shouts. The occasional few shots. Some cries of pain and anguish. I decide to wait until it's totally calm.

I haven't heard anything for at least half an hour. The shooting stopped first, but the crying and wailing went on much longer. There's been no movement around me. I still have my gun and several clips. I listen keenly, intently, straining to hear the tiniest of noises coming from the nearby echoless chamber.

Still. Nothing.

I stick my head above the parapet, there's nothing new to see. I climb down from my perch and skulk towards the door. I pause at the threshold, too scared to take a peek. I summon up the courage and make a darting peek and do. I don't pick up any real detail, but I know it's ugly, I certainly don't see anyone standing or potentially threatening nearby. I decide to jump right in and step around the corner to the full horror.

There is a thin blueish haze resting about 5 feet above the ground across the whole Store Room, or as far as I can see anyway. It looks dark, which is odd for the stark grey whiteness and perfectly even light inside 15. There is a heat coming from the room, barely noticeable but it's there, like body heat, the warmth of a bruise or inflammation but intensified. And a smell, one that can never be unsmelled; of blood and guts, of eggy sulphur and shit and sweat, of piss and phlegm and cordite and dirt, of burnt flesh and hair, of ammonia and metal. And it's acrid in the back of my throat, making me want to cough and spit. It's the smell of battle, of a bloody, disgusting battle, the smell of industrial death which I can see in all of its glory. Mangled, twisted corpses piled high, with huge holes shot right through whole torsos, pieces of flesh splattered across the ground. Limbs; a foot, a leg, an arm, a part, an unknown, unrecognisable portion of a body. Exposed bone, half a face. A body riddled with bullet holes next to another with just one. Empty bullet cases everywhere, shrapnel, machine parts, crumpled weaponry.

Then, as I pick my way through the killing field, I reach the truly nasty bit, which turns my stomach and makes me heave. The burnt bodies, hundreds of them scorched, unrecognisable, charred and conflagrated it looks like the Kruzians got hold of a flame thrower, and threw it. They had a little fire party and invited hundreds of avatars. I heave again, but it's a dry retch, there's nothing left. I hock up and spit on the ground by my feet. The smell is putrid and disgusting, popped eyeballs, blistered skin, scorched bones. I turn and pick my way back to the shelving units. I've got to get away, to not see this, to not smell this, to not taste this.

There must have been a few thousand avatars in this store. Many were inactive, just lined up ready to be used. I think the Kruzians fought off a few hundred avatars and toasted the rest. I suspect they did this in case they became active at some point. There is no sign of any of the Kruzians, no sign of injury and certainly none dead.

The racking is sprayed in bullet holes and blast marks. There was a hell of a lot of lead thrown in this direction, and I imagine at least the same amount was thrown back. There are piles of disposed used weapons. It looks like the Kruzians went gun after gun. Fire until it empties then pick up another and repeat. There are boxes of grenades, half full: a mortar, a tripod-mounted, heavy machine gun, handheld rocket launchers, pump-action shotguns, submachine guns, automatics - most classes, every maker, all represented.

Egalitarian death.

First time I was here I was nervous I'd be found by the avatars, that I'd be 'spotted' now I'm the only one standing in this vast room, with thousands of dead avatars around me. None is looking for me. I take my time in the racking. There is loads and loads of stuff, ephemera to look at and sort through, but there's nothing I need, not much that will help me. A bicycle pump, what good will that do? Almost everything is pointless. I find a knife and think about sticking it in my belt but then just leave it. I've still got this big fuck-off gun and plenty of ammo. I think I'm fine.

I walk back through the lines of racking and back into the piles of death. I'm getting used to the smell and desensitised to the sight. Still, I see the odd thing that makes me recoil and wince, but I walk on, and I walk to the ramp I fled down previously. I walk the same way top right corner diagonally across to the bottom left. At the base of the ramp, there's only the wall to corner around. As I do so, it happens again. I walk my face straight into the butt of Yerech's rifle.

Lights out (again!).

Stars. Stars and a few comets. Some starbursts and 'Pop', I open my eyes.

I see Yerech's face with a blood smear on his right chin and cheek. It's dried blood. His face has patches of dirt, soot, carbon.

"He's awake." A jab in the ribs from Yerech's boot. "Get up you fucker."

"*Oof*. Thanks." I recoil at the sharp pain in my side from the sneaky kick, my ribs ache. I sit up.

The three of them are there, looking a little battle-scarred but intact. Assey is the worst wounded.

"Took one under the ribs, was a through-and-through. Bleeding's nearly stopped. Hurts like hell but I'm OK."

Brito looks at me "You missed the fun, you fucking coward." He sneers at me. "I hadn't realised you were so yellow."

I baulk but play my part, "I thought we were all going to die. Sorry, I was scared."

"Unprepared. You fought in the Arena, but that's not the same as a proper battlefield. The mark of a real soldier is what he does when the bullets are flying around. You ran."

"I never said I was a soldier."

"No, you're a killer of innocent unarmed girls. There's something wrong with you."

I look at Assey, he's told them.

"I've paid for my sins imprisoned on this ship. Forced to fight. The longest prison sentence in the history of Humankind."

"You're still a yellow belly." Brito dismissively fires back.

Yerech is loving this. His hard-bitten, stony-face, is sporting a half-smile. The happiest I've ever seen him.

"What are we going to do?"

"We?" remarks Brito. "Whose side are you on today?"

"Look, I was scared, there were a lot of them. I thought we couldn't win. You three went to town on them. It's a bloodbath up there."

"We did our job. Nothing more, nothing less, and we will continue to do our job. We need to get into the Sphere Room."

"And?"

Assey talks now, "I've scouted ahead. The avatars have built a barricade with a bunch of large vehicles; they're inside and well-armed. I don't know how many, but a few hundred, I suspect."

Fuck, they're protecting it, at last, took them long enough to work that out.

"We don't know if 15 is back in control of them or if they are free-willed. Either way, they don't want us in."

"So do you have a plan?"

Yerech laughs and says "Yup, we're going in the hard way. Full-frontal, full-on attack, and we're going to keep going until every avatar is a burning hunk of flesh." he sneers.

"The flame thrower?" I say.

"I take it you saw Yerech's lovely work back there?" says Brito.

"Yeah, I saw it."

"Yerech is our favourite barbecue chef."

Yerech looks smug.

I know the dead are all avatars and not real people, just 'people-like' things made by 15, but I'm still appalled at Yerech and his actions. Just sickened. I don't like Brito revelling in his work either. Assey is quieter.

Chapter 35

IT LOOKS LIKE THE avatars are all defending the Sphere Room. However many of them that survived the Store Room massacre retreated here after Yerech went crazy with the flamethrower. We have no idea how many are left but undoubtedly many, many fewer than were in the Store Room originally. We can assume they're heavily armed and because they've built the barricades. They will have brought heavy guns - possibly even anti-tank weaponry into the Sphere Room to protect from attack. Taking this room out will be a very tall order, the avatars know we are coming. They have cover, we have little, but these three, along with me, are going in from the front. We are 'on', and there's no backing out this time. Yerech is behind me all the way, usually with the nuzzle of his gun poking between my shoulder blades.

There is a plan, though. It does involve four armoured JLTVs, the vehicles that replaced the Humvee in the battlefield for the US forces. The idea is to drive in a four-vehicle column, straight at the barricade. I will be in the front vehicle. Yerech in the fourth, and last vehicle.

If I veer off course, he will peel off the back and follow me, and shoot me dead. The plan is that as the front vehicle, I will provide cover for the other three. When my car is destroyed, they will only lose me – collateral damage. Something they won't lose sleep over. My car is full of live ammo, hand grenades, mines and any other explosive devices they could find. When I go up, I'm going up in style - and hopefully creating mayhem. I'm supposed to get as close as I can, but it's not expected I'll get anywhere near the barricade. My burned-out vehicle and burning corpse will provide cover to fire from behind and smoke, which will obscure the battlefield. This smoke may allow the Kruzians to get closer to the barricade in their vehicles where they will all decamp and attack in their unique way. Assey has an M240 belt-fed, medium machine gun mounted on the back of his truck; this gun fires 7.62 calibre spits of red hot lead that can rip apart vehicles, engine blocks, concrete or brick walls. Avatar flesh, by comparison, is easy meat. Yerech has his trusty flamethrower, fully refuelled and primed ready to roast and Brito has a few single-use hand-held rocket launchers plus a meaty RPG mounted on his primary assault weapon.

As we turn into the room preceding the Sphere Room, I see the three other vehicles form a line up behind me in my rear-view mirrors. Ahead of me, I can only see grey whiteness but in the far distance a thick black line. I know this is the line of vehicles forming the barricade. As I near, I start to make out the individual vehicles; different types of tanks, some half-tracks, a few petrol tankers (which I hope are empty), heavy construction trucks, a cement mixer, a long low-loader, light vans, 7.5-tonne trucks, 13-tonne trucks, panel vans and other light goods vehicles. Some big SUV/4x4 cars have been positioned separately in front of the barricade in an attempt to slow or stop, a 'battering ram' attack from a big heavy vehicle under speed, they're a bit like make-shift tank traps. I know the avatars have made a mistake here, these SUVs will offer handy cover and firing positions for the three in the JLTVs behind. But, just as I start to think I'm getting into range, and I fear for the worst, anticipating my sudden and swift end at any second - nothing happens.

I keep driving, getting closer and closer. I slow down from the 70mph I've been doing. I'm now only half a mile away and closing. There's something wrong here. Something unexpected is happening, or actually not happening. Not a shot has been fired. Were' only a quarter of a mile out, and closing fast. It's eerily quiet and making me scared. I start to think that maybe the entire barricade has been rigged and that any moment it's all going to go up, but I can see avatars in position. I can almost see the whites of their eyes, only a few hundred yards now - avatars, a few hundred of them, pointing their weapons, training them on the convoy. Now I'm slowing again. I'm nearing the SUVs the avatars placed in front of the barricade. I'm going to have to weave in and out of them to make further progress. I slow to 35 mph, then turn left.

The other three behind have to do the same if they are to follow me. As soon as I turn, the other three become visible to the defenders from behind me, the avatars open heavy fire on them, shooting fierce volleys at the following three vehicles. I pull away, and Yerech cannot follow me even if he wanted to.

I can see avatars along the barricade to my right, I am right in their sights, but they do not shoot at me. I turn right then left again, Brito and Assey are still behind me. I see Assey stop behind one of the parked SUVs and get out; he's found his position. I keep going right then left, ever nearing the barrier but no shots fired. Brito stops and jumps out firing and throwing explosives. I keep going; I'm nearly there. What am I going to do when I arrive? I pull up behind an estate car only 10 metres or so from the barricade. I jump out and, run backwards, away from the barricade, about ten metres, to get distance between me and my now abandoned vehicle. I know a bullet from either side could blow it to kingdom come.

I hit the ground around the back of a Mitsubishi Shogun. The noise of the battle around me is fierce. I can see Brito playing hit and run, he pops up and fires an RPG then drops back down, as soon as it explodes, he's off to find another position behind another car, then he repeats. He's knocking considerable holes in the barricades. Assey is still standing in the back of his JLTV and continually firing. I can see the bullet dents in the thick steel shield plates surrounding his weapon. He's bobbing and weaving from side to side to pick his targets from behind the shield; he rarely gets his body anywhere near a direct line of fire. If he does ever get hit, it's most likely going to be from an unlucky ricochet - so far he looks unscathed, unlike the avatars in his gunsight who are falling in their tens. I can't see Yerech, but I can hear him. For such a quiet guy, he's screaming and laughing, shouting obscenities as he toasts. I can smell the gasoline and feel the heat from the flamethrower. It's an odd weapon of choice. It has a range of up to 100 metres but has only a short burn time, so it's an excellent weapon to have, but only for a bit. Additionally, the operator is a pretty easy target for a sniping gunman. Yerech knows this. Flamethrowers are particularly effective against barricades and shielded positions. It throws liquid flame which is capable of bouncing off objects which opens up the stream up into 'spray fire', spreading through and down into the vehicles - causing colossal damage and petrifying any attackers near him. Then, when he reaches the burning barrier, he'll ditch the thrower and use the secondary weapon to mop up - dealing death, creating hell. He's some fucker.

Chapter 36

IT GOES ON AND on for what seems like an eternity. I hate every minute of it. I throw away my ammo reserves and fire a few shots off, but not aiming at any avatars until my weapon is empty. I throw away the gun. I need to look like I've taken part, but no bullets have come anywhere near me. I am not, and probably never have been, under attack.

The Kruzians are machines; when their small arms are exhausted, they go for their swords. They're like three angry hornets. Aggressive, bullish, but calm in attack. Thought through, rarely over-extended. Tight, capable - very productive. Finally, the last avatar standing is silenced; Brito sticks his sword through its neck. The battle is won, we have all made it to the other side of the barricade. Now, the Sphere is left unguarded. Although this army of avatars is dead, the Kruzians do not know if there are others, possibly millions, in another part of 15, that are heading this way. They need to take control again, which means moving the Sphere.

All three Kruzians are breathing heavily, their adrenaline, or equivalent, is running high, but they're tired. It's been an intense physical battle. Assey is sitting, catching his breath and laughing to himself heartily. Happy to be alive and enjoying the euphoric rush. Yerech is still sticking his sword through a few groaning, prone avatars to ensure they're done. Brito looks at me.

"See, that's how to fight. We're a superior race to yours in so many ways." He's still smiling, smirking, goading, laughing at Humanity, laughing at me. And he's still smiling as my kick, the hardest kick of what's left of Humanity in the whole Universe can manage, connects to Brito - dead centre in between his little legs. Hard, fast and with massive follow through. It is powerful and mean-spirited enough to lift him both up, and backwards, in the air. He flies for a short while before landing in a heap a couple of metres away. A rugby 'drop kick' that sends Brito flying across the room. It also loosens the sword from his grip, which I instantaneously whip up from the ground. He may not be dead, but it's the equivalent of being hit by a small car travelling at a low speed. It's going to put you out of immediate action and hurt like hell for a few weeks. He may even need surgery to put him all back together down there, but he's not dead.

Two left. Yerech is back to me in a heartbeat; he sensed the trouble. But I'm also good with a blade; one-on-one is my forte. I easily parry his first thrust and push him away. He's got a big smile on his face, "I've been looking forward to this." he snarls and swishes a wild uppercut, left-to-right which I quickly counter and push him away again, he stumbles and tumbles onto the ground. I can't see Assey until it's too late, and I feel cold steel in my back, just above the hip bone on my right-hand side. He's silently got around behind me as I've been fronting up to Yerech. The Kruzians are so good at fighting in teams. He rams the point in pretty deep. I see the blade tip appear out of the side of my stomach. Then he retracts it again - to stick me again. I spin around; the pain is intense and very uncomfortable, but not enough to get me to drop. I swipe at him to get some distance between us and then back up so I can see both of them. Yerech is now back on his feet. Assey looks focussed.

"You haven't got a chance," chuckles Yerech, "We're going to dice you up."

I try to manoeuvre, so I always have each of them in my peripheral vision, but they know this and whenever I turn towards one, the other slides away behind me into my blind spot, outflanking me. I know what they're up to so I take the fight to them. If I can't even up the odds, then they're going to take pot-shots at me from a distance until I'm unable to fight back. I've also got Brito in the back of my head. What if he can recover enough to join them? The decision is swift; I know what I've got to do and how to do it - it's just that I'm going to have to take some damage. I make a wild lunge for Assey, who, quick as a cat dances backwards out of range. Yerech sticks his blade into my backside, my gluteus maximus. It's a painful injury. Right through the muscle. He knows it's debilitating and painful, but he's a sadistic motherfucker, so I expect he's rather enjoying himself. I feel the blood oozing down the back of my leg and inner thigh, it's on the same side as the hip-high run-through I received from Assey. I'm now weak on my right side; I realise I'm tucking my elbow back into my body on that side to protect the wound. The two punctures have cut the length off my reach. I take a chance and run towards the Sphere, it's closer to me than the two Kruzians. I reach it before them and turn, so it is at my back.

Without saying a word, they split so there is one to my far right and one to my far left. I think the idea is that one is prepared to sacrifice for the other. If I grab one, the other is hoping to swipe in and kill me before I can do any further damage. Either is prepared to sacrifice themself for the success of the mission.

They stand back and wait for me to make a move. I'm bleeding pretty severely, but even though there's plenty of blood, I don't feel like there's been too much damage done. That said, the wounds are some of the most uncomfortable and debilitating I've had the pleasure to receive in my hundreds of years of fighting. I'm breathing heavily and let my sword hand drop. It's taken as a signal for their simultaneous attack. They haven't communicated with each other, but with years of on-point training, they both instinctively know that the first sign of any form of weakness or exhaustion is the time to go. They both leap forward simultaneously and swing at me - Yerech to my left, Assey to my right. I can only try to parry Assey's whistling edge with my sword hand because I'm also desperately pushing away Yerech's blade with my left hand. I can only focus on one attack, so Assey's blade avoids my defence and the tip slides straight into my belly, just to the left of my navel. It penetrates a good six inches. This is real bad news, but the good news is that I've got a hold of Yerech by the throat, something I've wanted for a very long time. He aimed his sword higher towards my heart, which I deflected upwards enabling me to grab and grip him. I pick him up off the ground and twist him around, swinging his back in towards my body. Assey backs up. I'm using Yerech as a shield. The wound to my stomach hurts - another one on my right-hand side. I'm beginning to look like a bloody pin cushion, not a bloody pin cushion, a 'bloody' pin cushion.

For the first time, Assey looks a little lost. Brito is on the floor moaning, and I'm strangling the shit out of Yerech who's thrashing about to no avail.

Assey is still backing away. Yerech is trying to tell him to do something but can't talk; he can't breathe. I throw him hard on the ground. His head contacts the floor first and bounces back up on impact. I kneel on his chest with all my weight and look down at him, my eyes are focussed on Assey, but he's not currently threatening.

I address Yerech, lying prone beneath my knees as I stare into Assey's eyes, "I might not be a soldier, but I've fought many, many warriors braver, stronger, *better trained*, and with better morals than you over two millennia. This is what I do, and I'm very good at it. I'm a Human from Earth, and this is how I roll."

I can feel Yerech's ribs crackling under my shins. I think the fractured bones will instantly damage most of his internal organs; he starts coughing, and choking on his colourless blood. I lock-on to Assey's eyes; I don't flinch as I squeeze the life out of Yerech. I want Assey to witness what I am capable of. I let him see Yerech's life slowly drain away. A nasty, slow, painful death. There's nothing glorious about it. It's graceless - nothing less than he deserves.

I still don't take my eyes of Assey as I get to my feet and circle around to Brito who's lying, groaning on the floor, disabled. I address Brito while Assey still looks at me, half 'sword up, in position, ever alert', half scared out of his wits.

"Brito! Mate. Buddy. All that fancy footwork and superlative sword skills then you get undone by a big haymaker to the bollocks. Poetic justice if you ask me." I smirk and then place my sword tip on his left temple. "Sorry 'Old Bean'. I will prevail."

I put my whole body weight on the sword hilt. It doesn't immediately penetrate the skull bone, so I push harder until it suddenly gives. The sharp sword tip and blade slide effortlessly down. I stare sanguine into Assey's eyes as he stares at Brito's head. I never look down, I know he's dead.

It's a very unpleasant sound and feel.

Now there's only two of us left. I turn my attention to Assey.

"You've seen what I can do. I've told you about some of my fights, you've seen the pictures, and you know I was a serial killer, in a previous life. Is this what you want me to do to you? Cause you're next."

His bottle has gone. His sword is up, but he's lost it.

"Do I have a choice?" a meek, squeak from a lion that's turned into a mouse.

I think for a moment.

"Sure, you do. Drop the weapon. And any others you may have on you. Then stand over there, away from all the dead bodies and sit and wait for me like a good Kruzian. If I see you move, I'll kill you - not in a nice way."

He does as I ask. I keep him in my field of vision as I walk, as upright as I can, over to the nearest group of dead avatars and find a loaded handgun amongst them. I'm still bleeding heavily, and everything hurts, but I'm never going to show it.

"C'mon. Over here." I gesture with the handgun for him to come closer.

He is obedient. When he arrives, I put my arm around his shoulder.

"You and me, we gonna be best buddies!" I smile at him. He's shaking.

Chapter 37

An hour later, I'm sitting in the Food Room with Assey. Everything's much calmer. Of the three, he's the one I've always liked the most. Actually, without the influence of the others, the brooding menace of Yerech and the stilting authority of Brito, he's more relaxed and more friendly than he ever has been but still sheepish and yielding.

He's still eating his bowl of green slop though.

"What's so great about that then? Why is it all you eat?"

"I wanted to ask you a similar question; you seem to eat lots of different things. I can't understand how they can all be good or nutritious. We eat one type of food because there is only one type of food. It is a perfect meal. Whatever we eat is utilised by our body. It has everything we need to survive. When you eat, you then have to excrete either solid or liquid waste product. We find this odd. I also find it odd that although your race does this, you have not, to my knowledge, needed to do so since we have been together."

"That's because there are a few things about me that you don't know about. Firstly, 15 has placed some very helpful little nanobots in my system. Having them means I don't have to eat at all for sustenance. The nanobots can just keep using and recycling all of my current cells to keep me in perfect order. I do not have to drink, to sleep, to shit - totally self-sufficient, I just do it because I like it. And if I get an injury, I'm not talking about a scratch here, but let's say a gunshot wound, the nanobots will fix it within a few hours." I think I'm looking a little smug as I'm explaining all this. I feel a bit special - Superman.

"Kruzian physiology does most of this without the aid of nanobots. As long as we remain alive, our bodies can regenerate even when we have extensive injuries. We don't need to sleep. We never need to 'shit'. We just need some fuel to keep the engine going."

He's right. I don't feel quite so impressive anymore.

"Could you eat a slice of pizza?"

"Yes, I could chew it and swallow it, but I wouldn't be able to digest it, the proteins in the meat and carbohydrates in the base are indigestible to me."

"So you'd get rid of it..."

"Chuck it up. The only way out."

A pause in the conversation. Assey takes a suck on his straw, and the level of greenness in his bowl drops about a centimetre.

"What other secrets?" Asks Assey.

I look down into my plate of Seafood Linguine. I say the words quietly, almost under my breath, "I turned the avatars against you."

He doesn't get outwardly angry, but I see his fists clenching and unclenching. He hisses. "You *bastard*."

"Brito let me tell the avatars to put the Sphere back. It was his mistake. He let his guard down for a second, and I took my chance. I told them to put the Sphere back on the '15 in control of avatars' indentation and to arm all active avatars. I told them to barricade the Sphere Room with 200 heavily armed troops and vehicles. They did what I asked. After that, it was just down to me to wait for the opportunity to try to overpower you three. My plan worked."

"You killed my friends and ended the mission."

"They weren't nice people, and your mission still exists. You still want to take over 15 don't you?"

"It's not the same." he sounds downhearted.

I think for a while. And then start to smile.

"I've got a little plan..."

Chapter 38

WE'RE IN THE STORE Room rummaging around the racking looking for the right tools. I'm in fresh clothes after using water from the Food Room to wash congealed blood from my skin and already repairing wounds. We've got a fire engine as our mode of transport. I've always fancied driving one but in all my long, long years had never actually tried until now. And it's fun. It's a classic British Dennis version. It's got a 'Nee-naw' siren rather than a 'Woo-woo' which makes me feel warm and nostalgic inside. When I explained this to Assey, he looked back at me blankly.

We pull a few things out and pile them all up, or attach them to the tender. I was going to bring the handgun from earlier, but it didn't feel right. I sense that the mission has changed; the threat has diminished. I left it behind.

We drive off out of the Store Room and into the 'Big Objects Room'. I'm no longer fearful. Every time I've previously been in this room, I've felt on edge and scared, always waiting for an attack. Now, it feels like a Sunday afternoon drive through the country. I do keep an eye out for stray avatars - although not for my safety. I'm way more relaxed now I know they are not inclined to harm me, but I am just a little worried that one might attack and/or kill Assey, and I don't want that to happen.

We don't see a single avatar in any of the link rooms between Store Room and the 'My Brain/Pipes Room'. I still struggle to look at the images of me on the walls. They're so big, so 'full contrast' colour and so graphic that I avert my gaze to avoid seeing them. Assey looks out of the window all the time occasionally trying to draw my attention to a particular image he spots; "You have great form in this one.", "That guy looks scary?" "How did you defeat that one?" sort of thing. My answers are always short, lacking detail. I'm not revelling in the death depicted around me. We reach the entry point into the dark area. We parallel park alongside and use the ladders to get across. The fire engine is almost tall enough to get to the bottom of the opening. The ladder ends up more like an angled gangplank than a ladder. I had tried to work out what the perfect vehicle would be for the dark area. A skateboard? A bicycle? We chucked a couple on, to be safe, in case our other options didn't work out. I wanted something powered though, to take the strain but loading other vehicles onto the fire engine and then up into the opening was going to be a problem for us. I looked at a quad bike - too heavy, as was a golf cart. In the end, we opted for a couple of petrol motor scooters and found the lightest ones we could - two of us, two scooters - double the chance of finding the hole. Getting the scooters onto the top of the fire engine was pretty easy as we used a cherry picker back at the Store Room. Pushing them along the rungs across the ladder was way more complicated, and we both made heavy weather of it, but soon enough we were up on the lip of the opening with all of our equipment - mainly lights.

The best tool in the box, though? Assey. As before, Kruzians have the 'homing pigeon' quality to them. I wouldn't exactly say that he took us straight to the spot, but he did get us close. Although Kruzians are very, very good at directions, I think the headtorch helped. Then we employed a grid system. We placed a group of powerful arc lights at our 'base'. From here we drove out in our four compass point directions trying to drive in a straight line and dropping a battery light flare every quarter of a mile as measured on the mileometers of our scooters. We did this for five miles and then returned along the line back to base. We could pretty much see each other as we did this because one could always pick out the other's scooter headlight. Once we had the middle 10-mile cross, we would go to the first marker out from the centre and try to drive a line parallel to the first one. We didn't have to do too many lines up and down before we found what we were looking for. The 'hole' still wasn't throwing any light from the space above, so it wasn't an easy spot, even when we were close to it. We then moved all of the arc lights to this spot. Next, we both drove back to the fire engine, with Assey as guide, dropping lights to our left and right to create a marked road back to the 'Big Hole'. Now, all we needed was a ladder, or ramp to get back up to 15. The fire engine had plenty of short ladders, so we brought a couple.

Chapter 39

IT WAS GREAT TO once again poke my head up out of the hole. I look around and see absolutely nothing but a acres and acres of heart-warming, welcoming, empty grey whiteness. I turned almost 180 degrees around until I see 15 directly behind me. The small, innocuous, traffic-bollard like column - still flashing red. I was hoping for a blue light! I pulled myself up onto the floor and sauntered over.

"Hey mate, how'ya doin'?"

"*hi.*", a pale, flat reply.

"Is that all you've got after I've just saved your big white ass?"

"*still not right*". 15 sounds very meek, sickly.

"But everything's back to normal. I've killed your enemies - well almost all of them. I've still got one of them here. He's coming up, and I don't want you to kill him." I shout, "ASSEY, COME UP HERE."

A moment or two later Assey's head pops up looking disembodied by the blackness. Then the rest of him emerges intact. He stands and looks around meekly but stays at the edge of the hole.

"I've got a prisoner!"

"Am I your prisoner?" Asks Assey, surprised.

"No. Well sort of. But not really. It was just something to say."

"i need more help. you need to fix me."

"What can I do?"

"there is a black liquid. it is crucial. some of it is missing. they stole it."

"No, we didn't." replies Assey.

"What's he talking about?". Like I don't know.

"He means the 'oil' I showed you, we took some, mainly stuck to the soles of our shoes, but we put it back. It found its way back to the black."

I remember the oil creeping its way back to the mass, and I realise what 15 is going on about. It's not the Kruzians who took the oil; it was me. And I know why he's not right. It's because I've left some in a flask 'captive' in the back of the battered van. I play dumb.

"What the fuck did you do lot do with the oil?" I ask Assey. Neither he nor 15 know I kept some in a flask, and I'm not owning up. "I take it you can't make ships and avatars, and function properly without it?"

"that is correct. i need the black back. find it for me."

"Don't worry. I'll get it back for you." I'm at my heroic best.

I look over to Assey,

"Back down the hole, prisoner." And I laugh at him.

It doesn't take us too long to retrace our steps. We now have a lit path back to the hole and the fire engine. We have to take the fire engine back with us as it is the only transport we have, but it's fun driving along at high speed 'NEE-NAW'ing as we go. I chat a lot with Assey about what he's going to do now.

"Return to the Kruzh Empire."

"How will that be received? You're defeated, your mission a failure."

"The Empire does not look favourably on defeat, but I have so much information about the workings of fleet ships. My knowledge and experience will be invaluable."

"I don't think that even if we do get 15 back to full working order that he's going to be happy going back to Kruzh airspace to drop you off. He doesn't turn around either. It's more likely that you'll get dumped somewhere."

Assey looks a little blank and dejected. I think he feels the burden of failure, especially as the only survivor.

Then he looks up at me, "What about you. What are you going to do?"

This hadn't occurred to me. What am I going to do now? Do I stay on the ship and go back to being Champion? I didn't want that from the start. I could just die. How long would I be dead for? Would 15 resurrect me at the first sign of trouble?

I put the whole conversation out of my mind. We're at the Store Room again. It's still a bloody mess - there are no avatars to clean the place up. We change from the Fire Engine; it's a bit too big. I find an undamaged two-door Honda Civic, quite a sporty looking black one, it's perfect for our needs, smallish, easy to get about in. I'm driving. Assey is good at driving, but we still have to modify cars for him because he's so short. I'm not totally at ease with him driving around with a wooden block tied to the accelerator and brake to allow him to reach. While I was with the Kruzians, I had no choice but to be driven. I'm not pointing a gun at Assey; in fact, he could grab any weapon from the racking and used it on me, but he doesn't. I think 'killing' time has passed. We're working together now.

We drive to where the avatars and Assey towed the old van after Brito crashed it into the Brain's forcefield.

I open the back doors and rummage around for the flask.

"You had it!"

"Yeah, don't tell 15."

"But it thinks that we had it."

"Just tell him Brito had it. He's dead, so no-one's going to know. Keep it on the hush-hush."

Assey seems OK with this. I just want to get the oil back to the Oil Room as soon as possible. We jump back in the car and hare off at a fair lick. Assey's navigating, I'm glad he's here as I'm not sure I'd find my way around on my own.

"I think you got your plan wrong," I say to Assey as we're driving.

"In what way?"

"I think messing around with the Brain was a waste of time. I think you should have got a bucket full of oil and gone back to see 15 with it. You could have ransomed it to make him do what you wanted. I think it's his Brain fluid. He can't operate without it."

"We were scared to return to the surface in case it used some of its weapons against us."

I see his point, their attack was just trial and error, to see what worked and hoping not to be killed finding out.

Soon we're back at the lake of inky black oil. I get the flask and start to pour the liquid back into the pool. It oozes thickly from the flask and drops out in a big lump. There is no splash, the black just smooths itself over the rest of the black and leaves no trace, no ripple - only blackness. I check the flask; there isn't a single drop or morsel of blackness in the flask, it's like every last drop was desperate to escape in one. I turn to Assey.

"Remember, Brito had it."

He nods in silent agreement.

"Is there anything else you want from down here, or anything you want to see? I suspect that if 15 is back to normal that we won't be down here ever again?"

I thought he might want to see Brito or Yerech again; he might want to say a prayer, he can't bury them, but may want to see them off somehow."

"No, I'm good."

We head back to the surface.

I'm pleased to see a blue light this time. In fact, I'm more than pleased. I'm hugely relieved. There is something else also. Although this place is noiseless, I'm sure I can hear a silent 'hum' or the feeling of a hum, but no hum - strange.

"Back to blue, that's a very welcome sight."

"I'm happy to be back and feeling my old self again."

"What was the stuff about the oil?"

"It is not 'oil', but it is necessary for me to function. It might be my 'essence'. It has to be whole. Without it, even a small drop, I am incapacitated."

I look behind me and see that the hole has closed up. There is no trace of it. I could look around for hours and not be able to tell you exactly where it was. No seam, no edge, no join, no discolouration. Back to normal.

"And the avatars."

"You'll be pleased to know the mess is cleared up. Very soon, everything will be back to normal. As if nothing happened."

"And you're back building ships again?"

"From the moment you dropped the fluid back into the lake and it re-amalgamated itself."

"You need to see this too. Turn around."

He's done it again, one of those "It's behind you moments when something pops into existence but out of my sightline so as not to be too weird.

I think my smile hit the bottom of each of my ears.

"My habitat!"

I motion to Assey, "Oi, come and look at this."

Assey follows me in through the invisible barrier. Straight away, I'm hit by the smell - fresh-cut grass. The last smell I remember is the filthy stench of after-battle; after that, this is a welcome joy. I also hear the birds twittering in the tree canopies, and the gentle breeze rustling the verdant leaves, the warmth of 'the sun' on my face.

"Is this what your world is like?"

"Yup. Whaddya reckon?"

"Kruzh is way more beautiful.

I rankle, "If it's so fucking great why don't you all spend some time enjoying it rather than pissing people off all over the galaxy?"

I kick off my shoes and run to find my woodland cottage, the last house I lived in. I see an avatar pruning a rose bush, "Mate, can you rebuild all the houses I burned down to their original state, please?"

"Of course, consider it done."

Assey and I hang around for a few days. I show him the mountains, the rainforest, the desert and the sea. He soon starts to enjoy pissing around in a jet ski. I spend a lot of time sitting down, and remembering how good it is to sit down and also in bed or lying on something soft, that moulds to your shape and is *comfortable*. But after a few days, I start to realise that this is limbo. I need to sort the situation out with Assey and more importantly with me.

Chapter 40

I'M GENTLY SWINGING IN a hammock; it's free-standing, i.e. has its own frame. It's delightful, having a gentle rock. I have a few questions for 15 about what happened inside him, a few loose ends I want to clear up. Assey is back in the habitat, he's discovered the ride-on lawn-mower and has taken over cutting the grass from the avatars, I can't believe how much he loves it.

"I saw the window frames, you had a go at building some."

"I'm not embarrassed, I think you're trying to embarrass me. I just wanted to test a hypothesis. It's very scientific."

"I think you wanted a window but couldn't make one. You should let me go down there and knock one out for you."

"Don't hold your breath on the invitation."

I chuckle to myself, then ask,

"So how would you move the Sphere under normal circumstances?"

"I would get some avatars to move it from one space to another for me. They are my 'hands' in effect."

"But that doesn't work, does it? You can move it to one spot which disables all of the avatars. If they're disabled, how can you get one of them to move the ball?"

"If such an incident occurred, then I'd ask the Champion to do it for me."

"Whoa, you told me no Champion ever ventured into your insides, no-one ever got 'below deck'. And if they did, there would be nothing to stop them from rolling the Sphere into the wrong indentation and taking control of the avatars and possibly you."

"They would not know that the other indentation would allow control of the avatars. They'd just do what I asked."

"But they might do it by accident?"

"It's not a discussion because I've never asked a Champion to move the Sphere. You are the first one ever to venture into my 'innards', so it's a bit of a silly hypothetical discussion."

"But the question remains. What if there was no avatar and no Champion and the Sphere became dislodged? I don't know, in the middle of a meteor shower or if the shockwave hit you from an exploded gas giant. In the whole infinity of space and time, this could happen. What would you do then?"

"Easy. I'd roll it back myself. "

I scoff, "How exactly would you do that with no hands?"

"I'd move forward and then hit the brakes and then slam it into reverse, I'd roll it out of one dent into another."

I laugh out loud. "You're fucking huge, sometimes planet-sized. The Sphere only has to move a few feet. You'd never be able to do it. The ball would roll off all over the place."

"Then I'd move to roll it back."

I form the image in my head. The idea of this colossal entity sitting in space and nudging itself up and down, left and right, to roll a small ball into a little dent - like a super-jumbo-sized teeter toy ball maze, is one of the most ridiculous things I've ever attempted to imagine.

Chapter 41

ASSEY HAS ALSO BEEN having conversations alone with 15. It took a while for him to get to the point where he felt comfortable to be alone with 15. He was sure 15 was going to kill or torture him for what he did. I think though, 15 likes Assey and if anything has been on a charm offensive, almost to prove that he (and his type) are not the devils that the Kruzian Empire think they are. He's not debating the 'cons' of the Empire - I think that might just end up in a fight. He's talking more from a Humanitarian standpoint, talking about how he's worked to save planets under threat. I've been keeping a low profile during these chats - I don't want to get involved. I do talk about the Kruzh Empire to Assey individually though. Usually later in the evening, around a fire on the beach, or when sitting out on the deck listening to the sea.

Like this;

"I'm not talking about individuals now, I mean I quite like you, but I don't like what drives the Empire. It's just the pure hatred of fleet ships and nothing more. 'Getting even' is not even the primary objective of the Empire, it's the only objective. An empire that abandons local and national politics, doesn't care about the arts or society. One that centres *all* of its resources; its ideology, its raison d'etre, against something or things that bear no grudge. They don't even realise they're your enemy or targets. The original Kruzians who first 'fell out' with a fleet ship aren't even around now, haven't been for thousands of years. It's ridiculous not to move on.

"I think the Empire should be focussing on its people, welfare, education, the arts, entertainment, having fun. Finding something it wishes to export to the Universe that isn't just military observance. I think the Empire needs to 'get a life', to go on holiday, to get pissed and wake up in the wrong bed with the wrong person now and again. To not always be shining its shoes until it can see it's face in them, sometimes it needs to wear a pair of sandals, and not over a pair of socks."

"You know, I could never see it. I was part of it. It was blind adherence. I was born into it, and until I escaped, I could not see the difference. I like 15; I like talking to it, I nearly said 'him' then like you do." Assey smiled.

"It's OK to call him 'him', or 'her' if you'd rather. In the end, it's neither, but I like to see the 'Humanity' in him. He's got an uncompromising side also, but generally, I think he's a benign force. Maybe not a force for good but generally a force for fairness."

I'm not sure what's going on in Assey's head, but he's definitely got something on his mind that he's mulling over.

Chapter 42

"I DON'T HAVE 'FEELINGS' BUT I can 'feel' you, the Kruzians and uncontrolled avatars running around in a part of me that is supposed to be inaccessible. I can 'feel' where each individual is, their footfall, their body heat, their air displacement, but I have no control of what they do, or where they go. The unpredictability is 'exhilarating'. I have a greater understanding of 'feelings' than I did before." I sit up at this, this is something new, and it's got my attention. 15 carries on.

"I don't 'feel' but I understand the sensation of it more, maybe 'touch', more than 'feel' and also what it is like to be tickled."

The thought of tickling a spaceship that could, on occasion, be about half the size of Earth intrigues me. 15 continues,

"To feel something, painfully pleasurable, and not be able to do something about it, to be unable to stop, to quite like it. The anticipation of the next footstep grounding, heel then toe or even severed limb falling from the ex-owner until it hits the floor. Blood splatters. Single large droplets landing with a meaty splash, to fine sprays, each minute droplet leaving an almost undetectable sensation as the mist of scarlet settles on the surface. It's almost the feeling of pleasure, feeling the wide arc gently touch down, and leave the faintest of colour changes like the brushstroke of the watercolour artists across cartridge paper, translucent, almost unseen yet the mark has been made, the pure white sullied by the palest of pinks. I know it's happening, but the anticipation is the nicest part. Is it 'feeling'? Is it in the way you feel things? Or is it just numbers crunching at such a tremendous speed that I anticipate the answer before it arrives." 15 stops, almost the poets trembling hesitation. Pause for effect?

I start a slow clap, "Well done, Byron, you've surpassed yourself, how wonderfully poetic! It's great to hear you talking like this and to know that after all these years of rolling around from galaxy, to star-cluster, to nebulae and back again that you've finally experienced something out of the ordinary, something you have no control over. It might serve to make you a better," I hesitate, "...thing, in the future. I do think you've felt something, but not in the same way I feel things? My sense of touch and therefore feeling is centred around nerves, on the skin, in fingertips, in hair follicles etc. You don't have these. You do though have an ability to calculate. I think that you've learned to feel as a result of what's happened."

"Now that we're all back to where you want us to be, meaning, not inside you, you're in control so whatever you 'felt' you've lost that ability again. It's the lack of control that gives *you* the ability to 'feel'. If I drop a ball on the ground now, you know what is going to happen. Not just where it is going to land, and how high it is going to bounce; but you have created every molecule of the ball, every molecule of air inside the ball, the floor it is going to bounce on, and the air that will be displaced as the ball falls from my hand to the floor. You've already worked out the velocity, the bounce, the air pressure, the temperature, the gravity, all of it. Nothing is a surprise. Inside you, you had no control of this. You could still work out all the stuff around the individuals, you still had the floor, the air, the pressure, gravity and temperature under control, but you couldn't control the protagonists and what they would do next. You can see an avatar's arm being severed, correctly triangulate its place in space, anticipate it's rate of fall, it's weight, it's mass, it's space-time position, and although you originally made it, you had relinquished control of it, so you didn't know what it would *actually* feel like until it hit your deck. You could run all the numbers and produce all of the calculations, but there was a bit you weren't in control of – a degree of variance or 'leeway'. The variance was not just in this example, 'how a severed arm would feel' but the unpredictability of the individuals inside you and their actions. Although this leeway was probably numerically minute, it gave you a frisson, it 'excited' you because it was something you didn't know. Isn't it nice to sometimes have something in your life that is beyond your control? I think that's part of what makes life worth living, something extraordinary, something spontaneous."

15 chimed back in, "I agree with you to a point, but I have always had that here, with you. You give me the 'frisson' that you're talking about. I get small amounts of 'variance' every day, and I think that's why I enjoy having a companion with me, but it's the barest tickle of unknown whereas I've just had an exceedingly large amount of unknown. I think that's why I've always looked forward to the Champion/Challenger fights. Each protagonist could kill or be killed in an instant. The fight, and the result, is always beyond my control."

"So what are you going to do to stop you from being attacked in the future?"

15 explained the Store Room to me. It was pretty much as expected. 15 builds lots of avatars for lots of situations. Then he parks them. I used to spend a lot of time 'going to work' in a fake, 'outer space London' that he created for me as part of my environment. Most of the avatars and the equipment in the Store Room were waiting for the occasion of me wanting to spend a day at work. He'd fire up the also-rans, the background cast, like the extras in EastEnders, to populate the scene. Just faces; people of different shapes and sizes, different sexes, ages, colours - whatever to make the scenario more believable. They

were 'spares', all based on real people though. 15 took 'shots' from my memory to create them in case required. He just quite liked making them. Some of the avatars, like the first four I killed; the woman in the toilets and the three work colleagues, happened to be people I knew or remembered - there were plenty of others too. Not my next-door neighbours but the people who lived at the end of the road. The lad who was on college work experience that worked at my office for two months. The lady who works in the sandwich shop, not the one I usually buy my lunch from but the posh one around the corner that I go to on the odd special occasion. It's a bit like Christmas tree lights. You buy a set and every year put them on the tree. A bulb goes, so you go out to buy a bulb - but you can't just buy one because they're so small, you have to buy a box of six. A few years pass and one day, with Christmas approaching, you see a charming new set of LED lights. These new lights are energy-saving, and there are loads of different flashing sequences to select - and you can control them with your phone. So you buy some and throw the old inefficient string out. Three years later, you find the box of replacement bulbs for the original string of lights; there's still five left. These avatars were the equivalent to the five replacement bulbs - surplus to requirements, sitting around; spare.

Chapter 43

I'M IN THE ENVIRONMENT, just pottering about, not doing much really when an avatar asks me to visit 15 for a chat. I can't find Assey, but when I get to 15, I see he's arrived before me - and is standing next to 15. 15 says,

"I wanted to know what your plans are for the future? I brought you back, but you didn't want to come back. What would you like me to do now?"

I think he means 'do I want to die again'. I did - especially when first resurrected, but that's past tense. Now I'm enjoying being alive again, spending time with Assey and having 15 in my debt.

"Erm, not sure. I'm sort of enjoying myself at the moment."

"It's just that, as you know, I don't take passengers. If I do, it's only for a short period."

"But I'm not a 'passenger'; I'm your Champion - and your saviour." I thought I'd add that for dramatic effect.

"It's just that since Assey has been here, with me, he's shown an interest in becoming my new Champion."

I'm astonished, I look at Assey, and then at 15, I think my jaw is hanging open. I feel suddenly empty, betrayed.

"But, but... I thought Assey was going to leave?"

"I asked him to stay, and he's accepted." Assey smiles at 15.

"But I'm your Champion."

"Brito killed you. You wanted to stop being my Champion, and then when you died, we agreed that was the end. You vacated the job role."

"You brought me back to help you!"

"Yes, and you did so. Very well, expertly in fact. But that was that. This is now. I need a new Champion."

"What if I want to be your Champion?"

"You made it clear that you don't want to be my Champion, and if I do relent and give you back the role, how do I know if you're not going to get upset again in a couple of years and become all petulant again?"

"PETULANT! How dare you!" I spit angrily.

"You became petulant and acted as a small Human child. We then agreed for you to vacate the role..."

I cut in...

"But then you brought me back, and I saved you. You ungrateful sod. And this little shit was one of the ones who tried to kill you." I point to Assey, who looks at the floor in silence.

"Only because he knew no better. Assey will be a fine Champion, he's young, well-trained, an excellent fighter."

"Well, clearly not as good as me. He's my prisoner."

"No, he's not. And he wants an environment that's Kruzian; he doesn't like your 'Earth' one."

I'm aghast; I feel as if I've been kicked hard in the stomach.

"It's decided, so the next issue is what do we do with you."

"Fuck this." I stomp back to the environment.

I don't see Assey again. 15 built a Kruzian environment. I don't want to go and see it. He's in there, keeping away from me, hiding.

After a couple of days, an avatar asks me to revisit 15.

"There are only two options on the table. You can choose to die again..."

I jump in, "So you can bring me back again at the first sign of trouble, or when it doesn't work out with 'Golden Boy'. FUCK THAT!"

"...Or there is a suitable planet nearby that I can leave you on."

"What does that entail?"

"It's a nice place, Earth-like in many ways. Very different flora and fauna but nothing particularly dangerous to you. I've scanned for all diseases and viruses and can inoculate you against everything down there. I will supply you with a habitat; a house to live in, a small self-sufficient fission plant for all your power needs indefinitely, this plant will also power a small number of avatars to help you, and all the supplies you'll ever need."

"Until I eventually die?"

"Yes, that's it. The nanobots in your system can be tasked to keep you alive

for as long as you want, but it's probably better to get old and die. That's what you always wanted - your death back in your hands. So it's down to you. Live your life out and die when the time comes."

"The planet; gravity, temperature, pressure all of that stuff?"

"Slightly different to Earth but not by much. It's perfectly liveable. It has some beautiful sunsets."

"Looks like you've made my decision for me."

"Can you suggest an alternative?"

I think for a few moments, that's all, a few moments.

"I'll take my chances on the planet. It will be nice to breathe real, unmanufactured air again."

"I'll make arrangements for your shipping. We'll be in the planet's range in two days."

So that's it, I walk back to the environment feeling dejected. I've spent 2,000 odd years on this spaceship flying from galaxy to galaxy, fighting aliens left and right. Eventually, I tire of my life and agree to die. This 'thing' brings me back in its hour of need to save it - which I do out of the kindness of my beating Human heart - and this is my payment - dumped off at the next habitable rock. See you later. So much for showing the Universe how great Humans are. I wish it'd left me to die in peace.

I spend the next couple of days walking around my environment, feeling sentimental, reminiscing, looking at what I'll miss. I look to see if there's anything I want to bring with me, but apart from some clothes, there's nothing. I saw the cherry wood staff leaning against the wall in the corner. Nah, can't be bothered.

Chapter 44

"RIGHT THEN, I'M READY."

There's no sign of Assey. I don't think it's that he's fallen out with me - I just think he's embarrassed. I can understand. Part of me wants to stay, and part of me is desperate to go. Could this be the start of my next great adventure? I've probably travelled further than any other Human ever. I'm going to live on a new planet that isn't Earth. It's a good thing. But I still feel a bit empty. This is the end of the road for 15 and me.

The 'other stuff' has already shipped down to the planet, and apparently, the new accommodation is ready for me to move into.

15 says, "Any famous last words?"

"Actu..."

And I'm shipped down to the planet.

Epilogue

A DARK BLUE LIGHT BLINKS on, and then off, in the whiteness.

Some time later, it does it again...

Acknowledgement

THANKS TO COVID 19 for giving me the free time to dedicate to writing the follow up to It starts...badly! The discipline of getting up to write every day gave me structure, purpose and mental stimulation during difficult and uncertain times.

Once again, thanks to the manuscript readers: my siblings Paula, Alison and Mick - and to John and Chris also. All of your input was listened to and mulled over, and occasionally, acted upon. Thanks to Ben Mascari for the cover.

Number 3 next.

Facebook: www.facebook.com/FrankNeary15
Website: www.frankieneary.com

Printed in Great Britain
by Amazon

26809296R00187